Blue Buddha

AN ADVENTURE IN JAPAN

Francis Abbott and Johanne Léveillé

BLUE BUDDHA
AN ADVENTURE IN JAPAN

iUniverse books may be ordered through booksellers or by contacting:

iUniverse
1663 Liberty Drive
Bloomington, IN 47403
www.iuniverse.com
844-349-9409

Because of the dynamic nature of the Internet, any web addresses or links contained in this book may have changed since publication and may no longer be valid. The views expressed in this work are solely those of the author and do not necessarily reflect the views of the publisher, and the publisher hereby disclaims any responsibility for them.

Any people depicted in stock imagery provided by Getty Images are models, and such images are being used for illustrative purposes only. Certain stock imagery © Getty Images.

ISBN: 978-1-6632-5138-1 (sc)
ISBN: 978-1-6632-5139-8 (e)

Library of Congress Control Number: 2023904292

Print information available on the last page.

iUniverse rev. date: 03/14/2023

A Twelve-Day Sojourn in Japan

Curator Madame Françoise René de Cotret travels to Japan to procure loans of Buddhist sculptures for a forthcoming exhibition to be held at the Cernushi Museum in Paris. She is reunited with her Japanese friend Itsue and learns about her troubled romance with a Korean national, Françoise in turn becomes attracted to a Buddhist monk. Later, as she travels around Kansai, our heroin is caught by gangsters when she finds stolen statues waiting to be exported by a criminal syndicate.

Co-authors Abbott and Léveillé weave a tale of suspense and romance together with historical and geographical locations.

Dedication

This book is dedicated to the people of Japan, those who befriended and taught us much as well as those who exasperated and frustrated us. They have provided us with the very material of which we write. We also dedicate this book to you people of Korea, we hope and pray your country will one day be united once more.

We express thanks to associate *Martin Nuttall* for exhaustive help during the early stages of this novel. Sincere thanks to *Barbara Jones* for many valuable comments after an early proofread, to *Christopher Sheen* for proofreading a later draft, to *Dr. Malcolm Parker* for painstaking work on punctuation, and to *Maya Miyazoe* for creating the illustrations. Our gratitude also goes to friends and colleagues who checked the accuracy of various facts and locations.

Francis Abbott / Johanne Léveillé
Kyoto Japan / Ottawa Canada
January 2023

Notes on Style

Note I

The Chinese character for temple is represented in roman letters by the suffix 'ji', (*sometimes 'tera' or 'dera'*) which if written with no space can be mistaken as part of the temple name, e.g. 'Todaiji'. On the other hand it is cumbersome to write it as 'Todai Temple'. We have therefore separated the final syllable from the name of the temple with a hyphen so that it reads clearly but concisely, e.g. 'Todai-ji'. Likewise the character for a Shinto shrine is represented in roman letters by the suffix 'jinja' or 'sha', we have separated the name of the shrine with a hyphen, e.g. 'Yasaka-jinja'. The same style is used for suffixes of -kun -chan -san -sama -sensei after people's names. Other definitions of Japanese and Korean words used can be found in the glossary.

Note II

B.C. Before Christ. & A.D. Anno Domini. B.C.E. Before Common Era. & C.E. Common Era. With or without periods seems to be a matter of choice. Complicating the issue is that AD is written before the date whereas BC, BCE and CE are all written after the date. Where it makes no sense to refer to Christianity many historians and curators now use the terms BCE and CE. However, following the lead of American journalist William

Safire we have opted to use BC for years before the birth of Christ, but to omit notation for years in the current calendar.

Note III

In creating the character of Françoise we questioned what language she would use to express thoughts to herself. We presumed a French person who usually interacts in French would think to herself in her native tongue and decided to use French in certain places to give the story a certain finesse. For those who do not read French, utterances in French have been paraphrased so that no understanding of the story is lost. French and Japanese words have also been *italicized* for clarity.

Note IV
Disclaimer

Temples and sites mentioned in this novel are genuine and can be visited. Historical details are factual as are descriptions of sculptures. Characters, circumstances and events however, are products of our imagination. Any resemblance to people living or deceased, and to situations past or present is purely coincidental.

Part One

The Cernushi Museum in Paris

September 8th Paris

On the top floor of the Cernushi Museum in Parc Monceau the curator Françoise René de Cotret reaches down, pulls open the bottom drawer of her desk and rests her right foot on its front edge. A still incomplete report file is displayed on the computer monitor to her side. Françoise leans back from the cluttered desk and reflects on her recent trip to Japan. Having become impervious to the squeaks of the metal swivel chair her eyes stare upwards as she reviews in her mind the various scenes of her escapade. Just how is she to explain gallivanting around central Honshu with a Buddhist monk, hunting for missing statues, being threatened by gangsters and to cap it all falling in love?

Lost in another world when, from beyond the thin partitions of Françoise's office the sonorous click of certain unmistakable footsteps coming down the hallway startles her into action. With the edge of her foot she briskly pushes the desk drawer back in, flips her seat forward straightens herself up and, anticipating raised eyebrows and probing questions, stares anxiously at the door as the director of the museum gives a perfunctory knock and strides into the room.

"Ah! You're back," the senior woman says. "At last."

Françoise raises her hand as much to hide behind as to stall the flow of questions.

1

"Before you ask, I... I can explain," she stammers. "I can justify everything."

"I sure hope so. The Cernushi can't afford to have its staff running around aimlessly on extended holidays. Put it all in the report," her eyes narrow, "but give me the bottom line first. Did you acquire the pieces you were searching for?"

"There are complications. I found a number of sublime works that you'll love but there are other sculptures that were, err... how shall I say... stolen? But even without them we should be able to put on quite an impressive show."

"Then you'll plan an exhibition for the summer of next year?"

"Yes. That should leave time enough to arrange things."

"All right. I'll convey your intentions to the trustees. We must make a decent return this time otherwise our jobs, indeed the Cernushi Museum itself, may be heading for extinction." The woman drops more papers on top of the pile of documents already on Françoise's desk and turns to leave. At the door she pauses and glances back over her shoulder, her stern face momentarily softer.

"Good to have you back," she says.

"Thanks," Françoise smiles.

Safely back in Paris, Françoise certainly felt relieved. Three weeks earlier, elated by the prospect of organising an exhibition of Buddhist Iconography, she proposed to her superior a display that would illustrate the changes in Buddhist art throughout the centuries. The museum director asked her to focus the show on explaining how artists of different countries modified their techniques to reflect the sensibilities of the times. To accomplish this task Françoise explained she would require a wide range of sculptures from the seventh century onwards and she knew just where to find them, for Japan possessed a rich collection of this type of work.

Cernushi administrators were aware that when the museum requested the Japanese Embassy in France for information about Buddhist sculptures the staff at the Embassy only provided brochures of works at famous temples. Consequently Françoise had been able to convince her superior that she should go to Japan herself to search out lesser known works of art from the temples around Nara, the city that was once the centre of ancient Japanese culture.

The humourless director agreed, she knew that Françoise had studied in Japan and the trip would probably provide an opportunity to meet old friends. Françoise was a trusted employee, and if she could perform the job with the assistance of personal connections so much the better. Françoise also welcomed the chance of two weeks away from her demanding husband Georges. After almost eight years of childless marriage Françoise clearly recognised that their relationship had soured. Too often these days she wondered how they managed to create such a monotonous existence.

"Better to go on the ninth," Georges told her. "Eight is unlucky for you."

Françoise had no reason to suspect the troublesome adventure that lay ahead of her and ignored his numerological prediction. "In Japan nine is homophonous with pain," she replied, but failed to realise that departure from Paris on the eighth meant that she would arrive in Tokyo on the ninth.

The whole trip had in fact been fraught with pain. Air France flight 304 from Charles de Gaulle left more than an hour late, *Oh ça commence mal*, Françoise thought as the validity of her husband's fortune telling crept into her mind, and had been anything but restful. Severe turbulence forced passengers to keep their seat belts fastened most of the time and people had been taken ill. The crew kept extremely busy with requests for blankets, water, even a doctor. Agitation and fear took many people to the restrooms, except for the man Françoise nicknamed Monsieur Moustache, for he had remained seated, nursing his free whisky, throughout most of the flight.

Later however, his breath stale with whisky and cigar smoke, his obnoxious face close to hers, as he stroked a forefinger down her cheek and glared into her eyes, his deep-voice almost a whisper. Even now in her cramped office at the Curnushi museum, Françoise shivered when she recalled his words, "… an attractive lady like yourself would be an especially suitable star…" the implications involved were all too clear. Françoise shook off the memory and eased her chair nearer to the desk intent on starting her report, but she could not focus; instead she re-lived the flight searching for signs that would have warned her of the troubles she was to encounter.

Françoise remembered how after boarding the plane she had first seen the heavily built man, his red passport clutched in one hand, he hoisted his bag into the overhead compartment with the other. He then took his seat across the aisle one row behind Françoise. As she in turn settled into her seat he studied her longish mousy blonde hair intently while he stroked his forefinger back and forth along his neatly trimmed moustachioed mouth.

Since then from the corner of her eye Françoise often saw Monsieur Moustache staring in her direction as he slurped at his whisky and water. Slowly Françoise became aware that he did not seem as interested in her as much as the reference book of Buddhist sculptures she was reading. Several times he leaned forward for a better peek at a particular picture. The book contained photos and descriptions of Chinese sculptures that police investigators of various countries uncovered in the last thirty years. Statues pilfered from Chinese tombs during and since the great Cultural Revolution resulted in a tragic cultural loss for the Chinese people. Françoise was taking the opportunity to catch up on the latest heists exported illegally to European dealers and from there all over the world. Would it have been different if she had questioned the man's interest in the icons she was studying?

Monsieur Moustache rose from his seat and Françoise turned slightly to see him march off towards the restrooms in the rear of the plane. Upon his return he ambled past her to the flight attendants' mid ship section and moments later came back to his seat with yet another double whisky clutched in his hand. Françoise could hardly blame him for the flight was dreadful and even though his teeth sucking drove her mad she noticed that the alcohol had not affected his still rigid confident gait.

Finally they neared their destination and the voice on the intercom signalled the end of Françoise's reading.

"Mesdames et messieurs, nous allons bientôt commencer notre descente sur Tokyo. Redressez vos sièges et bouclez vos ceintures s'il vous plaît. Nous sommes vraiment désolés de tous les inconvénients et désagréments qu'ont pu vous causer les turbulences. Il est maintenant 9h02 à Tokyo et la température est de 25 degrés avec un ciel nuageux. Tous les membres de l'équipage vous souhaitent un bon séjour à Tokyo et espèrent vous revoir bientôt sur un vol d'Air France."

A member of the cabin staff repeated the announcement in Japanese and Françoise closed her eyes as she checked her ability to comprehend the language she had not heard for so long. Prior to her enrolment at The University of Paris, Françoise spent a year at Nagoya Women's University. Thanks to her affable personality she easily made friends with Japanese students who in turn helped her acquire an advanced level of spoken Japanese. Reading however, proved too much of a challenge for one year's study. Françoise could not possibly memorise the two thousand Chinese characters her classmates mastered before they even left high school.

It was later, after her return to France, that Françoise developed her reading and writing skills when she pursued her studies for three years at The University of Paris. It was there that she met Georges, eight years her senior, a professor of Buddhism proficient in Sanskrit who travelled frequently to India. Enchanted with each other Françoise and Georges married soon after her graduation and honeymooned in Georges' favourite part of India the former French colony of Pondicherry. Afterwards they settled in Paris where Françoise found work at the Cernushi Museum while Georges became part owner of an antique shop.

Now, from her aisle seat, Françoise stretched towards the window and peeped out at the densely populated land below. Soon she would be immersed once more in Japanese culture this time in search of Buddhist sculptures. Françoise leaned back and fastened her seat belt as the plane began its final descent towards Narita International Airport.

Once on the ground Françoise joined the line assigned to non residents and read the sign 'Aliens.' She recalled how when she lived in Japan years ago people protested this appellation. Yet obviously those other than Japanese citizens were still officially referred to as aliens. Immigration procedures went smoothly, the officers asked routine questions, and with her passport duly stamped Françoise headed for customs to find herself in line behind Monsieur Moustache. He turned to face her she approached and stared brazenly while he studied her face, which made her feel slightly uncomfortable.

"So you like the Buddhist art, eh? You come to Japan for business? An art dealer maybe?" Monsieur Moustache spoke with a marked Japanese accent and glanced down at her passport. "France, eh? French," he nodded knowingly and stared at her for a long moment. "You like art work, eh? You love the artists: Monet, Manet, Matisse," he grinned as he ran off a list of French artists: "Gauguin, Degas, Renoir," Ha, ha, ha, ha. "Lautrec, Rouault, Utrillo. Do I miss anyone?" he said. Undoubtedly this was no ordinary Japanese man and Françoise stood dumbfounded until Monsieur Moustache turned back to the customs inspector, grabbed his bag and marched off towards the exit.

After Françoise cleared customs herself she came out through the airport doors and again caught sight of Monsieur Moustache as he climbed into the rear of a shiny black Nissan Sovereign President. A young heavy set tanned man in white sportswear gently closed the limousine's rear door and quickly got into the front passenger seat beside the driver. The tinted rear window slid down and the ruddy whisky loaded face peered out.

"Have a good day! Ha, ha, ha, ha," he shouted, and as the car moved off she noticed the phonetics of the registration plate, 88-88, matched the sound of his rough laugh.

Françoise hailed a taxi and went to her hotel. Two hours later, relaxed and refreshed, she emerged from the bathroom, wrapped a towel around herself and flipped open her suitcase. Seated on the edge of the bed she pulled her address book from her bag and called a number in Nagoya.

"Itsue?" she said as soon as she heard her friend's voice. "Yes. I'm in Tokyo . . . Fine. How are you? . . . No, I want to visit the National Museum here in Tokyo first . . . Yes, tomorrow . . . All right, I'll call you around six . . . That would be great, thanks . . . No, he's in France . . . No, we're still together," she laughed. "Au revoir."

Warm and drowsy as she dried her hair, Françoise recalled her first meeting with Itsue. Fifteen years earlier as an exchange student she stayed with a Japanese family. The mother Mrs. Tanaka was a friend of Itsue's aunt Mrs Kitamura the wife of the history professor at the university. Mrs. Tanaka introduced Françoise to Itsue and the two girls became good friends. They both enjoyed their professor's quirky lectures and asked Itsue's aunt to introduce them to him on a personal level. Since then they often visited the outspoken Kitamura at his antique shop to question him on what he called the True History of Japan.

Throughout the year Françoise's stories of Paris persuaded Itsue that she should see France for herself. Itsue was accepted at the University of Paris where she studied French language and sociology, while Françoise continued her Japanese studies. The two developed a habit of interacting in English, which established a cultural neutral ground. With that and the gurgling radiator pipes in their tumbledown apartment they enjoyed exhilarating days that strengthened their friendship. Filled with these happy memories Françoise looked forward to seeing her friend and dropped off to sleep.

一

September 9th Kasanui

Two stations north of Yamato Yagi station on the Kintetsu railway's Kyoto line lies the town of Kasanui. There, just before sunrise, in the shadowy interior of the main hall of Honkomyo-ji, Shigehiro Kurosawa glanced over the three square purple cushions placed orderly on the wooden floor in front of the statue of Sho Kannon. Offerings of rice and sake were arranged in front of the prized icon, while on either side piled in miniature pyramids shiny oranges and polished red apples created serious splashes of colour. Shigehiro looked up at the lustrous golden ornaments that hung from the wooden ceiling just above his head, then knelt on the left side cushion. He had just begun to recite the morning sutras when his father Yoshihisa entered the hall, placed two sticks of incense in the burner and knelt on the middle cushion. The deep rasp of his father's chanting soon competed with his own.

As usual the cushion on the right remained unoccupied, for these days grandfather Hiro, Yoshihisa's father, chose to devote his time to finishing his latest work in the storehouse near the main gate. Shigehiro silently wished he could be in the storehouse with his grandfather instead of in the main hall at his father's side. He had long yearned to enjoy the devotion his grandfather had shown as a sculptor. Even now Shigehiro still hoped for a miracle that would allow him to dedicate his life to sculpting. He knew he did not belong to the world of monks and had at first refused the religious order. Yoshihisa had urged him to follow in the footsteps of his ancestry, told the boy that affection for his grandfather clouded his thoughts and that he did not possess the skill or talent for such an artistic commitment. Eventually Shigehiro succumbed to his father's will and accepted the responsibilities that would keep his family content. The day to day care and management of the temple Yoshihisa had worked hard to maintain would become Shigehiro's destiny. The same temple grandfather Hiro had neglected in his passion for sculpting.

That morning, just like other mornings since Shigehiro officially became an adult at the age of twenty, he acted the part of the devout Buddhist monk. Day in and day out father and son performed the religious ceremonies with hardly a glance at each other. The rituals masked the tension. Seated on designated cushions, backs straight, legs tucked underneath, hands held in their laps, Yoshihisa's formal black kimono worn over a plain white silk under kimono contrasted sharply with Shigehiro's comfortable baggy trousers and loose fitting jacket of a blue samue. The younger man, although of similar build to his father, was slightly taller and a little overweight yet with their narrow eyes and wide visages their physical likeness was immediately obvious. Yoshihisa's balding head and Shigehiro's cropped hair added to their similarity as did the gold framed glasses of identical design and the gold wrist watches that accented their otherwise drab appearances.

The two men dutifully concluded their prayers, stood, bowed and walked out of the main temple building. Shigehiro followed his father the abbot of the temple more out of custom than of respect. As they neared the private quarters Yoshihisa spoke without the slightest turn of his head.

"It seems the statues that were to be displayed at Horyu-ji have disappeared."

Shigehiro took two quick strides forward and caught his father's arm.

"What statues are you talking about?"

"Statues made by your grandfather that as a gesture of goodwill I loaned to some of the other temples here in the Ikaruga area."

"What happened to them?"

"They were collected from the temples I loaned them to and were to be delivered to Horyu-ji for an exhibition at the end of last month, but they have not arrived." Yoshihisa paused for a moment then added. "I have called the man I dealt with and he is coming to see me this morning. That's all I know at the moment."

"Does grandfather know his works were to be taken to Horyu-ji?"

"No. He does not. They have been at the other temples for some time."

"But if you had not lent them out in the first place they would still be where they are supposed to be here with us."

Yoshihisa stopped, turned and fixed his gaze on his son's chest. "I know you cherish those statues, but clinging to objects of desire is not the call of a true Buddhist disciple. You are no longer the boy you were when your grandfather sculpted them. The yearnings of the child must surrender to the mature adult. Let go of your worldly possessions and ambitions."

"Forget your spiritual lesson," Shigehiro fumed.

Yoshihisa raised his eyes and stared at his son full in the face. A tense silence reigned between them. Yoshihisa knew Shigehiro had strong recollections of the times he spent with his grandfather and envied their attachment. Pangs of jealousy prevented him from appreciating his son's sensitivity towards his own father's art works. Grandfather Hiro's statues represented an artist's prayers but Yoshihisa failed to comprehend the emotional significance of meditative creation. He breathed deeply to calm himself while his gaze remained expressionless. His neutral visage revealed nothing, no anger, no sadness, no regret nor pain. The mask he had learned to wear maintained the harmony that pervaded much of Japanese society. Personal feelings were to be kept covered for the good of everyone. Slowly he let the air from his lungs and without another word returned his gaze to his son's chest, turned and continued towards their living quarters.

Shigehiro stayed behind in the grounds. He loved the gentle gardens where he had grown up. Set on a narrow road between common residences the temple and its surroundings formed a peaceful tableau for monks who studied with Shigehiro's grandfather when he was abbot of the temple. Shigehiro had spent much time with the monks studying in the teahouse and exploring the bamboo groves at the rear of the temple. Now as he strolled past the storehouse he remembered the early mornings when he had watched his grandfather at work on what was to be his last oeuvre.

As a child, soon after he awoke, Shigehiro often sought out his kindly grandfather. He would slip into the main hall and creep quietly under the barrier that separated the other monks from the abbot's sacred space and sit at his grandfather's side. Grandfather Hiro never missed a word of his chant nor did he falter in his rhythm on the mokugyo, the wooden gong carved with two fantail goldfish, used to give the mantras a steady beat. At times his head would turn slightly for a glimpse of his grandson as he prayed, hands pressed together while his eyes flitted silently over the Buddhist image of Kannon. As Shigehiro became a teenager grandfather Hiro did not always show up at the main hall. He had handed control of the temple over to his son Yoshihisa who would thenceforth conduct all the prayers. Shigehiro would then find his grandfather at work in the storehouse at the edge of the temple complex near the main gate. He would hear the irregular tapping of the round wooden sculptor's mallet on the head of the chisel and would enthusiastically run to the stained rustic shed. His face creased with joy he would ease open the shed door and peer inside. Day after day he watched silently as grandfather

Hiro rhythmically chipped away at the shiny ebony wood. He formed first the body then the face and painstakingly brought the youthful statue of Buddha to life. To the young Shigehiro this Buddha created by his grandfather seemed so real that he believed Buddha's soul would indeed penetrate the statue.

Shigehiro remembered one particular morning when, as an ever inquisitive ten year old, he had found his grandfather at work.

"Hello Grandpa," Shigehiro announced his presence.

"Hello little one. You're up early today." Grandfather Hiro put down his tools and stretched out his arm to the boy.

"I heard you banging."

It was only 6:00 am but the sunlight was already streaming in through the open doorway of the storehouse. Shigehiro, no taller than the statue on the workbench, stared at his grandfather's creation.

"How do you like it?"

"Kind of scary. Funny blue colour," he had said to his grandfather.

Grandfather Hiro had laughed. "Blue Buddha it shall be! This is a rare piece of wood Shigehiro and will be valuable one day."

"Where are you going to put it?"

"Oh! Too early for such a question, anyway that will be for you to decide," grandfather Hiro added as he wrapped the statue back in its sackcloth and knelt to place the bundle under the workbench. Shigehiro still remembered his grandfather's words clearly as he spoke still knelt beside him.

"Shigehiro can you keep a secret?"

"A secret? Just you and me?" his eyes brightened.

"Yes! A secret just between you and me," grandfather Hiro repeated the words slowly and firmly. "Shigehiro I don't want anyone to know of this statue. I'm going to give it to you. It'll be yours but not a word to anyone. Do you promise?"

Shigehiro had not understood his grandfather's wisdom but felt the urgency in his voice and affirmed that he would.

"Okay Grandpa. I promise."

Grandfather Hiro pushed the bundle further back under the workbench and Shigehiro helped him to his feet.

"Thank you," he said as he put his arm around the boy's shoulders. "I think you will be a good monk one day. Let's go and see if we can find some breakfast."

Shigehiro had kept his pact for he never mentioned the statue to anyone and as these memories reverberated in his mind he walked aimlessly across the grounds and out of the main gate. He strolled down the lane beside the adjoining Shinto shrine to the bamboo groves and stood awhile deep in thought. Sometime later a glance at his watch showed ten o'clock, he turned and headed back towards the temple. A short cut across the shrine grounds meant he did not see the black Nissan Sovereign President parked a way down the narrow street. However, as he slid open the outer door and set foot inside the monks' private quarters he could not fail to hear the visitor's loud forceful voice resonating from behind the thin partition of the guestroom.

"You will have your share at the end of the month. I can't pay you before we have the money, can I? Ha, ha, ha, ha."

"You assured me those statues would be... that they would be delivered to Horyu-ji but nothing has... I called and nothing has arrived... They said they are still wait..."

Shigehiro caught the hesitation in his father's voice.

"Now why did you have to go and check on me? You don't trust me? That doesn't make for a good business relationship, does it? The statues are stored safely until we procure others, then we will deliver them all together, which will be very soon and you'll receive good payment for lending them out."

So that was it, Shigehiro thought to himself. His father wasn't simply lending the statues his grandfather had made to Horyu-ji.

14

He was actually making money out of them. How much had he been promised, he wondered?

"Now. You said on the phone that you had another statue…" The deep forceful voice continued but Yoshihisa's voice cut in.

"I'll loan it to you after the others have been delivered to Horyu-ji. I…"

"Now listen," The rasping voice took on a distinct threatening tone. "I've just returned from Europe. I've had a long flight and I'm tired. Where is this statue?"

Grandfather Hiro, disturbed by the raised voices, emerged from the kitchen at the opposite end of the hall and made his way towards the guestroom. He nodded to his grandson stood just inside the main entrance then swiftly opened the door and stepped into the room. Shigehiro took three quick steps along the hallway and got to the door just as his grandfather started to close it. He excused himself into the room turned and gently closed the door behind them. As he turned back to the room he saw that grandfather Hiro had seated himself in one of the easy chairs opposite the black suited stocky man, knees spread far apart, perched on the vinyl covered couch. The two men who stood behind the couch, both of whom wore flashy vests with tasteless logos emblazoned down one side, did not seem to intimidate grandfather Hiro at all.

"You will be aware honoured guests that this is a sacred place," grandfather Hiro eyed the man on the couch carefully, "a place where believers meditate and pray." The visitor opened his mouth slightly as if to speak but grandfather Hiro continued with calm self-assurance, a skill acquired after decades of meditation. "I would respectfully ask you therefore to refrain from this passionate conversation while on these premises."

Their eyes bored into each other's. Neither admitting the slightest emotion nor displaying any move until the man on the couch slowly raised his hand and brushed his moustache gently from side to side with the back of his index finger.

"Furthermore," grandfather Hiro continued. "Since a misunderstanding of sorts seems to have taken place I humbly request you to respect our family name and give us time whilst we attempt to sort this issue out. I sincerely hope you will do us the honour of visiting again on a more auspicious occasion."

The two men of opposing persuasions stared at each other for what felt like an eternity. Shigehiro's gaze dragged to his father's face and the men behind the couch raised themselves to their full height but the old monk remained calmly seated without the least sign of aggression. Indeed he exuded such dignity that the demanding guest had no choice but to respect the situation as the host had requested. He heaved himself to his feet and as Yoshihisa scrambled to stand, made a short curt bow in his direction. "I will see you another time," he growled and strode from the room, and his two aides hurried after him. The three monks left inside the room remained silent and motionless.

As the sound of the car engine receded Yoshihisa eased himself back down into the easy chair and caught the gaze of his father looking questioningly at him.

"Just what is it you have done?" grandfather Hiro asked quietly.

Yoshihisa adjusted his kimono around his knees. He could see the confrontation with the gangster had tired his father and he looked across at him apologetically.

"I've been trying to raise money to buy the plot of land behind the temple that is overgrown with bamboo. I wanted to build an extension to the temple so we could exhibit your statues. You know we can't get enough donations to acquire that land for ourselves so when Yamamoto offered to help I went along with him. I thought we could build a showroom while the statues were on loan and when returned we would be able to display them right here on our own premises."

"Just what exactly was his offer?" grandfather Hiro asked.

"He told me that Horyu-ji was trying to boost its cultural heritage ranking and needed more treasures to exhibit on their premises, that he could provide me a loan to build the extension ready for when the Horyu-ji exhibition was over, and the loan could easily be repaid from profits received from entrance fees."

"Why didn't you go to Horyu-ji directly?"

"Yamamoto told me he had been asked by the abbot at Horyu-ji to organize everything and that he was doing so. He had transportation available. He would collect the statues from the other temples and take them to Horyu-ji personally. He said the project would boost tourism in the area and he would also make a personal donation."

"And you went along with that without checking further? You trusted him. A monk dealing with a trickster."

"I had no reason not to. It wasn't until I called Horyu-ji two days ago that I found out the statues had not been delivered and they were still waiting to hear from him. It was then that I started to doubt him and asked him to come over to explain things."

"Why didn't you talk this over with Shigehiro or me?" grandfather Hiro asked.

Embarrassed by his mistake Yoshihisa's tone became defiant. "You handed over the responsibility of this temple to me. I saw no reason to discuss it."

Shigehiro's thoughts raced. What he had overheard before, when he stood just inside the main entrance suddenly began to make horrible sense. "...You said on the phone that you had another statue..." Shigehiro slipped quietly out of the room, walked quickly down the polished wooden floored corridor, passed the kitchen where his mother was preparing lunch and headed for the side entrance of the house. He stepped down onto his wooden sandals and crossed the gravel pathway to the storehouse. It was unlocked. The door stood slightly ajar. He eased it fully open and stepped inside. The room was neat and ordered. Grandfather alone cared for the sacred objects stored there along with his tools and work. The Blue Buddha had been concealed with other paraphernalia under the workbench for many years. This piece more than any other represented Shigehiro's heritage, a piece that had been created for him, it should remain within the temple. Shigehiro knelt to check on its presence but marks in the dust showed signs that something had been disturbed. He squatted back on his heels and stared at the space where the sackcloth bundle had been. He realised now that his father had no compunction whatsoever about using anything he saw fit, including grandfather's artwork. But he remembered he had overheard his father say that he didn't want to loan it until after the others had been delivered. He looked all around. Nothing.

Certain that the Blue Buddha had been taken, Shigehiro rushed back to the house to join his father and grandfather who were still discussing the situation. He knelt beside his grandfather looked across at his father and took a deep breath before he spoke.

"Grandpa. The statue is gone." Grandfather Hiro's head turned swiftly to his grandson, a frown creased his forehead and he turned back to his son.

"You had no right to lend that out. I gave that to Shigehiro."

"Don't worry. I was going to let Yamamoto have it. I took it out this morning and put it on the bench. Yes, I knew where it was kept, but I changed my mind and told him so. It's on top of the workbench."

"It's not on the workbench or under it. I have just checked."

Yoshihisa's eyes opened wide. He took a long deep breath of air then let it out slowly with a sigh. An expression of genuine regret crossed his face. "I left the door to the storehouse unlocked. They could have seen it on their way out."

Grandfather Hiro studied his son for a long moment then slowly, without another word, raised himself to his feet and left the room. Moments later the steady rhythm on the wooden mokugyo in the main hall could be heard throughout the temple. Kneeling in prayer before the statue of Sho Kannon, the Bosatsu of compassion, Grandfather Hiro offered prayers of much intent. He sought answers.

~

三

September 10th Tokyo

During Françoise's experience as a student in Japan she had been reminded numerous times that first impressions counted. Uniforms, suit colours, cosmetics, even voice pitches, were constantly modified to match age and circumstances. Françoise had therefore packed her favourite crease resistant outfit, a mustard yellow ensemble printed with autumn leaves. Now, after her unpleasant flight, she had spent a restful night in the Tokyo hotel and was satisfied to see in the full-length mirror that the slightly flared jacket made her attire neither too formal nor too casual for the occasion. She took her Cernushi Museum name cards out of her briefcase, inserted them into a delicate lacquered case, and slipped it into her pocket. Ready for business with a spot of sightseeing along the way.

Still plenty of time for a leisurely breakfast Françoise took her bag down to the front desk, asked the staff to keep it until later and went along to the restaurant. At the entrance she frowned at the poster advertising a Viking Breakfast 7:00 am to 10:00 am as she imagined hoards of Viking sailors breakfasting, but she knew it simply referred to the self-service smorgasbord or buffet style breakfast served at many hotels in Japan. Around the sides of the dining hall the sight of western and Japanese food laid out so early in the day made the process of selecting what to eat a confusing task. Eventually she combined eastern and western dishes and filled her tray with a menu that included scrambled egg, crispy fried bacon, a bowl of miso soup, a packet of dried seaweed, a slice of bread that she toasted at the grill provided, creamy Hokkaido butter and some Japanese green tea.

After breakfast Françoise decided, rather than a taxi, she would take the once familiar subway. She confirmed directions from the bellhop, and strode off towards the nearest metro entrance. A network of national and private railways that reach the remotest parts of the country made the Japanese railway system the most efficient provider of public transportation in the world. A ten minute ride may be expensive but the trains proved reliable in the extreme. Françoise purchased a ticket at the vending machine, descended the designated escalator and gasped as the platform came into view. Dozens of black haired, dark blue suited expressionless businessmen with brown briefcases stood at regular intervals down the length of the platform. White circles painted on the platform indicated where the doors of the train would open. Each queue was formed religiously vis-à-vis these circles and, as she elbowed her way down the platform to the 'Women Only' section, she realised she was truly back in disciplined Japan.

The train arrived already crowded. *"Ah, c'est trop tôt, c'est encore l'heure de pointe. Je prendrai le prochain train,"* Françoise murmured to herself as she glanced at her watch. However, before she could step back from the crowd she was herded into the train by the throng of passengers. Within seconds and without control over her own movements she found herself in the middle of a packed carriage with every part of her body pressed against someone else. Her nostrils assailed with the odours of cheap perfume and deodorant. *"J'étouffe!"* she exclaimed aloud. The women around her seemed exhausted. *Comment peuvent-ils passer par cette folie jour après jour,* she wondered.

Just before the stop at Ueno station the conductor's voice from a speaker above her head apologised for a delay at a red signal.

Thirty seconds later the train began to move. *Qui s'inquiète de trente secondes de retard?* Françoise thought. *Il devrait faire des excuses pour l'entrée grossière et non-pour un retard si insignifiant.* Finally the doors opened and Françoise exited the train in much the same way she entered. Herded towards the platform with the other passengers she was ejected into the daylight of Ueno station and stood for a moment in the stifling heat. Françoise took a deep breath, straightened her jacket and headed for the museum.

Prior to Françoise's departure from Paris her secretary had contacted the major temples in Asuka, Nara and Kyoto and also requested appointments at Tokyo National Museum in Ueno Park, and Nara National Museum in Nara Park. The Tokyo museum was holding an exhibition of sculptures usually kept at Horyu-ji in Nara. Since Horyu-ji was one of the most prestigious of the temples in the history of Japanese Buddhism, Françoise eagerly anticipated a preview of these exhibits while she had the chance. Although she would not have time to visit the entire museum, for the Tokyo National owned more than ten thousand works of art, she would settle for a visit to the Horyu-ji room. Perhaps she could learn something useful before visiting the temple itself.

Françoise sauntered leisurely across the park and arrived at the museum a short while after it opened. Her briefcase tucked under her arm she approached the two grey suited women stood behind the reception desk.

"Bonjour. Mon nom est Françoise René de Cotret."

The two receptionists bowed. They knew immediately who the tall female foreigner was as soon as she marched through the entrance doors.

"Ohayo gozaimasu," they responded in unison. "We expecting you," the older woman continued. "I call research assistant. Please take seat over there."

The woman spoke English with a marked Japanese accent but it was easy enough to understand and while the older woman spoke on the phone the younger woman came around the reception desk and took Françoise to the waiting area. The woman departed, reappeared a moment later with a cup of lukewarm green tea on a tray, placed the cup gently on the table, bowed and left. Françoise had time for one sip before the elevator doors opened and a breathless young Caucasian man stepped out and hurried towards her. Françoise took a name card out of her lacquer box and handed it to him.

"I'm sorry I don't have my cards with me. Not used to carrying them around all the time. I'll dig one out before you leave though. For now just call me Martin."

"I'd rather expected a Japanese person," Françoise hesitated.

"Naturally." Martin replied and continued unperturbed. "I hope you don't mind if I show you around though. I'm primarily employed for the tedious work of translating research papers from Japanese into English. Any chance I get to guide visitors through the museum is a welcome break."

"I understand," Françoise smiled.

Martin gestured and together they walked towards the interior of the museum. As they neared the Horyu-ji room Martin explained how the level of humidity was extremely variable during the summer months and the construction of an atmospherically controlled space to keep the sculptures at a constant temperature had been a challenge, but finally the administration was justly proud of their success and in the dimly lit room a stunning sight awaited Françoise. Forty-eight identical plinths perfectly aligned in straight rows with two-foot square glass cases on three-foot high black bases. Each work of art identified as a precious icon. Françoise opened her handbag took out a powerful miniature pocket flashlight and studied each statue in turn. Martin continued his narration of how researchers now believed the original owners of the statues had been wealthy families who venerated their gods in their own homes. Then, sold off by later generations, the statues eventually ended up in Horyu-ji, which in turn had leased them to the Tokyo National Museum.

Some way along the row stood a plinth from which the glass case had been removed. Françoise shone the beam of her flashlight on the empty black base.

"Yes, I'm afraid we had some works stolen," Martin said. "Just a few days ago."

"A theft! Here in Japan?"

"Certainly the first time anything has been taken from the Tokyo National Museum…" Martin gave a wry chuckle, "…and we are in big trouble with Horyu-ji."

"Any clue of who's behind it?"

"Not really. The police suspect an export racket."

"Yes, that happens," Françoise acknowledged.

"The Tokyo police checked thoroughly as well as inspector up from Nara who felt it was his duty to investigate the theft since the statuettes belonged to Horyu-ji. He questioned the staff as to whether we had seen anything or anyone suspicious but to no avail. It was lunchtime when the employees rotate and go upstairs so no witnesses were present, and the thief was out the door before anyone realised why the alarms were ringing. The Tokyo police explained that unless clear evidence surfaced not much could be done but the Nara inspector seemed more hopeful and asked us to contact him personally if we remembered anything."

"What was it they took?"

"Oh! Only the most desirable pieces of the entire collection," Martin sighed. "A set of four miniature figurines of Queen Maya giving birth to Buddha from her armpit and of her three kneeling attendants. A beautifully crafted set."

"I have seen pictures of these treasured pieces. I do hope they find them."

"Well. They can't easily be sold without raising suspicion. They have to surface sometime, don't they? When, where, and in what condition though is anyone's guess?"

With that Martin excused himself and Françoise looked over a selection of masks, then wandered into the calligraphy section.

Martin returned with his business card, she thanked him for his help and told him not to give up on the return of the statuettes. They shook hands and before she left the museum she stopped in at the souvenir shop to purchase postcards of the exhibits. Françoise found two different colour pictures of the stolen pieces and bought one of each.

Queen Maya and Attendants

Françoise strolled back through Ueno Park and headed for the station. Fewer passengers, now mostly middle aged women busily chatting with their friends, made the ride back much more pleasant than the one she'd experienced that morning. By the time Françoise emerged from the station near the hotel it was time for a late lunch, she spied a noodle shop on the other side of the road and crossed over. *"Irrashaimase,"* the staff members welcomed her in unison as she entered. Lack of space obliged her to share a table with another customer already slurping his noodles. Françoise ordered cold buckwheat noodles and while waiting her eyes fell on a poster advertising the Horyu-ji exhibition at the Tokyo National Museum that featured the statues of Queen Maya and her attendants. *Les gens ne pourront pas voir ces précieuses statues pendant quelque temps,* she thought to herself. *Et qui sait, peut-être jamais.*

The noodles came with pickles and a cup of green tea. Françoise relished the meal and then paid her bill at the cash register by the door.

"*Gochisoosama,*" she said as she left the restaurant.

"*Arigato gozaimashita,*" echoed several times behind her, thanking her for patronage.

Françoise strode back to the hotel, thanked the staff for keeping her luggage, and went outside to get a taxi. The bellhop with a wave of his hand called to a driver who was dozing in the front seat of his cab, engine idling to keep the air conditioner running. The car with white lace edged coverings on the seats pulled up to the entrance. Controlled by the driver, the rear passenger door opened. Françoise slid into the back seat and told the driver, who studied her in the rear view mirror, to take her to Tokyo station.

"Nihingo jousu desu ne?" He said.

"*Merci,*" she replied and hoped the French response would confuse him.

When enrolled at the Japanese language school Françoise had often expressed her frustration with people who complimented her on her language skills even after she had made an obvious grammatical error. This time the comment was simply superfluous for the driver had only heard a brief sentence of her rusty Japanese and without further comment he eased the taxi into the flow of traffic and wound his way through the busy streets to the station. Françoise stared out at the new edifices that had sprung up since she had last been in the metropolis and shook her head as she reflected on how Tokyo constantly found space for yet another building.

At the station, rather than going through all the options displayed on the Shinkansen ticket vending machine, Françoise purchased a reserved seat ticket to Nagoya at the ticket counter, then made her way to the platform and searched for a public phone to tell Itsue the time of her arrival.

"Yes, of course it is. Don't worry," Itsue replied after a brief hesitation when Françoise confirmed if it was all right for her to stay at Itsue's apartment. Françoise read out the schedule number of the train and time of arrival printed on the ticket and Itsue said she would be at the central ticket barrier to meet her. Yet something in the tone of Itsue's voice worried Françoise. Was her friend troubled about something? Françoise put the handset back on the hook and checked her watch. *Bien,* she thought to herself. *J'arriverai à la station de Nagoya sous peu, ainsi je saurai bientôt ce qui se passe.*

Françoise purchased a bag of mixed nuts from a kiosk, checked the number of the carriage printed on her ticket, and stood in line at the designated place on the platform. When the sleek blue and white train pulled in she boarded promptly, found her place and settled back in the comfortable reclining seat. The journey would take one hour forty minutes and she looked forward to a peaceful trip in the air-conditioned carriage.

The front of the train no longer bullet shaped resembled an aerodynamic duckbill and although passengers hardly felt any motion as the train left the station they were soon travelling at a speed approaching 300 kilometres an hour. In the quiet interior of the pressurised compartment Françoise watched as the massive skyscrapers of Tokyo gave way to an endless array of factories, gasoline stations, warehouses and drive-in stores that flashed past the window in rapid succession. Thirty minutes later the young man across the aisle leaned over towards her and pointed out of the window.

"Mount Fuji," he said.

Françoise dragged herself from her thoughts, looked out of the small window, and saw in the distance under the clear blue sky the almost perfect triangle of the most famous of all Japanese symbols. She turned back to the young man.

"It's beautiful," she said.

"Lucky to see it so clearly," The man said. "It's usually rather cloudy around here. Where are you..." He was about to continue but a woman in a green uniform and white apron had entered the carriage and proceeded to push an aluminium cart down the aisle selling lunch boxes, beer, coffee and snacks. The woman now pushed the rather large cart between Françoise and the young man. Françoise asked the woman to stop and bought a paper cup of coffee for 300 yen, placed it in the holder on the back of the seat in front of her, tore open her packet of nuts and turned slightly in her seat towards the window. Françoise hoped the young man would not try to socialise further, she was in no mood to talk with someone who wanted to practice English with a French woman.

四

September 10th Nagoya

At Nagoya station Françoise took the escalator down to the exit, passed through the automatic ticket barrier, and waited near the kiosk. Before long Itsue was walking towards her smiling confidently. It had been years since the two women had met and they greeted each other enthusiastically, kissing lightly on each cheek and laughing childishly when Françoise's dangling earrings caught in Itsue's hair.

"Are you sure I'm not being a nuisance," Françoise said.

"You're welcome to stay as long as you like. It's wonderful to see you again."

"The same kind, helpful Itsue," Françoise smiled at her friend, still holding Itsue's hands. "You haven't changed at all."

"I've lost weight and I have more wrinkles," she laughed and reached for the handle of Françoise's bag. Françoise protested but Itsue waved her away and they strolled down the long concourse to the exit. Itsue unlocked her dark blue Honda Civic parked illegally near the entrance, deposited the bag on the back seat, and gestured for Françoise to sit in the front. Itsue got in behind the wheel and they drove off.

"So. How are you?" Itsue asked. "It's nice to come on business, huh?"

"Yes. As I wrote in the email the museum I work for is preparing an exhibition to trace the history of Japanese Buddhist sculptures from the 8ᵗʰ Century. We want to show the evolution of the artistic styles during the period when Buddhism was introduced into Japan from China. I'm here to arrange loans with monks and private owners. If I can find sculptures that are relatively unknown, so much the better."

"You remember Kitamura-sensei?"

"Our old Japanese history professor, your uncle? Yes, indeed."

"I arranged for us to visit him. He knows people who understand Buddhist sculptures and maybe he can give you an introduction. He's looking forward to seeing you again."

"That's great. Thank you so much, Itsue."

"*Douitashimashite.*" Itsue responded.

Itsue neared her home and parked at the lot two blocks away from the apartment, picked Françoise's wheeled bag from the back seat and together they dragged it to the white stucco edifice. At the entrance Françoise read the sign embossed in roman letters.

"What does '*Yamato Heights*' mean?" she asked. "This is not a hill."

"It's a tall building," Itsue said. "I live on the fifth floor and there is no elevator. You might find it appropriately named once we've climbed the stairs."

"No elevator! In this weather?" Françoise exclaimed.

"Elevators aren't compulsory in buildings of less than six floors," Itsue laughed and led the way. As they went up, they stopped at each bend in the stairs and took a turn with the case. In the humid climate, by the time Itsue took the keys out of her purse and unlocked the door, Françoise did indeed feel as if she had climbed more than five floors.

Itsue opened the door and gestured for Françoise to enter, followed right behind her, and held the door open while they removed their shoes before stepping into the slippers tidily arranged at the entrance. The cosy one bedroom apartment displayed a Japanese and western mood but Itsue's arrangement of golden yellow chrysanthemums on the table gave the place a distinctly Japanese air. The four adjoining panels that separated the lounge from the bedroom were open and Françoise espied a hanging scroll of Japanese calligraphy in the room beyond, a poem by Basho the most respected of Japanese poets, and recited it out loud.

kono michi ya	*this road here*
yuku hito nashi ni	*no traveller comes*
aki no kure	*an autumn evening*

"You can still read kana then," Itsue said

"Very rusty I'm afraid, but I try to practice whenever I can."

Although Itsue had not written this piece herself Françoise knew that her friend excelled in the Japanese kana style, and reminded of her friend's delicate hand she opened her bag and placed the present she brought on the kitchen table. A cut glass stand for ink and fountain pen she found in her husband's shop.

"Will grilled eel be all right, or is it too soon for seafood?" Itsue asked.

"That's fine. You know I eat just about anything."

Itsue tore the cellophane wrap off a packet of prepared smoked eel, placed two pieces under the grill, then took a seat at the table opposite Françoise.

"Tell me about your new man," Françoise urged. "How did you meet him?"

Itsue remembered the incident that brought her Korean boyfriend into her life.

"I got my bicycle wheel caught in railway lines at a level crossing."

"You're joking," Françoise exclaimed.

"No, it's true. I fell off rather badly, then the barriers started to come down and I was just going to scream when Chulsoo suddenly appeared, helped me up, grabbed my bicycle and marched me to the side of the tracks just as the train sped by."

"My God! Were you all right?"

"Yes, I was fine. My tights were all torn and my skirt was dirty but no serious damage. The wheel on my bicycle wouldn't go round though and Chulsoo carried it back here."

"Then you asked him in and the rest is history as they say."

"No. You go too fast. I thanked him and he left."

"You let him leave?"

"Yes," Itsue smiled. "Then a couple of days later I saw him on the street near here. I thanked him for what he had done. We talked a bit and he asked me out."

"You just 'happened' to see him?"

"Turns out he has an aunt here in Nagoya he stays with sometimes, but I think he'd been hanging around the convenience store on the corner."

"And you've been going together ever since." Françoise stared at her intently.

"Yes, and don't smile like that."

"I'm not smiling."

"You are, too."

"I can't wait to meet him."

"You won't have to wait long. He'll be over in the morning to take us to see Kitamura-san. It's only a short drive but my car is not comfortable in this hot weather."

Itsue reached for her bag, rummaged inside, and handed Françoise a photograph of herself standing next to a rugged man in white sports wear.

"This is Chulsoo."

"Wow! A strong man! Is he an athlete?"

"A taiko drummer. You can keep that photo if you like."

"So when's the wedding?" Françoise asked as she slipped the picture into her handbag.

"There may not be one. As you know, he's of Korean descent and my whole family is against it except for Uncle Kitamura. I despair of ever persuading Mother and my elder brother who both say they will never agree."

Françoise's smile faded as she reflected on the inconsistencies involved regarding intermarriages in Japan. When Japanese and Europeans become romantically involved, their families may protest, but at the same time there is curiosity and eventually tolerance wins. The intermarriages of Japanese and other Asians on the other hand, particularly Koreans, present deeper cultural and historical problems. The smell from the grill took Itsue from the table, but she continued the conversation over her shoulder while she prepared the meal.

"Actually I hoped we would be able to overcome all that one day, but now I'm... well, I'm stunned by what Mother has done. It seems she must have paid to have Chulsoo's family registration records investigated. Mama just called to tell me he was born and raised in Tsuruhashi, Osaka, and she wants me to have nothing more to do with him."

"Why is being born in Osaka a problem?" Françoise queried.

"Well, Chulsoo told me he lived here in Nagoya, but Mama says he lives with his uncle in Osaka, and his uncle is reputedly a gangster in the Osaka area." Itsue leaned back against the sink, arms folded, her head on one side.

"Have you spoken to Chulsoo about this?" Françoise asked.

"Not yet. I've only just found out." Itsue regained her posture and shrugged. "I'll have to deal with it in the morning..."

Françoise gathered her thoughts. The issues were complex. Over the years, hundreds of people of Korean descent had settled in Tsuruhashi. Japanese people thought them troublemakers and the pejorative term was difficult to shake off.

"...Well, let's celebrate our reunion, shall we?" Itsue opened a cupboard under the sink, and lifted out a 1.8 litre bottle of Shochikubai sake, decanted the liquor into two ceramic tokuri and popped them into the microwave. While they warmed she transferred rice from the cooker onto two dishes, placed grilled eel on top of each and complimented the meal with Japanese pickles.

"Oh! *Natsukashii*," Françoise exclaimed as she espied the meal. "This looks good and bizen yaki too, my favourite pottery."

Itsue placed two pairs of chopsticks on the rests in front of the bowls and the two women put their hands together with heads gently bowed.

"*Itadakimasu*," they said in unison.

"*Umm... Très bon*," Françoise enthused after the first mouthful.

"It's not much I'm afraid but I'm glad you like it. So how was your flight?"

Françoise immediately grimaced. "*Ah. Epouvantable. Absolument terrible.*"

Then while they ate, Françoise related the story of Monsieur Moustache, the way he slurped his whisky, his interest in her book, and his goodbye at the airport.

"I hope he's not a stalker," Françoise concluded.

"Did you get his name," Itsue asked.

"Yamamoto something," Françoise replied. "I saw it on his case at customs.

"The limousine you described and the man's audacity are typical of Japanese gangsters, but any rough man could have acted that same way…"

The microwave bell rang and Itsue still talking retrieved the sake.

"You're just not used to that behaviour from a Japanese man. I guess he was having fun intimidating a female. There's nothing to worry about. You'll never see him again."

Itsue brought the sake to the table and as she poured it into the tiny ceramic cups Françoise saw small golden particles floating around in the clear liquid.

"What is this?" she asked.

"Flakes of gold. Let's drink to our good fortune."

Itsue raised a delicate choko in front of her. Françoise took the other choko and lifted it to Itsue's. *"Kanpai!"* They laughed, and together savoured the liberating liquor.

As they drank their laughs became louder, and their talk more personal.

"And what of your love life? Are you and Georges still together?" Itsue asked.

"I sometimes think of divorce but I haven't said anything. He gets angry at the least inconvenience, but I'll put up with him for now. These days he spends more time at the antique shop than he does at the university. It wouldn't surprise me if he wasn't involved in some illegal dealings of some kind, but he denies it. I asked Fabrice, his business partner, about it but either he knows nothing or is a good liar." Françoise made a grimace. "How about you? Any regrets about leaving your husband?"

"No, not at all. He was too heavy on Japanese traditions like the rest of my family. We both wanted out and there were no children so it was a family court settlement. We signed the document, paid the fee and went our separate ways. He never understood my liking for western things and hated me talking about France."

"Good job I never met him then."

They laughed noisily and after more drinks, prepared for bed.

五

September 10th Yamato Yagi

Yoshihisa stood between his desk and the chair, pulled several cards and scraps of paper out of his wallet and spread them out. He reached over to the phone, took the handset off the rest, looked at one of the business cards and punched out the number. A male voice answered.

"I want to speak to Yamamoto."

Yoshihisa said his name as requested and a moment later the deep rough voice he had last heard in the guestroom of Honkomyo-ji came on the line.

"This is Yamamoto," Cheong said. He hated to use his Japanese name but it was easier to do business with a Japanese name.

"We have to talk," Yoshihisa blurted out. Cheong tried to interrupt him but Yoshihisa continued irately. "You took a cherished possession from the temple without consent. I want it back. You told me those..." Cheong interrupted again louder this time and warned him about being so explicit on the phone.

"Those other... items," Yoshihisa stammered. "You promised to deliver them. What have you done with them? I want them back or I'll go to the police."

There was a pause and then Cheong, his voice now quiet, suggested meeting at the exit of Yamato Yagi station at one o'clock.

"I'll be there," Yoshihisa replied and slammed the phone down. His notes whisked off the desk by the sleeve of his kimono fluttered to the floor as he headed to his private room where he changed into a formal black suit. He strode back along the corridor, took his shoes from the rack in the entrance, and left the temple without telling anyone.

As soon as Yoshihisa appeared at the station exit a shiny black Toyota Lexus drew up with Cheong in the front passenger seat. The rear door opened and as Yoshihisa prepared to enter a hand reached out from the further side and pulled him into the velvet interior. The car sped off which threw Yoshihisa back into the seat. The man reached across and pulled the door securely closed then slowly pulled on a pair of white cotton gloves. Yoshihisa remembered him as one of the men who had been with Yamamoto at the temple. The driver glanced behind; they then headed out of town.

A white gloved hand moved smoothly along the upper edge of the seat, reached behind Yoshihisa's head, and flicked his far side ear.

"Ouch!" Yoshihisa turned sharply towards the man who grabbed Yoshihisa's jaw and pulled it down towards his chest. He stared straight into Yoshihisa's eyes and a faint smile spread slowly over his face. His white-gloved thumb forced its way between Yoshihisa's lips and moved back and forth over his lower teeth. Yoshihisa grabbed the younger man's arm and tried to force himself free, but the arm tight around his shoulders held him in a vice like grip. Yoshihisa ached. The thumb found a suitable spot and pushed. The pain was unbearable and Yoshihisa screamed. The driver glanced in the rear view mirror and winced as two teeth cracked and collapsed into Yoshihisa's mouth. The white-gloved man grinned at the blooded mouth of his handiwork.

Cheong spoke. "Yoshihisa-kun I gave you my phone number to contact me if you had more business to offer, not to threaten me. If you threaten me, there can be no business between us." Cheong turned around to make sure Yoshihisa was still in pain. "Is that clear enough?" He added. Pronouncing each syllable slowly and distinctly. Blood spilled from Yoshihisa's mouth as he responded with a grunt.

"Dump him!" Cheong commanded.

Without slowing down, the driver pulled to the side of the road, the bloodied white gloved hand reached across Yoshihisa's chest, the door opened and the man lunged heavily against his victim. For a second Yoshihisa hung motionless in the air aware only of a fading laugh, then the sudden jar of his shoulder told him he had hit the ground. He rolled sideways into a ditch tumbled head over heels and came to rest with a sickening thud against a wooden telegraph pole. His feet in the mud alongside a paddy field his eyes rolled upwards, his head sunk to his chest and Yoshihisa passed out.

~

In the office on the second floor of Kashihara police station Inspector Sasaki invited Shigehiro to take a seat across from him, he then seated himself behind the grey metal desk. Behind Sasaki six desks formed an oblong, at the head of which a man with hunched shoulders, arms folded firmly across his chest, elbows planted on the desk, watched the room with narrowed eyes. The dirty beige walls desperately in need of a fresh coat of paint and the exposed grime covered pipes suspended under the ceiling created a gloomy atmosphere. In front of a row of lockers on one side of the room three policemen reached for their helmets and gloves as they readied for duty on their motorcycles. With good-natured banter between them they adjusted their belts and gun holsters, pulled on their boots, and descended an outside staircase to the garage.

With one arm rested on the edge of the desk inspector Sasaki listened to Shigehiro's complaint. The inspector's other hand tapped the pad on which six pictures Shigehiro had brought with him had been laid out.

"So you believe this man who came to your temple, the man your father had been doing business with, has made off with all of these statues. Is that right?"

"That is correct," Shigehiro answered.

"All right. Let me have the details again," Inspector Sasaki intoned.

Shigehiro sighed and began once more.

"I want to report the theft of this statue from the premises of Honkomyo-ji," Shigehiro repeated. "And the loss of these other statues from Matsuo-dera, Yata-dera…"

"Just a minute," The Inspector cut him off. "I need to have the names of these temples written down." The inspector reached for a pen. "All right. Continue."

"The temples are Matsuo-dera, Yata-dera…"

"Wait, wait, Matsuo-dera… Yata-dera…" He wrote slowly checking the Chinese characters with Shigehiro.

"Jiko-in…" Shigehiro continued, "…and Horin-ji."

"Oh, I know those temples. They are all here in Ikaruga.

"Well, Horin-ji is but the others are outside the area. Both Matsuo-dera and Yata-dera are quite a way in the mountains."

Inspector Sassaki was taken aback at being corrected, and it showed in his face.

"The statues were all made by my grandfather and have been on loan to those temples for several years." Shigehiro continued. "Just recently my father had arranged with this man to send statues to Horyu-ji for an exhibition. They should have already been delivered, but the abbot of Horyu-ji told me they have not received them. My father phoned the other temples and was told the statues had been collected some…"

"The monks did not take these pieces to Horyu-ji themselves?" the inspector cut him off. "They entrusted them into the hands of this man, you don't even know the name of."

"My father did. Yes. He knows his name. As I told you, it seems they negotiated a deal but it has turned sour."

Inspector Sasaki looked down at the photographs. "And this other picture?" he asked.

"The other statue is what we have called the Blue Buddha. It is a representation of the Buddha at birth. It has been taken from Honkomyo-ji without our consent."

"And without your father's consent?"

"There is some confusion but no agreement was made."

As Inspector Sasaki studied the pictures a frown slowly formed on his forehead.

"You say this Blue Buddha statue is the Buddha at Birth. How is that possible? It seems to me he is already a boy."

Startled by the question Shigehiro looked at the inspector benignly.

"It should not be taken too literally," he replied.

"But I saw pictures in Tokyo recently of another statue called the Birth of Buddha and in those statues he is coming out of his mother's sleeve. How is that possible?"

"There are various interpretations. Other artists portray things differently. I'd be pleased to provide you with an explanation of the various Buddhist statues at another time, but I think we are straying from the issue."

Sasaki was annoyed at the rebuff and continued running his finger back and forth under the photos.

"So this statue was taken without consent, but these were collected from other temples but not delivered to... Where was it? Horyu-ji? And you think they have all been stolen. Is that correct?

"Yes, all of them were sculpted by my grandfather and now not one of..."

At the further end of the room a door suddenly burst open and all conversation stopped. Framed in the doorway was a man on wooden crutches. Sasaki turned his head and watched as the man ambled slowly forward with a ten millimetre thick rope tight around his waist, the other end tied to the wrist of a police officer behind him.

"Do you think he is going to run away with all these officers around?" Shigehiro asked Sasaki as soon as the man was out of sight.

"We don't know what he might attempt. That man is a dangerous thug and accused of a very violent attack. Listen! Stealing works of art is an ongoing affair and as you can see we have many other situations to deal with. Unless somebody is injured or killed it is difficult for us to give priority to your problem."

"Can't you do anything?"

"We will do what we can, but without better evidence..." The inspector raised his voice. "Unless someone comes up with a real lead there is nothing much we can do," he paused and leaned forward on the desk.

The two men glared at each other. "I understand." Shigehiro said, stood and turned towards the exit. Down the cold marble stairs he went outside and held his fist fast to his chin. If this involved just one or two individuals the police would move quickly, informers may have even ferreted suspects out and tipped the police off. But here we have an organized gang, and likely someone being paid to drag their heels. If the police won't do anything, what can I do? Shigehiro reflected.

~

Cheong grunted as the black Toyota pulled away from the roadside back into the lane. "Let's go and see the advisor," He directed. Without a word the driver swung the Lexus left at the next traffic signals and took off in a new direction. In the back of the car the other man cleared his throat and swallowed heavily. Peeled the bloodied gloves from his hands and dropped them from the window.

The three men drove in silence for almost thirty minutes before they arrived at the country home of Ha Joon Lee, the syndicate's senior advisor. Second only to the head of the organization, it was the advisor who held significant power. His residence was ostentatiously a rice farm at the edge of a village, cared for by a group of employees. The estate had high roofed walls, a hillside at the back, open rice paddies at the front and a small bamboo grove that hid the property from the road. The houses and barns stood so near together that the corner eaves of one building jutted under the eaves of another. The two main houses were typical Japanese homes. The one nearest the road a classic innocuous thatched farmhouse covered with brown metal roofing; the other house a luxurious two-storied wooden framed residence with traditional curved grey slate tiles.

The three visitors were shown into an immaculate tatami room at the back of the house. The austere room welcomed them with a rectangular table of mahogany surrounded by six dark blue silk cushions. Cheong took a seat cross legged beside the table. The two younger men stood slightly apart from each other near the glass doors of the veranda that ran the entire length of the room.

The syndicate to which Cheong belonged operated under rules written three hundred years ago. Formed with strong links between fathers and sons, families consisted of a tight knit organization of extended relations. Like most they controlled gambling and loan firms in their area, but Cheong's group had invested massively in the export of art treasures of which Cheong was in charge, thus he came to report on the situation.

Cheong moved uncomfortably on his cushion. His dislike for his host was never well disguised and he had not seen Hyuun Pak the oyabun for six months. Cheong was just one year younger than his cousin, they had attended the same school, and the two thugs had earned a veritable reputation as extortionists. Once, during a scuffle with some rival gang members, a knife headed in his cousin Hyuun's direction had instead imbedded itself in Cheong's fleshy posterior. By merit of age and the loyalty of those under him it was Cheong's cousin who had became oyabun and the ostensible head of the organization. Legal advice however, was required and it was an uncle of the oyabun that held this senior position and guided the organization in their exploits. Ha Joon knew of Cheong's animosity towards him and he in turn thought Cheong unnecessarily ill mannered. But Ha Joon knew that Cheong was committed to the interests of the organization and that the oyabun was indebted to Cheong for saving his life, and the advisor respected Cheong for that.

Footsteps approached. HaJoon Lee threw the door open, strode across the room and seated himself crossed legged at the head of the table. Cheong bowed and both men greeted each other formally. The senior advisor studied the papers Cheong placed on the table. From Ha Joon's demeanour Cheong assumed that criticism would follow. The advisor however, was pleased.

"Good work, Cheong," he said as he looked up from the papers. "But I have to put a hold on your operation for the rest of the year. We've had word from our police connection that French customs officers are on the rampage. They are making a search of all antique dealers in Paris. Your connection there might unwittingly provide a lead to us. We can't be too careful."

"Those noted in the reports have already been shipped," Cheong said. "I have just a few at the museum. I will put a hold on them."

"Good," the advisor said curtly. "That's all."

Cheong bowed deeply and stood to leave. Chulsoo and Kouno turned from the glass veranda doors, bowed to the advisor, and followed Cheong out.

六

September 11th Nagoya

Late the following morning in Nagoya the sound of a doorbell roused the two women from their slumber. As Itsue lifted her head from the pillow she immediately regretted the amount of sake she had drunk the night before, she got up, wrapped a gown around herself, and shuffled to the front door. Françoise heard two male voices, a whispered greeting, and pulled the quilt over her head. A panelled door slid open and closed. Françoise eased the futon down, opened an eye, and saw Itsue kneeling on the other futon folding her bed sheets.

"*Bonjour,*" she muttered.

"*Ohayo,*" murmured Itsue.

Françoise winced and put her hand over her eyes. "Chulsoo's here?"

"Uh, huh, and his friend Kouno. They are just outside those doors."

A worried expression creased Françoise's brow. "Is there another way to the bathroom?"

"You can go out on the balcony and back in through the room next door but it is all right to go through the kitchen, they won't bite."

"I'd rather go out on the balcony."

"I'll go and unlock it."

Françoise bundled her clothes under her arm, slipped out onto the balcony and into the next room, gave a schoolgirl grin to Itsue and disappeared into the bathroom.

As Françoise emerged from the shower she heard a high pitched voice from the kitchen that sounded like the tail end of a heated conversation.

"Why didn't you tell me this before? Did you plan to tell me but it slipped your mind? Is that it?" Itsue demanded. In the silence that followed Françoise returned to the bedroom, dressed, then slid a partition door open to join the others. The two muscular men at the kitchen table made the room seem smaller than the previous evening. Similar in stature, dressed in blue and white sportswear they appeared to be brothers. One of them removed his sunglasses and placed them on the table with his white gloves.

"You are Françoise?" he asked.

"Yes, I am. And you are Itsue's fiancé Monsieur Chulsoo?"

A smile beamed across his face. "Yes, I am Itsue's secret lover."

"Stop it! Kouno," Itsue sighed exasperated and turned to Françoise. "That's Kouno," she said. "This is Chulsoo."

Kouno laughed at his brief deception and Chulsoo hesitantly extended his hand.

"My name is Chulsoo," he confirmed. As he spoke Françoise had the strange feeling that she had seen him somewhere before… at the airport perhaps?

"Bonjour Monsieur Chulsoo. Enchantée," Françoise greeted him.

"Nice to meet you," Chulsoo responded. "Kouno is a friend since junior high school."

Kouno and Françoise bowed to each other and uttered Japanese greetings.

"Hajimemashite. Yoroshiku Onegaitashimasu."

"Call me Ken," he said. "Kouno is my family name." His relaxed easy nature lightened the heavy atmosphere of first meetings.

"Would you like breakfast?" Itsue asked.

"Just coffee's fine," Françoise replied as she took a seat at the table.

Itsue skilfully avoided the eyes of both men as she put a pot of hot coffee, a mug and two thick slices of buttered toast on the table in front of Françoise.

"*Merci* Itsue. What time do we meet Professor Kitamura?"

"I'll be ready in fifteen minutes. Then it's about a forty minute drive or so."

Itsue headed for the bathroom. Françoise poured some black coffee for herself, had a sip, and a bite of toast, and then looked up at Chulsoo.

"Congratulations on your forthcoming wedding," She said.

"Thanks but I think Itsue may have just changed her mind."

"It's just a lover's quarrel. She'll calm down." Françoise changed tack and addressed Kouno. "You are Korean, Ken-san?"

"Yes, but born in Osaka. I met Chulsoo when he moved from Nagoya as a kid."

"Why did you move to Osaka Chulsoo? Because of your father's business?"

"No..." Chulsoo hesitated. Pressed his lips together and then explained that his father had disappeared when Chulsoo had been five years old. His mother had been afraid to raise her son alone and took him to live with her older brother in Tsuruhashi.

"That's what Itsue's mother has so cleverly just found out." He concluded.

"Had you been raised in Nagoya, would you not have any problems?"

"Problems yes," Kouno cut in, "but not quite the same prejudices. Chulsoo's problem is that his uncle has a company in Osaka that makes taiko drums and Japanese think the people who work for him are disreputable and don't want to be associated with them."

"Why should that be?" Françoise asked.

"Taiko drums are covered with animal hides. People who help make the drums come from the same families of Burakumin that have dealt with leather for generations."

"Oh!" Françoise exclaimed. "Yes. I've never made a connection between taiko drums and leather workers before but, Umm... now you mention it, I understand."

"Not only that," Kouno added, "Only Japanese drummers can give public performances, Koreans who build the drums are not allowed to join the Japanese drummers."

"But, that has changed," Chulsoo said," now that Kouno and me have become accepted drummers. I guess that is some kind of progress."

"Why don't you take Japanese nationality? Wouldn't that help?"

"Why should we go through a lengthy process to obtain Japanese nationality?" Kouno responded sharply. "We are proud of being Korean. Why can't we have the same rights as Japanese citizens, the right to vote for example, without having to change our nationality? We were born here and we pay taxes." Kouno ran out of steam and Chulsoo took up the thread, while Françoise stared at her coffee.

"You see, both our grandfathers were brought over to Japan as conscripted labour and our parents were born in Japan. We are the second generation in our families to be born here. Yet it's still hard for Koreans like us to find a job at Japanese companies and impossible to obtain work in local government. All because people like Itsue's family won't have anything to do with us. Our only chance of convincing her parents to let us marry is through Kitamura-san and his wife.

Kouno wandered to the window. Françoise sighed, took a last sip of coffee, and placed the mug and plate in the sink. "But you are not teenagers," she said over her shoulder. "You don't need your parents' permission to get married."

"It may seem strange to you as a European," Chulsoo said. "But respect for family is strong in both Korean and Japanese societies. Japanese parents have been known to cut all ties with children who have married into Korean families even to the extent of not acknowledging their own grandchildren. It can be that painful. But if we obtain even a reluctant approval from our families, we can avoid such unpleasantness."

Françoise turned to face Chulsoo and she saw why Itsue had fallen for him.

"I sure hope things work out and that you'll come to France for your honeymoon."

Before Chulsoo had a chance to reply Itsue strode into the room ready to leave.

"All right. Let's go," she said.

"To France?" Chulsoo queried.

"No. To Kitamura-sensei's," Itsue sighed. "And what's so funny?"

"No. Nothing. Come on let's go," Kouno replied.

As they ambled down the endless flight of stairs Kouno courteously waited for Françoise at each turn in the stairwell. Chulsoo's white Nissan Cima parked in the strong sun was hot inside. The two men got into the front and as soon as the air conditioner began to cool the air the women settled back into the spacious if rather garish maroon interior. Chulsoo behind the wheel drove slowly.

Itsue leant closer to her friend and spoke quietly. "I'm just not sure if I should go for this cross cultural marriage thing."

"You're both born and raised in Japan," Françoise objected as she puzzled over how Japanese seemed so nice to westerners yet so sharp to Asian peoples.

"It's the same in Europe," Itsue protested. "Europeans who fall in love with Orientals are easily tolerated yet those same Europeans may cast a critical eye towards Europeans who fall in love with Europeans of a different nationality."

"Where did you learn that?" Françoise asked with raised eyebrows.

"When we lived in France. Many Parisians expressed such opinions. Europeans are bemused when they deal with Asians and Japanese people are bemused when they deal with Europeans. The exotic partner does not belong to any of the local social classes and allowances are made for cultural misunderstandings. That can work very well for friendship and even for marriages if each partner genuinely develops the ability to merge the two cultures. But our marriage is between people from cultures that have in the past been severely antagonistic to each other. How do you think it would it be if you were to fall in love with a German or an Arab?"

Itsue got a tissue from her bag and wiped her eyes.

Françoise reached out to hold her friend's hand. "You do have a problem," she said.

"We know," Chulsoo interjected. "We just can't do anything about it."

"Chulsoo, just drive, will you?" Itsue retorted testily.

He had been driving carefully but listening to every word.

七

September 11th Nagoya

As Chulsoo pulled up in front of Kitamura Antiques, Itsue and Françoise waved at their Japanese history teacher seated outside his shop on a wooden bench. The professor stood to welcome his guests as the two women rushed to him. Kitamura, typical of Japanese old men seemed quite frail but, with not an ounce of fat on him, was as fit as a fiddle. He greeted the women and then turned to the men.

"And how are you, young Chulsoo? Staying out of trouble?"

"Trying to. Thanks," Chulsoo responded. "You are well?"

"I'm all right for my age and this is?" He raised questioning eyebrows towards Kouno.

"A friend from school days. Ken Kouno. Helping me look after Itsue and Françoise."

"Umm… and they'll need some looking after," he winked and the three men laughed.

Greetings exchanged, Kitamura called to his wife who had already heard voices and shuffled her way through the shop wiping her hands on her apron before greeting them.

"My, my, my," she beamed as she laid eyes on Françoise. "How you've grown."

"Hello Auntie. Yes it's been a long time, hasn't it?"

Kitamura's wife, Kyoko, was the elder sister of Itsue's mother and as such everyone called her Auntie, even her own husband.

"Come in. Come in. Come through to the house," Aunt Kyoko beckoned the two women to come through the shop to the living room in the rear.

"Won't you come in, too?" Kitamura enquired of Chulsoo and Kouno who stayed back near the car.

"Please go ahead," Chulsoo replied. "Françoise needs to talk with you and we are happy to have a smoke outside."

"As you wish," Kitamura replied, and followed the three women into the shop. Cluttered with lamps, bric-a-brac beyond description, gourds and curios that hung from every available beam, the darkened interior held nostalgic memories for Françoise.

"This place hasn't changed a bit," Françoise exclaimed as they entered the store. "Don't you ever sell anything, Sensei?"

"I just sold those two statues up at the back there, old Fugen and Monju," he replied. They laughed and went on through to the private living room at the back of the house.

Itsue went with her aunt into the kitchen and helped prepare some refreshments. Françoise and Kitamura seated themselves at either side of a low wooden table while the television provided background noise for their talk of old times. Françoise, enamoured by the vitality of this aged couple that procrastinated retirement, asked after their daily life. Countless numbers of similar small family business dotted the country and Françoise wondered how the pensioners found energy enough to run them. Of course, old people are skilled at getting assistance from others, so perhaps Itsue's mother helps them with their accounts and taxes.

Itsue and Aunt Kyoko rejoined Françoise and the Professor and brought iced wheat tea and a tray of sweet red bean savouries that had been steamed earlier that morning.

"Well, what brought you back here? Are you here for long?" Kitamura asked Françoise.

"It's just a short business trip. The Cernushi museum is preparing a third exhibition on the development of Buddhist art and we hope to borrow some sculptures with different artistic styles from the time when Buddhism was introduced from Korea, or should I say, Kudara as Japanese called the peninsular at that time?" Françoise quickly corrected herself as she remembered how the professor always insisted on using the terminology of the period to which people referred.

"Well, I don't know if you'll find many temples willing to lend out their ancient treasures," Kitamura said. "People that administer such things can be quite stern. These days they are more concerned with protecting the copyright image of their statues than with promoting historical information. You best go to see my old friend Kurosawa in Nara. He's an expert on that period. It's been a while since we've met but I haven't heard from any of his relatives, so he should still be alive. I'll call him and tell him you were a student of mine."

In their youth both Kitamura and his friend Kurosawa planned to live as monks but Kitamura gave up. "I was too interested in worldly pleasures," he explained. Kurosawa however, became abbot of the temple where he lived, then after his grandson was born passed the responsibility over to his son.

"Is the temple easy to find?" Françoise asked.

"Easy enough," Kitamura replied. "It's in Kasanui, near Kashihara City. Near the most famous Shinto shrine in the area Kashihara Shrine."

"What's the name of the temple?"

"Honkomyo-ji. Wait a minute. I have a map here somewhere."

He turned to a cabinet in the corner of the room pulled open the bottom drawer and flicked through files indexed according to Japanese Hiragana. The syllable YA appeared with several maps related to the Yamato area. Colours faded over the years but the paper was still in good condition. The old professor spread a relevant map out on the floor, leaned over it, and gestured for

Francoise to take notes. Itsue meanwhile noted the location on her mobile phone.

"See here," he began. "Take a Kintetsu express train to Yamato Yagi, then a local train to Kasanui, here's the station just two stops north. Ask a station attendant where the temple is, he is sure to know. Nowadays it will take perhaps thirty to forty minutes as opposed to one that would have taken a few days not so very long ago."

While Françoise noted station names and train connections Kitamura felt transported back to the classroom. "Ancient Nara, Heijo-kyo as it was called, was an expansive city that covered most of the northern part of the Yamato plain. It spread westwards as far as Saidai-ji and nearly as far south as this temple here in Kasanui."

"After the Asuka period, right?" Françoise asked.

"That's right. Between 710 and 784." The professor beamed and looked at her over the top of his glasses. "I'm pleased you remember your history lessons."

Delighted to be teaching again the professor continued his musing. "See prior to the Yamato era people inhabited an area further south around the village of Asuka. We know little about them except that they lived near to the mountains underneath straw roofs over shallow pits."

"Were they the indigenous people of Japan?" Itsue asked.

"Ah," Kitamura turned to his niece. "Itsue's young man likes to think they came from Korea and he could well be right but all we have are legends. There is no record of their origins. As far as historians are concerned there were two groups of people, the indigenous Jomon and the immigrant Yayoi. It's not possible to know which group took over the other or whether one was assimilated into the other. All we know is that in time people moved away from the protection of the mountains into the plains of northern Nara prefecture where they established Heijo-kyo. Still later they followed the rift between the mountains further northwards and found another great plain and established Heian-kyo. The modern Route 24 is probably the same route travelled by our ancestors. That was to be expected since only the northwest of Nara prefecture is flat and workable. Three quarters of the area is mountainous with peaks of nearly two thousand meters right there in the centre.

"Actually, Mount Koya in Wakayama prefecture," Kitamura continued, "was the perfect place for Kūkai to establish his temple. You remember learning about Kūkai?"

Françoise acknowledged that she did.

"It's well worth a visit if you have time. It's the centre of Shingon Buddhism and since the original Garan temple was built around 820, a secluded temple town has developed around the sect's headquarters. There are now more than a hundred temples, a town hall and a post office. They even have their own university. Many of the temples offer overnight stays where guests can experience the aesthetic life of the monks, and of course it is the site of Okuno-in, Kūkai's mausoleum."

"His ashes remain up there?" Françoise queried.

"Well, not quite. As Kūkai approached the end of his life he stopped consuming food and water and spent his time in meditation. At midnight on the 21st day of the third month of the year 835 he died at the age of 62, but Kūkai was not cremated. In accordance with his will he was entombed on the eastern peak of Mount Kōya.

Some time later, when the tomb was opened, Kūkai was found to be the same as before, his complexion unchanged and hair grown by a centimetre or two. Legend now has it that Kūkai has not died but has entered into eternal samadhi, awaiting the appearance of Maitreya. Monks bring food offerings to him twice a day but no one, except monks of the highest ranks, are allowed to view his body."

"It sounds a fascinating place. How long would it take to get there?" Françoise asked as she contemplated changing her plans.

"Indeed it's one of Japan's holiest places." Kitamura began. "From Osaka it would take you more than two hours by train, then you have to take a cable car to reach the top and about now it begins to get quite cold. There's a rather difficult multi day trek called the Kumano Kodo, which is a UNESCO registered pilgrimage route. A scenic 70 kilometre hike through the mountains that ends up at Mount Koya. However, now I think about it you wouldn't be able to go that way. That region still keeps some of the pilgrimage routes open only to men and..."

Sign on Mount Omine Nara Prefecture

"What do you mean?" Francoise interrupted somewhat rudely.

The professor chuckled. "I mean that some weeks ago a group of female teachers accompanied by a male teacher dressed as a women went there and the monks were very annoyed to see them on their territory. If you, a foreign woman, tried to enter the trails you would certainly be told to turn around."

"I can't believe it," Françoise shook her head.

"I know what you're thinking," Kitamura replied. It's not legal to stop people from using public land, right? On the other hand, not allowing people to practise traditions and customs because of modern rights is also questionable. When progress conflicts with traditions, people challenge ancient privileges with the law, but modern Japan is alive with ancient beliefs, and who is to say we should question them? It upsets people when new ideas erase the old ways without proper consideration. Auntie's sister for example, Itsue's mother, is convinced that Japanese people have a pure bloodline and will accept no argument to the contrary."

Aunt Kyoko began to fidget and Kitamura realised he may have said too much.

~

Outside in the heat the two Korean taiko drummers, Chulsoo and Kouno, stood conversing near the car, engine left idling to keep the air-conditioned interior cool. Kouno opened the front passenger door and reached inside the glove compartment for a pack of cigarettes just as his mobile phone rang. He dropped the packet on the seat, clicked the door closed, and ambled away from the car as he took the call. After repeating yes, yes, yes, several times the call ended and he returned to where Chulsoo leaned against the Cima.

"Cheong wants us at the Museum at nine o' clock tomorrow morning."

"What the hell for?"

"He didn't say." Kouno opened the car door, and retrieved the cigarettes from the seat.

"That uncle of mine is a pain," Chulsoo muttered.

"You are the pain," Kouno said as he lit himself a cigarette.

"Kouno, I need to stay here tonight. I want to talk with Itsue. I'll drop you off at Nagoya station and you can take the Shinkansen. It'll only take an hour to Osaka."

"And you? What will you do?"

"I'll take the highway early morning."

"You'll never make it through the morning rush hour. If you don't return to Osaka tonight, you'll never make it to the museum in time."

"Don't worry. I'll be there."

Kitamura heaved himself to his feet, called to the two men waiting outside and then addressed Françoise.

"Would you like to see the two statues I've just sold?"

"I'd like to, yes," Françoise said.

"They've been in the shop for years but I finally sold them to a British tourist. I told him they were not that old and probably artificially aged but he was taken with them and we made a deal."

"What kind of aging treatment?" Françoise asked.

"Probably buried in sand for a couple of months then dug up, washed off and left in the sun to crack. It's a simple process."

Kitamura turned, opened the street door, and beckoned to the two young men.

"Chulsoo," Kitamura began as soon as Chulsoo and Kouno stepped into the shop. "I need to get those two statues out of the window. Could you and your friend get them down for me?"

Françoise smiled at the way Kitamura so easily got the assistance he needed. Age did have certain advantages it seemed. Chulsoo slipped off his shoes and stepped up into the show window. He picked his way slowly between the pottery and iron antiques until he was near the statues.

"They might try and resist," Kitamura joked. "They've been there a long time." He spoke of the statues as if they had a will of their own, but Chulsoo easily lifted the first one then the other and handed each across to the muscular Kouno who with a firm grip lowered them carefully to the shop floor.

"Fugen and Monju Bosatsu," Kitamura muttered as Françoise cast a critical eye over them. "Otherwise known as Samantabhadra and Manjusri, their Sanskrit names. Sculpted in pairs they always travel together, one seated on an elephant, the other on a lion. This one represents emotion, the other intellect."

"Well, but still in excellent condition despite having been artificially aged," Françoise said. "I hope you got a good price."

"Well, they're not paid for yet. The gentleman is coming back at the end of the week to pick them up." He turned to the two men. "Thank you, both of you. You have saved me a lot of trouble. Come into the back and let's see if Auntie can find you both a drink."

"We really should be on our way," Chulsoo declined the offer. "Kouno here needs to get back to Osaka earlier than planned so we better leave soon."

Itsue was visibly surprised, but finally agreed it was getting late and they gathered outside the shop to say their goodbyes. Kitamura told them to drive carefully. Aunt Kyoko fussed that they would be all right. Françoise thanked them both. Itsue promised she would see them soon and they were on their way back across the river to Nagoya.

"What is this sudden rush?" Itsue demanded.

"Sorry Itsue," Kouno apologised, "but I had a call from our boss and he wants to see us both early tomorrow morning. Chulsoo should come too but he's going to…"

"We'll drop Kouno off at Nagoya station," Chulsoo interrupted, "and then I'll take you both back to your place."

They pulled into the forecourt of Nagoya Shinkansen station. Kouno got out of the car and put his head back in at the window.

"Goodbye Françoise. It was nice to have met you. I hope we can meet again sometime." He looked across at Chulsoo. "Nine o'clock at the museum. You'd better be there!"

"I'll be there. Don't worry."

"You're crazy." Kouno stepped back and Chulsoo drove off.

"What did he mean by that?" Itsue asked as they left the station precincts.

"He's angry because I wouldn't go back to Osaka with him, but I want to explain to you why it was that I was brought up in Tsuruhashi."

"Chulsoo, we need to talk but not now. I have a guest."

Chulsoo concentrated on the road without answering. When he pulled up outside Itsue's apartment she leaned forward and put her hands on the back of the front seat. "Chulsoo, I will call you as soon as I have time."

He turned and slid his arm along the back of the seat and grabbed her arm. "Can I come in for a coffee?"

"No, you can't! Go and stay with your aunt!"

He released her and got out of the car.

"I'll call you," he shouted across the Cima as the two women got out of the car.

"No! I'll call you. It's better that way. I need to think."

He let out a frustrated sigh, nodded to Françoise, got back into his car and drove off.

Itsue and Françoise started up the stairs to the apartment. Françoise, still not used to the number of steps, lagged behind. Finally they reached the fifth floor, Itsue unlocked the door and they stepped into their inviting slippers.

"Oh! Françoise, it's so infuriating. What am I going to do? He admitted he was brought up in Tsuruhashi. What did he want to explain? What if Mother's right and his uncle is a gangster? Would that make him a gangster too?"

"Do you know anyone in that taiko group?"

"No. The only friend of his I've ever met is Kouno."

"What if he is a gangster? Would he have to stay with them?"

"I don't know.… There are lots of things I don't know.…" Itsue slid open one of the fusuma panels and stepped into the room beyond. "But if you are going to go to Yamato Yagi tomorrow you better get some sleep." Itsue opened another panel in front of a built in cupboard, pulled out the futons, and laid them neatly on the tatami floor. Françoise's bedding nearest the tokonoma, considered a place of honour for the guest and a tradition resolutely practiced by most Japanese.

~

Out on the Meishin highway heading back across the river towards Osaka Chulsoo consulted his navigation system. Instead of returning to Osaka that night and taking the Kintetsu Express in the morning, as Kouno would do, he could go straight to the museum at sun up. He would drive south to Kameyama Junction leave the highway at Hisai Interchange, join Route 165 and, allowing for heavy traffic, he could easily be there on time. So, tired and hungry, he eased his Cima into the Oyamada Service area, strode into the restaurant and ordered a bowl of pork soup ramen noodles with a side dish of kimchi. He took the food to an empty booth and slurped away at his evening meal. Afterwards, alone in the booth he stretched out on the bench seat, checked his mobile phone for messages then began to play a downloaded baseball game. Minutes later he was sound asleep.

~

Part Two

Hollowing out a Buddhist Icon

八

September 12th Sakakibara-Onsenguchi

"Where is he? This fool nephew of mine," Cheong exclaimed as he paced the office of the syndicate's headquarters. It was 9:30 and Chulsoo had failed to show up.

"You say he spent the night in Nagoya?"

"I can't be sure," Kouno replied. "We spent a day together in Nagoya with Itsue and her friend from France. Chulsoo dropped me off at the station in the evening and said he was going to take them to Itsue's apartment. He may have stayed in Nagoya."

"His woman had a French friend with her?"

"Yes. Françoise. A sexy name don't you think?"

Cheong cast the younger man a sideways glance. "I'm not interested in your erotic fantasies. Call him on your mobile."

"No response," Kouno said, his phone still ringing Chulsoo's number.

Cheong's breathing became irregular. He had an appointment in Mie prefecture with two important leaders of affiliated families in Nagoya, and being late made him anxious. There were statues packed and stored and he had to ensure they were shipped on time. Being behind schedule was simply not acceptable. Why hadn't his nephew come with Kouno? And why didn't he answer his mobile?

"The love sick lad is losing his mind," Cheong muttered. "Go get the car, Kouno."

Kouno took the keys from the desk, hastened briskly to the parking lot, unlocked the black limousine and got behind the wheel. Only Kouno, who still possessed a clean drivers license, was allowed to drive Cheong's treasured Sovereign President. He eased the car slowly around to the front of the building and waited for his boss. Cheong strode out of the office, climbed in the back behind the black tinted windows, and tossed his newspaper onto the seat beside him. Without a word Kouno eased out into the traffic.

They followed the route towards Nagoya then took the road to Sakakibara Onsenguchi, a spa town on the Kintetsu railway line. The black Sovereign President squeezed tightly through a narrow railway underpass and turned sharply to the right. They passed a couple of farmhouses and a derelict structure that was once a thriving restaurant in the days when tour buses visited the area.

Cheong's limousine cruised slowly past life sized replicas of the winged goddess Nike and other plaster cast statues that stood on the outside corners of a museum building, around a half dozen vehicles in the parking lot, and pulled up outside the entrance to a temple complex. At the further end of which, set against tree-covered mountains, a thirty-three-metre gold-plated statue of Kannon Bosatsu cast benevolence down on the innocent and guilty alike. There was no sign of his two colleagues and Cheong sighed with relief.

"Kouno," Cheong began, "take the car back down to the entrance and wait for the guests. When they arrive take them to the office and tell them I'll be there soon." Cheong then strode off towards a prefabricated workshop at the top of a slight incline. As instructed, Kouno drove back down to the narrow country road and stopped in front of a black Mercedes 900 and a Mercedes 850 already parked on the side of the road just below the elevated

Kintetsu station. The drivers stood beside the cars while Cheong's guests approached Kouno.

"*Irashaimase,*" Kouno bowed and addressed them respectfully. "*Kochira no hou, dozo.*"

The two men nodded and followed him up the slope, into the museum and up the stairs to Cheong's office. Kouno closed the door behind them, peeled off his white gloves and went in search of his boss.

At the prefabricated building Cheong found the door unlocked, and charged straight into the room. Lights blazed overhead. Five Buddhist statues stood along one wall others of European origin against the opposite wall. A workbench and an overhead winch were near the back wall and bundles of packing material littered a corner. Two men in their late twenties, who were playing Koi-Koi on an improvised table set between them, jumped to their feet when they saw Cheong approach, the Hanafuda cards fell to the floor. Three others who chatted and joked stopped abruptly.

"Why is that door unlocked?" Cheong demanded as he neared them. "Why is there no one outside keeping visitors away from this area?"

Stillness filled the workshop. The calm tone in which the question was articulated meant reprimands would soon be made.

"Shou... should it be locked when we are in here?" One of the men stammered.

Cheong jabbed a finger in the man's chest. "I told you to make sure no one could see what was going on in here. I just walked in as easy as walking into an Izakaya. Get someone outside to watch that door. Now!" Cheong pushed the man away from him and approached the statue on the bench; a replica of Samantabhadra seated on an elephant. Manjusri seated on a lion was already securely packed and stacked on a pallet.

"Have they both been hollowed out and loaded?" Cheong asked.

"Yes sir."

"How much?"

"Five bundles in each."

"Any problems?"

Cheong ran his fingers over the delicate wooden sculpture. He procured the two statues himself and knew that his contact in France would be able to get a substantial price of which he would get a handsome cut. Suddenly he frowned and glared at the man opposite him. A crack snaked across the elephant's back and up the side of the icon.

"This is cracked!" Cheong said in astonishment.

"Err... it got... err... it cracked during the hollowing out and..."

Cheong's facial muscles tightened as he leaned towards the man. "What happened?"

"Err... we took out the insides from the back then, when we turned it over, we found this crack on the outside."

There was a pause as Cheong let out a deep sigh.

"What about the other one?"

An icy finger ran down the man's back.

"Was it damaged?" Cheong demanded.

"Ah... a little. Not as bad as this one."

Cheong gave the man a sideways glance. "Unpack it!"

⁓

Kouno ran across the parking lot, approached the man now stationed at the workshop door, and inquired after Cheong. The man acknowledged with a simple nod that Cheong was inside. Kouno went in but stopped near the door, and watched as three men at the far end of the room hoisted a packed statue onto the workbench, cut through the bindings and peeled off the packing material. The exquisitely carved statue lay exposed before them and Cheong's eyes opened wide as he studied the hairline fracture that ran down the side of the statue straight across the lion's face.

"Do you idiots have any idea how much these statues are worth?" Cheong asked.

"We were doing our best…" one of the workers began.

"*Urusai!*" Cheong growled as he smashed his fist into the side of the man's face. Cheong turned, ignored Kouno as he strode out of the room, and marched diagonally across the parking lot. He entered the temple complex by a side door and took a back route into the museum and continued up the stairs to his office on the second floor. Cheong's two guests found the Hanafuda cards kept on Cheong's desk and were engaged in a game when Cheong walked in. He greeted the two leaders, apologized, and slumped down into his chair clenching and unclenching his fist.

Kouno who followed Cheong at a discrete distance went to the window overlooking the parking lot and reached into his pocket for a pack of cigarettes when he saw Chulsoo's car burst from the short tunnel under the tracks, screech around the corner and pass within inches of the two black Mercedes and Cheong's limousine parked on the side of the road.

"Here comes Chulsoo now," Kouno said still looking out of the window. The white Cima charged across the parking lot and pulled up next to Kouno's shiny black Lexus. Chulsoo leapt from his car, slammed the door behind him, and ran across to the main temple entrance. Minutes later Kouno saw him emerge from the temple and head for the prefabricated workshop. Then, after an exchange with the man outside, turn and head back across the parking lot towards the museum.

Cheong still rubbing his hand, finished telling his colleagues what happened.

"You're getting too old for physical fights," one of them joked. "You may end up with more than bruises one day."

"You may be right," Cheong acknowledged, "Anyway holding off on the exports as the advisor has ordered will give us time to find someone to repair those statues."

Kouno heard a chance to boost his worth. He turned from the window and asked for permission to speak.

"What is it Kouno?" Cheong asked.

"Those statues are Bosatsu Fugen and Bosatsu Monju, right?"

Cheong raised his eyebrows and nodded. "Yeah, they are known as Fugen and Monju."

"I know where to find two replacements. They may not be exactly the same but…"

"And where would that be?" Cheong interrupted.

"They are in an antique shop in Nagoya owned by Chulsoo's fiancée's old professor."

Cheong grinned at the idea of stirring up discord between the two lovers.

"They're inside the front door waiting collection by a…"

"Never mind," Cheong heard Chulsoo on the stairs outside, and cut him off. "What's the address?" Kouno quickly described the location and Cheong looked at his colleagues.

"We can find it," one of the senior men assured him.

"Thank you Kouno," Cheong said as he heaved himself from the easy chair. "Perhaps I will enjoy my game of golf after all."

Chulsoo burst through the door as his uncle and the others were about to leave.

"So you finally managed to tear yourself away from your lover."

"There's no excuse, Uncle. There was some trouble getting down here and…"

Cheong snarled and forced him back against the wall as the senior men went out. "Come on," Cheong shouted from the bottom of the stairs. We are going to have a round of golf. You can caddy for me. Ha, ha, ha, ha."

Humiliation was the reprimand. Chulsoo's lateness embarrassed his uncle in the presence of the other leaders. Now his uncle would humiliate him to save face. Chulsoo would have to tag along with the middle-aged women hired to pull the golf carts.

On the way to the cars Kouno, several paces behind the leaders, turned and gave Chulsoo an inquisitive stare.

"Some idiot ran into me at the highway interchange and called the cops. I had to..."

Chulsoo could not finish his explanation. The drivers waiting by the cars flicked their cigarette butts into the open ditch at the sight of the five men that strode towards them. Cheong took out a cigarillo and Kouno stepped forward with a lighter. Cheong accepted the light, turned and got into his prized Sovereign President. Chulsoo got in the front passenger seat and Kouno slid behind the wheel. The other mobsters boarded their autos and, as the train above pulled out of the station, the three limousines moved off down the narrow road.

Two hours later on the green of the eighteenth hole at Prince Lakewood Golf Club Cheong lined up his putt and sank the ball from just under seven yards. He retrieved the ball marked his card and handed it to Chulsoo. He retired to the edge of the green, waited while his colleagues finished their putts and the three men then marched off laughing towards the clubhouse.

Chulsoo accompanied the two other caddies to return the trolleys and other goods they borrowed. He checked the card and saw his uncle marked himself one short on three of the holes, he suspected the other senior members probably knew but thought it better to humor their host. They enjoyed the game anyway and Cheong was always in a better mood when he won.

After the group had enjoyed a drink at the bar, the waiter personally escorted these special customers to a table looking out over the greens. During lunch, much to Cheong's enjoyment, Chulsoo endured the jibes of the two senior men about his skills as a caddy. After the meal Cheong leaned back in his chair, stretched his arms, made his neck crack as he rolled his head around on his shoulders, and announced that he wanted to go to the spa.

The younger men went across to the golf club car park and brought the cars around to the front of the clubhouse. The two other mobsters took their leave and drove off. Then, with Chulsoo in the front and Kouno behind the wheel Cheong's Sovereign President slowly cruised along the country roads headed for the hot spring.

Upon arrival at the spa the three men met the stern faced manager of the spa who took a few seconds before he welcomed them with the usual *'Irashaimase'*. The manager was uncomfortable in allowing them into the premises but he had done so before and could now hardly refuse them entry. Although people with tattoos were forbidden to enter the baths, Cheong had previously explained, somewhat forcefully, that since it was early afternoon, there would only be a few visitors, so no one would be offended by his tattoo.

The three men went to the changing rooms, stripped and secured their clothes in the lockers. They wrapped the orange plastic straps that held the locker keys around their wrists and with long narrow towels held modestly in front of their privates entered the steamy baths. Chulsoo and Kouno seated themselves at shower cubicles and soaped up from head to toe. Cheong approached the largest of the baths, squatted beside it, scooped a hand basin in the water and doused himself two or three times before he got into the forty-two degree Celsius water to relax.

Ten minutes later Cheong left the bath, testicles elongated by the heat swayed gently under his bloated belly as he stepped over the wet tiles towards the two younger men. He squatted precariously on a small plastic stool, dropped his wet hand towel into Chulsoo's lap and turned his back towards him. Chulsoo picked up the towel, handed it to Kouno and strolled off to soak in a bathtub.

Cheong turned slightly and cast a dark frown over at his nephew. Kouno laid the long white towel across his thigh, rubbed a bar of soap over it several times, slapped it on his boss' ample back, and started to wash the entwined chrysanthemum and nude figures tattooed on the fleshy canvas. From the base of Cheong's neck the tattoo encircled his arms to his wrists, covered his entire back, and extended below his waist onto his upper buttocks. Kouno knew the exquisite pain of the Japanese tattooist's needles they experienced little by little over the years. His own tattoo; a weasel fighting two snakes covered most of his back from below his neckline, and encircled his upper arms to the elbow. In time, more tattoos would cover his back completely. Chulsoo's meager tattoo however; a leaping carp, only spread across his shoulder blades and the backs of his upper arms. It would soon need to be embellished.

The hot mineral waters of the spa helped the men relax and two hours later they left the hot spring and headed for the office in Kashihara. Chulsoo opened the rear door for his uncle but Cheong indicated for him to get in the back and then climbed in beside him. With Kouno at the wheel they drove off. Cheong leaned heavily on the armrest between Chulsoo and himself.

"Ondore ahondara ka na! Kesa do nai shitan ya!

"You're a damn fool idiot," Cheong addressed his nephew with disdain. "What happened this morning?"

"A car ran into me at the highway interchange. The cops were there and I..."

"Ha, ha, ha, ha. Trouble with the law, eh?" He interrupted. "You know how much I hate people who are late and you know how much the people I deal with would like to trip me up for any reason at all." His voice low and calm coupled with his powerful frame instilled fear. "Next time, keep driving! Don't hang around for the law like a stupid schoolboy waiting for his mother."

In the front seat Kouno's head eased inconspicuously back towards the headrest. In the back Cheong leaned over to his nephew.

"That woman in Nagoya will be your downfall. Terminate your relationship with her!"

"That's an unreasonable request," Chulsoo retorted as he turned to face his uncle.

"I'm not asking you. I'm telling you," Cheong continued unperturbed. "Your alliance with her has already caused me enough problems. Dump her!"

"Other organization members have women," Chulsoo protested.

"A strong leader must rid himself of soft feelings. Why do you think I never married? Discord between you and a woman will make you unfaithful to the organization." Cheong paused to let the point sink in. Chulsoo faced forward.

"I've had women but I never let my brain rest in my pants. I knew what I wanted. I enjoyed my time with them and said goodbye. Women are fickle and if you upset them, one way or another they'll get back at you, so never give them a chance." He paused again, this time with a stern look at the side of Chulsoo's face.

"Have I said enough?"

"You have made it clear Uncle. Yes."

Chulsoo stared straight ahead. Did he know what he wanted? Would it be possible to make a life with Itsue away from the organization he grew up with? If he wanted to break away, now was the time.

九

September 12th Nagoya to Yamato-Yagi

The high speed Shinkansen trains from Nagoya that head for Osaka travel northwest through several built up industrial areas before crossing the border into Shiga prefecture. They then turn southwards alongside Biwa-ko, the nation's largest lake and on to Kyoto, the ancient capital with its countless temples and shrines. Then to Osaka, the second most important commercial centre in Japan. Here passengers could transfer to a local train and travel back eastwards to reach Nara. There are however, other interesting alternative routes.

Françoise travelled from Tokyo to Nagoya on the Shinkansen two days earlier but had not been able to notice when the train left the sprawling capital. The mass of factories and residences seemed endless, and there were never so few of them for her to make a clear distinction between city and rural areas.

Now on her way to Nara, Françoise decided to follow the advice of her old teacher, Kitamura and enjoy a more leisurely journey on the Kintetsu line. This course would take her through two designated quasi-national parks. The train would run southwards along the Pacific Coast, then swing inland and travel westwards across Nara prefecture to Osaka, on the opposite side of the Kii peninsula.

75

After a late breakfast Itsue drove Françoise to Nagoya Kintetsu station where she would become part of the usual Sunday morning passengers: young couples, groups of hikers, and middle aged women headed for shopping malls. Itsue bought a platform ticket and accompanied her friend to the door of her carriage. Françoise paid almost double the ordinary fair for a reserved seat on an express, but Itsue assured her it was worth it, the local train would take far too long to reach Yamato Yagi. So Françoise boarded the yellow and blue train, found her place, eased the reclining seat back, and from the upper deck of the two-floor vista car began to enjoy the panorama of the Japanese countryside. If it had not been for the cackling women further down the carriage behind her, the journey would have been far more enjoyable.

The train sped south along the coast past the fishermen's homes that lined the wide Kiso and Ibi estuaries. The sea remained hidden behind two and three-story tile roofed houses; only the expressionless sky with its invisible horizon belied its existence. The rarity of high-rise structures contrasted greatly with the full-blown areas of Tokyo. Even the busy port city of Yokkaichi just southwest of Nagoya, with its conspicuous red and white industrial chimneys, was blessed with some unoccupied land between houses.

Françoise gave a wry smile as the train passed a handful of ornate hotels with fairy tale towers and painted out windows. Tourists perhaps perceived them as abandoned buildings, but these facilities were designated love hotels. In an overpopulated society where parents and children lived together in close proximity with bedrooms sometimes separated only by paper sliding doors, renting a room on occasion for a few hours privacy, without revealing identity, was convenient for many couples.

After brief stops at Shiroko and Tsu, the train reached the major junction of Ise-Nakagawa. Françoise quickly changed to the waiting yellow and white express from Ise, bound for Osaka, and settled back in her seat. The train pulled onto the line that looped around westwards and headed across a vast plain of rice paddies towards Yamato Yagi. Here Françoise would change trains and go to Asuka. Other art professionals would perhaps have selected a visit to Nara and the temples, designated as World Heritage Sites, that were of appeal to historians, religious leaders and artists alike. Françoise however, wanted to experience the ambience of the unpretentious village of Asuka for herself, the village where the people of Paekche introduced Buddhism to Japan and left behind so many sculptures, ancient tombs, and ruins.

As Françoise pushed an empty can of wheat tea into the net pocket on the back of the seat in front of her the train emerged from a tunnel and stopped at a station. Her eyes widened in amazement at an imposing collection of statues on the opposite side of the tracks and, along with other passengers who left their seats for a better view, Françoise went to the carriage windows on the other side of the train.

At the far end of the lush green valley that extended away from the station stood an enormous golden statue of the Kannon Bosatsu clearly visible above the treetops. It faced a square white edifice surrounded by other sizable sculptures. A replica of Aphrodite of Milos, the Greek goddess of love and beauty on one corner, and a replica of the second century BC Greek statue, the headless winged Nike of Samothrace on another. Behind the building Françoise could see the wings of yet another copy of Nike that faced away from the train and, off to the side a replica of New York's Statue of Liberty. The statues seemed to have been dropped from nowhere into the middle of this luxuriant valley. Stranger still the architect had modelled the pyramid shaped roof after the Louvre Gallery in Paris.

Qui a voulu déranger la campagne avec ces caricatures impaires? Françoise thought to herself. *Est-ce que c'était exotique?* Except for farmland and a forlorn restaurant there was nothing in sight. Japanese artists usually show a great sense of aesthetics, but this combination of replicas erected amongst the serene natural beauty of the countryside bothered yet intrigued her.

Her attention was drawn to two men slouched near highly polished black limousines parked below the station. Their leisurely manner came to an abrupt halt as a group of other men came into view along the side of the white building. The men near the cars threw their cigarette butts into the open ditch and accompanied two of the older men to the front two cars. The other three stopped at the last car. One of them, an older heavily built man, reminded Françoise of Monsieur Moustache and she leaned forward to gain a better look. At the same instant, one of the younger men obscured her view as he stepped forward to light the older man's cigar. The older man then turned and the men got into their respective cars. Within minutes, just as her train started to pull out of the station, the three limousines moved off down the narrow country lane. Françoise quickly read the name of the station as the board slipped past the window. 'Sakakibara Onsenguchi' printed in Chinese characters and Roman letters that indicated a nearby spa. *Quel long nom,* she thought as she wrote it down in her notebook. *Une ville avec une station thermale, c'est sûrement une attraction touristique alors,* she concluded.

As Françoise settled back in her seat she remembered that during the 80's, the so-called bubble years of Japan's economic growth, landowners made a killing on golf club developments and the astronomical membership fees. Pressured by their superiors, businessmen joined golf clubs and gangsters reaped a nice percentage of company expenses. Idly she studied her map of the area and counted fifteen golf courses cut into the countryside, a further twenty of them spread between there and the city of Nara. In a booming economy the complex relationships between government, business and the underworld helped the wheels of society run smoothly and a cooperative lifestyle had been accomplished. However, with the decline of the economy Japanese companies could no longer afford such huge expenses for employees' recreational activities, consequently underworld organizations also suffered and turned to other enterprises.

The train trundled through a long tunnel and, as it emerged into the light, Françoise looked out at the Japanese countryside. The tracks followed the curve of a mountain range that ran east to west. On the left, mountainous peaks while on the opposite side of the tracks hillsides dropped away to lush valleys. From the cool interior of the air-conditioned train, the sun ablaze on the rich green panoramic tapestry of ripening paddies called for a moment of contemplation.

After a brief stop at Nabari, the picturesque villages nestled in the narrow valleys began to alternate with clusters of cultivated Japanese cedar trees and skilfully tended bamboo groves. The high walls of thatched farmhouses and storage barns contrasted sharply with the lower walls of modest homes and the open fronts of village shops. Eventually the train slowed as it approached Yamato Yagi. The rice terraces became smaller and abruptly the scenery shifted to fewer paddies and more homes. It was here that Françoise was to change trains but, as it was such a beautiful autumn day, instead of catching the local train north to Kasanui, she would keep to her original plan and welcomed the idea of spending the rest of the day exploring Asuka. Françoise closed her bag, pulled her case from the overhead rack, then walked to the end of the carriage and stood in line with the other passengers waiting to disembark.

As Françoise checked the hotel reservation Itsue had given her, she found the business hotel booked for her was in Kashihara city. *Pourquoi alors suis-je descendue à Yamato Yagi?* she wondered, but after she confirmed directions to the hotel with the station clerk, she found that Professor Kitamura had failed to clarify that Yamato Yagi was only the name of the station, this was indeed Kashihara City. Françoise walked the short distance to the Kanko Hotel Kawai where a white painted façade and an open door greeted her. A casually dressed male clerk in his mid thirties checked the reservation and asked if she preferred a Japanese or western style room, she chose a Japanese room with shared bathroom. The tatami floor would give her extra space to sort out her brochures and documents before the futon was laid out in the evening. The sparsely furnished room had a low table with tea making utensils and a wide screen television, but was perfectly adequate for her needs. Françoise left her case in the corner of the room and returned to the station, bought a ticket for Asuka, and went to the platform to wait for a train that would take her four stations southwards.

$+$

September 12th Asuka

As soon as Françoise walked out of Asuka station and descended the short flight of steps to the road, a man in his seventies walked towards her.

"Hi. You want rent bicycle?"

Bonne idée, Françoise thought. "How much?"

"One day, one thousand yen. I have a good map for you."

Françoise nodded and followed him to a nearby kiosk. The man handed her the map and pointed to an easy bicycle route to follow. Françoise recognised names of locations as she searched for the specific destinations she wanted to visit.

"Tachibana-dera where Prince Shotoku was born is where?"

"Oh! It is here," He pointed it out on the map. "You know more than Japanese people!"

"No, I don't think so. Where is Asuka-dera?"

"Here!" He pointed to the map again then led her across to the cycles, pulled one out from the rack and stood it on its stand. He thanked her for the thousand yen bill she handed him and wished her a pleasant day. He then rushed back to the station steps, eager to catch another potential customer.

Without further ado Françoise set off down the narrow paths between open rice fields on her way to encounter the ancestry of this tranquil village. Temples, palace remains, tumuli, archaeological ruins and unusual stones awaited her among the sites. Her first stop was the curious *kame ishi* or tortoise stone, a carved granite stone of the seventh century. Françoise recognised the face of a turtle right away. Enchanted by the work but pressed for time she continued to Tachibana-dera where she stopped, locked the cycle and entered the temple precincts. Just inside stood a statue of Prince Shotoku's proud horse. Before he founded Horyu-ji in 607 Prince Shotoku travelled regularly from Tachibana to Asuka-dera in order to engage in his studies of Buddhism. Inside the temple Françoise studied the eight statues and regretted not having contacted the temple earlier. There was no one in sight and she judged it inappropriate to disturb the residents without an appointment, instead she made a note of two sculptures that would be appropriate for the exhibition with the intention of contacting the temple later.

Françoise cycled on to Asuka-dera and there found a representation of Prince Shotoku as a young man to which the sculptors had given a rather feminine appearance. Along with other kannons there was also a rather special bronze Buddha, and Françoise was facing this statue when a female monk in grey kimono arrived and introduced herself as the current abbot of Asuka-dera.

"An interesting statue, isn't it? Half of the visage shows great gentleness while the other half presents a more severe countenance," the abbot explained. "Viewed from one side it seems peaceful from the other it appears annoyed."

Françoise quickly took the opportunity to inquire about the loan of statues, she explained who she was, about the Cernushi's forthcoming exhibition, and asked if a European museum would be able to borrow sculptures.

"*So desu ne...*" the woman hesitated. You would need to write or call the main temple of the sect. I do not have authority to deal with a project of that scale. I will give you the address and phone number," she turned and went back into the temple.

While Françoise waited for the contact information a scroll written in Korean Hangul script caught her eye and when the abbot returned Françoise asked about it.

"Oh, a gift from Paekche monks centuries ago," the abbot explained. "It was a Paekche emperor who urged Japanese to adopt Buddhism. Their artisans built our first temples right here in Asuka. In those days we Japanese did not have such advanced forms of architecture or sculpture and we relied on the people of Kudara to erect temples and statues. Perhaps you are aware that the adoption of Buddhism came slowly and painfully to Japan. It took fifty years of conflict before Buddhism was truly established. The new religion brought many cultural ideas from other countries. It was only after numerous battles and civil wars that Buddhism began to shape our society."

"What affect did that have on ordinary people?" asked Françoise.

"Buddhism remodelled our lives, our social structure, and most importantly the instigation of writing with Chinese characters."

"So the whole country went through a kind of culture shock?"

"Umm... an interesting expression. I have only heard that term refer to overseas travels but you're right. It must have been a tremendous upheaval for citizens of that period. The new cultural teachings brought contradictions, insecurity, anxiety and a major threat to our own indigenous Shinto religion. We could have abandoned it and converted to the new faith but Buddhism defined the gods of Shintoism as incarnations of counterpart Buddhist deities, incorporated them into the new teachings and now both are still practiced in our society. People take their babies and children to a Shinto shrine to be blessed, but opt for a Buddhist funeral. That may sound strange, but for us it is natural, a way to promote harmony, don't you think?"

"It got more complex when Christianity came along though?" Françoise said.

"We did not do well then," the abbot acknowledged. "Our emperor did not like the idea of someone more powerful than he. There was persecution. Christian converts hid or were executed, but nowadays Buddhist and Shintoist respect churchgoers, indeed most Japanese have a Christian wedding ceremony, even they are not Christian."

Françoise glanced through the open temple doors. The green hills and bamboo groves beckoned her to pursue her tour of the multiple ruins and religious sites of the region. She bade a gracious farewell to the abbot, went back to her bicycle and cycled back to the road she had taken from Asuka. The temperature was now almost 30 degrees Celsius and, as she contemplated whether to go next to Asuka Folk Museum or the Historical Museum, an ice cream vendor in a parking lot across the street caught her attention. Françoise cycled over and pointed to an advertisement for green tea flavoured ice cream. The man nodded, gave her a generous portion, and attempted conversation.

"*Nihongo wakarimasu ka?*"

"*So desu ne,*" Françoise replied.

"What did you see in Asuka?"

Françoise enumerated the places she had visited and mentioned the tortoise stone.

"Some people say it looks like a toad."

"Do you know what it was used for?" Françoise risked a difficult question.

"Oh, we have theories but no one knows the secret of these stones. Some may have defined boundaries of fields, bigger ones may have been monuments or tombs and others might have formed part of a dam. Who knows? If you are interested there are other granite stones at Asuka Historical Museum."

That suggestion ended Françoise's dilemma. She thanked him and rode off, steering with one hand and holding her green tea flavoured ice cream in the other.

In the gardens of Asuka Historical Museum Françoise strolled among reproductions of ancient works, the *Shumisen Seki*, Mount Sumeru Stone, with its carved pattern of mountains and waves, symbolic of the inaccessible mountain at the center of the universe, that probably served as a fountain in a courtyard some thirteen hundred years ago, and others, all of them with unique characteristics. Françoise recognised the *Nimen Seki*, Two Faced Stone that represented forces of good and evil, for she had just seen the original in the precincts of Tachibana-dera.

Françoise entered the museum and as she walked around began to understand the historical importance of Asuka a little more. She had not expected to be so enthralled with stones, and there were other places she wished to visit, but her tour of Asuka would have to remain incomplete. She considered a request to her boss for more time but decided against it. She purchased a can of tea from a vending machine and looked over the pamphlets in the rest area. A leaflet about the Japanese book of Man'yoshu caught her eye. It was comprised of a series of poems much related to Asuka, she took a seat near the exit, opened the leaflet, and read one of the lyrics.

Composed by Yamabe-no-Akahito on ascending Kamuoka.

The old capital that was our teacher
In Asuka
We had intended
To make our visits here always
Thinking it would be without end
And continue from generation to generations
Like the Tsuga trees that grow lush
Extending their many branches
Over the Mimoro no Kabunamiyama
The old capital with its hills seen tall
And its magnificent river
The mountains especially pleasing to see

On a day in spring
The streams so especially clear
On an autumn night
Cranes winging confusedly in sunrise clouds
And frogs croaking in the evening mists
Now whenever I see the place
I cannot but weep aloud
Remembering old days

Françoise was touched by the self-composed and noble expressions with which artists had so aesthetically created the works around Asuka. Stone works dating from the seventh century and temples built in the early eighth century made Françoise ponder human nature's need to create such works. There was no end to the exploration of the Yamato area. The most crucial thing perhaps was not to see everything or to remember all historical events, but rather to experience sentiments attached to such a rich culture, embedded in an environment that inspired peace and tranquillity. *Si seulement je pouvais reproduire ceci chez Cernushi,* she thought.

It was three o'clock and the extreme heat made the coolness of the mountains at Yoshino appealing but her visit to Asuka had taken longer than expected. The idea of climbing up to Kimpu-jinja and Kimpusen-ji would have to be abandoned, unfortunate because the latter was the second oldest wooden structure in Japan. Since centuries past, pilgrims on their way up Omine Mountain stopped at this temple to pray for safety. Then Françoise remembered the professor's comments about women not being allowed to ascend to the top, so perhaps it was just as well. Françoise decided instead to return to Kashihara and catch up on her paperwork. She cycled back to the station. A sullen teenager with dyed orange hair left in charge of the rental cycle stand took charge of the bicycle. Françoise ascended the steps to the station and bought a ticket to Yamato Yagi.

十一

September 12th Kasanui

From kindergarten to senior high Shigehiro and his friend Toshio attended the same schools, then their roads diverged. Shigehiro pursued theology and Buddhist history while Toshio studied economics and business administration, but they had forged a relationship that stood the test of time and even now, in spite of their opposing professional interests, they continued to appreciate each other's friendship. As usual in late September Toshio came up from Osaka not only to help with the harvest, but also to enjoy the pot stew and beer that would be served after a day of intensive labor.

While their Grandparents talked inside the grounds of Honkyomo-ji, the two younger men wandered out of the temple gate down the country lane and stood on the narrow grassy verge at the side of the path. Shigehiro stared at the rice fields while Toshio narrated the intimate details of his affair with an older married woman.

"You don't expect me to tell you to deny yourself such passions, do you?" Shigehiro said. "I believe we should experience life to the fullest. Of course, if an experience leads to another's pain or misfortune, one would need to question his or her behavior, but I don't want to give advice and I don't want to seek advice. I want to lead my own life."

Toshio turned to his friend. "What's on your mind?"

Shigehiro glanced up at the full moon and then back at the rice fields.

"I've got to get away from Father's influence. I've got to do something, just not sure what. Perhaps join the Yamabushi and live at Yoshino. Hard aesthetic training would keep my mind off things that trouble me. Maybe spend some time at the temples of mount Koya, or take the pilgrimage of eighty-eight temples around Shikoku."

"Sounds to me like you need a love affair yourself," Toshio attempted to lighten his friend's dark mood, for he knew Shigehiro to be overly serious at times. Perhaps he really did need more experience in the outside world.

"Well, we have a busy day tomorrow," Toshio said cheerily, "So let's retire."

Before sunrise Shigehiro would sit in the main hall of the temple to pray for an abundant harvest. Soon afterwards he would join Toshio and others to assist in the season's communal labor. As rice crops neared maturity local farmers kept a keen eye on the skies and examined their crops daily. If harvested too soon, the rice ears would not be fully developed. If left too late, a typhoon could flatten a crop and render it useless. Two typhoons had already approached the southern coasts of Kyushu and Shikoku, so tomorrow was designated the day for harvesting. It was a demanding but rewarding job and every year the local farmers asked all their neighbors to help in the surrounding paddies. Even wives and grandmothers would be out with hand-held scythes to cut the rice from awkward corners and search the ground for odd ears of rice.

"Is something else troubling you?" Toshio asked as they walked back into the temple complex. They turned and Toshio helped Shigehiro push the heavy wooden doors closed.

"Father has been missing for two days and no one seems worried."

"Do you know where he's gone?"

"Yes, I do as a matter of fact. At least I think he has gone to see a gangster he was dealing with. He was very quiet after grandfather talked with him."

"Go and see the police if it concerns you."

"I've already been to the local police station to inform them of the missing statues, but they weren't helpful. The inspector I spoke to said that without a real lead there was nothing they could do. I think they drag their heels on purpose, but what can I do?"

"Tell them about your father. They might be more sympathetic towards a missing person than a missing statue."

~

Itsue's father was seated at the head of the low wooden table. Itsue seated across from her mother and brother in their old family home just outside Nagoya.

"Mama, you don't understand how I feel."

"What's to understand? He's a gangster! There's nothing more to understand."

"He's not a gangster!"

"His uncle's a gangster. That's bad enough."

"He's a good man, Mama."

"Have you slept with him?"

"Mama! How can you ask such a thing?"

"You should never have left Satoshi-san. He was a good husband to you."

"He was alcoholic and abusive! He hit me more than once."

"I never saw any marks on you."

"Oh! No, of course not. He never hit me where sweet Mama would be able to see."

"Well, I don't know about that, but he worked for a good company and he had a good job. You could have had a good life and a nice house, but no. You wanted to go and throw it all away.

Now you want to marry a gangster. What is wrong with you child?"

"I am not a child!" Itsue shouted, "And for the last time he is not a gangster! He has a normal job and he performs with a taiko group in Osaka."

"That's another thing. Only Koreans play those drums."

"Mama, you don't know what you're talking about. That's not true any more.

"Look! I'll not have the good name of Nomura associated with any Korean name."

"Nobody would know. He has a Japanese name."

"Don't be so stupid. His real name is on the register at the Osaka city hall. How do you think I found out about him in the first place? Your name would have to go on there as well. Anyone who wanted to could go and check."

Itsue's father raised his eyebrows.

"Mama! Those documents are for official use only. No one is allowed to see them unless it's for a legitimate reason."

Itsue's mother just grunted and Itsue turned to her father for help.

"Papa, why don't you say something?"

Her father cleared his throat. "I suppose your mother is right. We don't want to have any trouble with the neighbors."

"That's enough!" Her mother slammed her hands down on the table. "Come to your senses young woman. If you ever think of marriage with that man, I will have nothing more to do with you. I will disown you and that's my last word."

Her mother collected the cups, banged them on the tray, and stormed into the kitchen.

"That goes for me too," her brother said as he stood up.

"Well, you've never been much help to me," Itsue retorted. "Always on Mama's side."

Her father put his elbow on the table and rested his forehead on his hand. Itsue stood up, "Bye bye, Papa," she whispered, and let herself out of the house.

That evening, alone in her apartment, Itsue took the bottle of Shochikubai from the cupboard and, in tears after several glasses of cold sake, reluctantly accepted that there was nothing she could do but to concede to her mother's demands.

Kagami Mochi and the Harvest Moon

As the amber harvest moon rose above the horizon Kurosawa Hiro walked across to the shrine that abutted Honkyomo-ji. Although ten years senior and a Buddhist, grandfather Hiro often went over to talk with his old Shinto friend, Miura, Toshio's grandfather. This particular evening an offering of rice cakes was set up near the open window. The moon was full and clear and the mythological rabbit, pounding rice in a pestle up on the moon's surface, could easily be seen. Both men seated on cushions set on the floor toasted each other with warm *sake*, and took turns writing haiku about this auspicious September night. The hot summer neared its end and a welcome breeze wafted smoke from a mosquito coil in its holder on the floor between them. The evening grew late, but the outside screen doors remained thrown open, and thin wispy clouds floated across the silver orb as the two men discussed the missing statues.

"Aren't you at all concerned about where they could be?" Miura questioned the old sculptor's nonchalant attitude towards his statues. Grandfather Hiro leaned forward to rest a forearm on his crossed leg.

"What's gone is gone," he replied. "No use concerning oneself. We should not care for material matters."

"Humph. Your statues have spirits though. They may want to return to where they belong." Miura grunted. An irascible man, he loved to challenge his Buddhist friend and remind him of the Shintoist approach.

"That's a thought," grandfather Hiro intoned. "No. Letting go is safer than being involved with thugs and searching for statues that may never be found. However, you do make me worry and I do hope no one is being hurt over them. I would not like the idea of my work being a reason for violence."

"Treasures of our civilizations have always attracted thieves," Miura mused. "Asia has been stripped of precious artifacts for centuries. We have experience of these crimes but since the down turn of our economy criminals have chosen new paths to make a living. Except at the most famous of major temples artwork is completely unprotected. Temple and shrine workers may be reliable at first but when financial difficulties strike, an offer of a significant amount of money can justify lifting a light piece off its pedestal and putting it into the trunk of a car. It has been known to happen."

Kurosawa made no response and Miura continued.

"Don't you remember that police officer at the airport who arrested some Frenchman caught in the process of bribing a customs official? The 18th century Buddha statue he wanted to keep came from a temple in Kyoto."

Kurosawa still made no response.

"And three years ago Chinese officials uncovered some ancient statues stolen from a collection at the Palace Museum in Beijing and that were supposedly on their way to Europe for an exhibition that didn't exist."

"What is your point?" grandfather Hiro asked.

"Perhaps your statues have absconded to Europe."

Kurosawa said nothing while Miura studied him through wisps of mosquito coil smoke.

"This is all because of those American hippies who came to study Japanese in the 60's and 70's and returned to California with Japanese wives. They became successful and now want to purchase ancient Buddhist sculptures to decorate their homes with."

"Very tempting to blame westerners, but we made it easy for them."

"Go to the police," insisted Miura.

"Something taken from a temple is stolen for sure, but from whom? We have laws banning the export of antiques, but how can the police enforce them?"

"What is your son doing about this? Come to think of it I haven't seen Yoshihisa-san for the last two days. Where is he?"

Kurosawa made no comment. Miura looked out through the open screen doors across the courtyard. The summer with its humid days of thirty-three degrees Celsius or more had worn them out. From trees in the temple complex the incessant sounds of cicada reverberated throughout the days. Lizards stood near motionless on rocks lifting first their front right and rear left legs then alternate opposite limbs.

Shigehiro and Toshio had returned through the temple gate, turned and pushed the heavy wooden doors closed. Grandfather Hiro and Miura watched as Shigehiro took a wooden beam and dropped it into the iron brackets bolted on the inside. The two stood awhile talking, then walked across the courtyard to the open screen doors and greeted their grandfathers. The evening's quota of rice liquor exhausted, and without rising from his seat Kurosawa swung himself around to the side.

"You will be so good as to help me home," grandfather Hiro's hand on his grandson's shoulder as he put his feet to the wooden geta on the flat stone outside.

"Oyasumi," he said to Miura who grunted in reply.

"Oyasumi," Toshio shouted after them.

"Oyasumi," Shigehiro responded.

~

十二

September 12th Tsuruhashi

The brutal consequences of being a descendant of Korean stock had not affected Chulsoo unduly. A blanket of indifference tightly bundled around his soul immunized him against the discriminatory and derogatory remarks he faced from the media and in his personal relationships. As he grew into a young man however, the blanket thinned in places and on lonely nights, as he pondered the limitations society imposed on his caste, both anger and sadness penetrated his being. It was then that he longed for the indulgence of Itsue's arms.

During the first half of the twentieth century Chulsoo's grandparent's along with other Koreans had been coerced into leaving their country and serving Japan. Told to deny their cultural background, and during the Pacific War had to use Japanese names. Later generations of Koreans born in Japan continued to live according to their parent's adopted identity and many viewed their Japanese name as a kind of protection from the discrimination they would otherwise have to face. Third generation Koreans born after the Second World War like Chulsoo, found it difficult to comprehend the complexity of the issues between older Japanese and Koreans. The younger generation had demonstrated for equal rights as citizens of Japan and as a result could now use their Korean names on official documents, and apply for government as well as teaching positions. It must be possible to find a respectable job, mused Chulsoo as he made his way from Kintetsu Imazato station to the warehouse where his uncle Cheong ran his only legitimate business, manufacturing taiko drums, and where the troupe, *Tamashi Taiko*, held their weekly practice.

Once the rehearsal began, with shutters at the front of the warehouse thrown wide open, the deep resonant beats of the taiko would echo out into the evening air with a heavy pulsing sound. Here the drummers sweated away their cares in a passionate rhythm of sound. For drummers of Korean descent like Chulsoo performing on these drums had been a recent development. In this island nation conservative beliefs and customs, no matter how unjust, were handed down generation to generation. Koreans needed leather for drums and in turn became identified with those that supplied it, those who worked in the abattoirs, those that cured and treated leather, the Burakumin of Japanese society. Since they belonged to the lowest class of society they were not allowed to perform publicly at the prestigious festivals of Japan. This deprivation lasted until the *Tamashi* troupe of drummers had decided to break the rules.

"*Oi, Osoi ja nai ka!*" You're late, enounced Kouno.

"Yeah, I know. Things on my mind," Chulsoo retorted as he headed for the locker room.

Kouno grunted and walked over to the drums stored along the side of the warehouse to check on their tuning. The large drums with heads nailed to the body could not be tuned, but certain drums had black metal hoops fixed around the middle of the drum. Positioned at intervals on this metal hoop, faced in alternate opposite directions, were bolts attached to the edge of the skins that covered either end of the drum. Tightening or loosening these bolts changed the tension and thereby enabled some tuning. Smaller shime-daiko with heads stretched over a hoop and tensioned with ropes also allowed them to be tuned, and still smaller higher pitched drums were used to establish and keep the beat for the group. Satisfied with the sound of each drum Kouno moved over to one side of the large drum set in the centre of the warehouse. Then Chulsoo rejoined Kouno and, naked except for a white loincloth, took up his position at the other side of the oke-daiko drum. The body of the drum carved from a single log of the zelkova tree was by far the most expensive the troupe owned. Other mid-sized drums called nagado-daiko, made from the wood of the Bubinga tree, were less expensive. Other drums were of laminated construction and although by no means cheap, of a smaller budget than the others.

Drumming in the oppressive humidity, even in September, required a high level of fitness and endurance. Most residents of Japan used their energy just to stay cool and dry and did not wish to exert themselves more than necessary. However, even after weeks of practice in the heat, fatigue had not affected the strength of the drummers. Their ability remained intact and they readied themselves for the September festivals. In fact they played with the same vigor at any time of the year, stamina and concentration kept the young men's spirits high and they lived up to the name of their troupe for 'tamashi' meant soul. They enjoyed popularity with local people and had several bookings for the coming autumn. One booking was scheduled for the following day at a shrine in Kashihara City, thus this final workout.

The leader tapped on the side of his drum to call the drummers to order. He then initiated a steady beat on a high-pitched black metal-hooped drum. The rest of the group, legs bared, chests naked, pounded on the drums in time with the leader's rhythm. The intensity of vibrations increased gradually until the speed and variations initiated by Kouno and Chulsoo on the oke-daiko required full concentration by the other players to keep pace with the rhythm the two friends pounded out. They hit with such vehemence that the walls of the warehouse vibrated. Gradually the beat softened then a final flourish followed by a crescendo that ended as everyone stopped on the same count. The sudden silence swelled the warehouse. The leader grunted and the others gave a cheer. It was an enjoyable practice. After they showered and changed, Kouno and Chulsoo exchanged farewells with the other members and walked together to Imazato station where they took a local Kintetsu train just one stop to the home of the largest number of ethnic Koreans resident in Japan.

"Ah! The delightful aroma of Tsuruhashi," Kouno said as they exited the station straight into the Korean market. They worked their way slowly through the hustle and bustle of the narrow crowded alleyways that heralded the informality of the distinctive Osaka community. The rapid-fire sound of the Korean language was everywhere. Stalls offered teas, kitchenware, household commodities and countless traditional food provisions. Other stalls offered meals such as chijimi with a range of fillings. The particularly pungent aroma that Kouno referred to came from a traditional delicacy, namely kimchi. This popular staple food of Koreans consisted of vegetables fermented with copious amounts of red chili peppers that accompanied meals three times a day. The ramshackle stalls offered different kinds, each with a distinct spicy flavor of its own. Kouno stopped at one such kimchi stall and bought three small packs, cucumber, spinach and radish. Chulsoo guessed they would be for his uncle, and while Kouno chatted to the woman, he turned aside to a tofu stall and purchased a block of grey sesame tofu for his own breakfast. When he turned back Kouno had moved on into the midst of pushy Korean wives haggling for the best bargains. Chulsoo turned his head this way and that until he saw Kouno several stores further down. He elbowed his way through the crowd and joined Kouno outside a brightly lit open fronted hanbok clothing store. An assortment of traditional jeogori and silky chima of every imaginable hue packed the three walls. Kouno joked suggestively with two middle-aged women seated on a raised carpeted floor where they unpacked and folded garments just delivered. The women laughed and invited the two men in for tea but Chulsoo was not in the mood for idle chatter nor for tea. He wanted food and a cool beer, much needed after a workout with the drums and he pulled Kouno away before he could accept their invitation. Chulsoo had something more important to talk about.

A couple of alleys further on they arrived at a restaurant they frequented. The modest decor and functional design of the tables with a gas ring set in the centre for grilling beef suited their needs perfectly. They took stools at a corner table and ordered two dai-jokki of beer. Within minutes a young waitress brought the two heavy glasses of beer along with two portions of kimuchi, courtesy of the house. The men took deep gulps to quench their parched throats and then ordered pulgogi and pibimbap, barbecued beef with a mixture of rice, eggs and vegetables.

Chulsoo leaned back against the wall.

"Kouno, I have to leave the organization," he announced.

Kouno, dai-jokki halfway to his open mouth, looked over the brim, continued to take a long swig at his beer then slammed the jokki down on the table.

"*Omai, nani yuton ne!*" Kouno shouted. "Cheong will never let you."

Other customers in the restaurant cast sideways glances in their direction.

"I will convince him. I have to, otherwise I cannot marry Itsue."

"Ahh... So your woman in Nagoya has put you up to this," Kouno shook his head. "Don't you realise the problems you'll have if you marry a Japanese woman?"

"Kouno, I am aware of the security the organization gives you, but I want out. I know many people will try to block us at each and every turn, but I'm sure others will help us. I have to take this path. I will face Japanese society with Itsue beside me."

"Oh... How romantic! Chulsoo, you are an idiot! You are Korean! Commitment to our Korean community is your duty."

"Commitment to Uncle Cheong's organization you mean."

"Commitment to the people who raised you," Kouno countered.

"My commitment now is to another person!"

Kouno sighed heavily and turned his face away from his friend just as two women dressed in traditional hanbok entered the restaurant and found seats at a nearby table. The men, grateful for the disturbance to their heated conversation, ordered two more dai-jokki and watched as the women ordered two portions of chijimi filled with shallots, and a bottle of beer to share between them. Both in their early thirties the women leaned towards each other and giggled in discreet conversation. One of them smiled at Kouno, he winked and turned back to his friend.

"Chulsoo, I know our organization has constraints but don't leave. I have known you since we were kids. I'd trust you with my life. Please think about this. You'll be just like your father who deserted those that would have helped him."

"Kouno, don't make it harder for me than it all ready is," Chulsoo replied.

Kouno leaned heavily on the table, almost pushing it over, stood, grabbed his beer and walked over to the two women who had just arrived. He pulled out a vacant stool at their table and was greeted by the women's friendly laughter.

On his way home Chulsoo wondered if his father ever frequented the Tsuruhashi market. People described his father as a thoughtful, sensitive person. A man who would always return even the most insignificant of favors, but thoughtfulness and duty now become confusing concepts for Chulsoo. Kindness had been combined with obligation, and the spontaneous act of giving had been negated by tradition. If he left the organization, there was no doubt that other members would curse him like they had his father. In their eyes he would be deserting them, and it would reflect badly on his uncle and on Kouno. If he were to go through with it, he would have to pay a heavy price that would be demanded of him, but what else could he do?

十 三

September 13th Kasanui

Two stations north of Yamato Yagi, Françoise stepped from the
9:43 train onto the platform of Kasanui station. At the exit she
approached the station attendant's window, handed over her
ticket, and asked for directions to Honkomyo-ji. Eager to perform
his duty, the fresh faced youth rushed out of his four by seven foot
cubicle and gestured to the level crossing a short way off.

"Down here, go over crossing and up slope, err..."

Françoise asked for the information in Japanese but she
understood he either wanted to show consideration or practice
his English. A pity to tell him she was French.

"err... slope on other side of railway. Go straight up narrow
road, turn left at top and go that road to tobacco shop..." Françoise
began to move away but he was not finished.

"...*Chotto!* Wait! Turn right at tobacco shop. Go down road,
over river, and cross Route... err... 24 at traffic signal. Walk down
road on other side, Honkomyo-ji on left side, next to shrine. About
ten minutes."

Françoise thanked the attendant and started off towards the
level crossing, crossed over, went up the slope opposite, and at
the top turned left onto a narrow road. A couple of cars drove
slowly past her as she walked along in front of traditional wooden
Japanese homes neighbored by modern houses. Both styles

architecturally pleasing, but bamboo fences and concrete walls next to each another seemed somehow incongruent.

Françoise found the tobacco shop on the corner, turned right and walked down the narrow lane, crossed over the river, and waited at the traffic signals of a major road. As soon as the lights changed she trotted briskly across and continued down the narrow road opposite. Two hundred meters further on Françoise came to a roofed temple gate. The Chinese characters on the stone pillar erected at the side of the entrance were difficult to read, but she knew enough to confirm that this was the temple Kitamura had told her about. Further down the lane she noticed the entrance to the shrine mentioned by the station attendant. Between the temple and the shrine a quaint hand pulled fire wagon stood behind the wire mesh of its shed doors. Françoise approached the temple gate and entered the premises. Behind the fire wagon shed, a row of sparsely planted two meter high conifers marked the boundary between the two premises, but the space between the trees enabled anyone to move freely between the two properties. In the grounds of the shrine, workers were erecting trestles. An aging Shinto priest dressed in a graying white gown stood watching them. As Françoise came in sight he came over to meet her.

"Hello, my name Miura. You interested in Shinto shrines?" he inquired.

"I have come to meet a Monsieur Hiro Kurosawa who I believe lives at this temple."

"Kurosawa-san? Yes, he lives over there. Why you want see him?"

"He is a sculptor, I believe. I'm interested in seeing some of his works."

"Oh, I see. Yes, he makes statues. Many statues. Come. I will take you to him."

He led her across the temple grounds to the residential building slid the door open and beckoned for her to enter the entrance.

"A visitor for Hiro-san," he called out in Japanese.

Down the hallway a door opened, a dignified middle-aged priest came into view and indicated for her to enter. Françoise slipped out of her shoes and stepped up onto the polished wooden floor, she bowed her thanks to the old priest who lingered in the entrance and followed her host down the corridor to the modest guest lounge. He closed the door behind them and gestured for Françoise to sit down.

"You are Françoise err..." he pulled a scrap of paper from the copious sleeve of his kimono and read her name aloud, "René de Cotret," and looked up. Françoise nodded while he continued speaking. "Professor Kitamura in Nagoya called to say you were a student of his and wished to talk with grandfather Kurosawa about..."

"I presume then you are Kurosawa-sama's grandson?" The priest had not yet introduced himself so Françoise interrupted his flow of speech.

"I'm sorry. Yes, Kurosawa Hiro is my grandfather. My name is Shigehiro."

Françoise explained her mission and Shigehiro went to tell his grandfather that the guest had arrived. While Françoise waited, an elderly woman came in, bowed, placed a cup of green tea on the table in front of her, bowed again and departed. The ceramic cup was undoubtedly selected to suit the season but before Françoise had time to appreciate the pattern of hand painted autumn leaves Shigehiro returned and announced that his grandfather was ready to see her.

As Shigehiro led her along the wooden passageway Françoise could not hold back her inquisitiveness about the woman who served tea and enquired about her.

"That is my mother," Shigehiro replied.

"I thought Buddhist temples were only for men."

"Not in Japan. Here we live as a family. Mother helps out as any other housewife."

At that moment Françoise realised this was not just a visit to a temple but also a welcome into a Japanese home.

Shigehiro stopped outside a door and put a finger to his lips.

"Please. I'm afraid my grandfather is rather frail these days. He likes to talk but it tires him. May I ask you not to keep him too long?"

"Yes, of course." Françoise caught the tenderness in his voice as he gently knocked at the door and slid it open.

It was an eight mat tatami floored room with Kurosawa Hiro seated in a wicker chair next to glass doors that looked out onto a stone garden. He turned his head as his guest stepped into the room and made a formal Japanese bow. Grandfather Hiro replaced the bottle of water he had just taken a sip from onto the table at his side, and beckoned for her to come nearer.

"Come and sit down. Forgive me for not rising. I've had a strenuous week."

Françoise walked slowly across the tatami floor as Shigehiro quietly closed the door.

"I do hope I am not being a nuisance," she said.

Grandfather Hiro gestured to a chair on the other side of the table, and Françoise seated herself gingerly on the edge of the seat.

"Please relax," he said. "I'm not such an old relic you have to handle with delicate manners. I am versed in the ways of the world. Kitamura tells me you have an interest in Buddhist sculptures. What would you like to know?"

Françoise told him of the Cernushi Museum and the director's plan to organise an exhibition to show changes in Buddhist sculptures during the influx of Buddhism to Japan. Françoise explained how the museum had already held two previous exhibitions in relation to the history of Buddhist artifacts. The first dealt with basic facts of Buddhist origins. Themes related to the birth of the historical Buddha named Siddhartha Gautama and the village of Lumina where he lived.

"Yes," Korosawa verified. "It seems certain he lived near the Indian/Nepalese border. An area that was once considered an important intellectual and spiritual center."

"That would have been between the 5th and 6th centuries BC. About five hundred years before the birth of Christ." Françoise concluded.

"Umm… It is curious to date years back from the birth of Christ even when we talk about Buddhism. It is something of an anomaly that we Japanese do not accurately date years of antiquity. We are accustomed to dating periods according to the Emperors. Prior to the emperors there are simply historic periods: Jomon, Yayoi, Asuka, etc. When we need to be specific Kigenzen refers to the western period BC and Kigengo to the current period. Our legendary first emperor Jinmu dates from 660-585 and we don't normally need to go further back than that."

"In fact that period also covers three succeeding Japanese emperors, Suizei, Annei, and Itoki." Françoise was happy to remember her studies with Professor Kitamura.

"You are well informed," Grandfather Hiro acknowledged, "and what you say is correct as far as we know. We must remember though that Buddha's life story is interwoven with legends and traditions. The turning point prior to his enlightenment was his realization of the spiritual and moral futility of extreme asceticism, and his adoption of the quieter methods of meditation. His teaching aimed at the common people who were not expected to lead a monastic life. His life provides us with an idealised portrait of what Buddhists should strive for, but please continue…"

Françoise described how the second exhibition brought forward the history of the Silk Road from the third century BC through to the sixth century and the spread of Buddhism throughout northern Asia.

"Not only Buddhism," Grandfather Hiro interjected. "The Silk Road enabled the spread of all kinds of things: Spices, cloths, fashions, fables, myths, art, everything made its way back and forth between the various peoples who lived along its routes and the copying of sculptures would have been no exception. Certainly, since the end of that first millennium, according to your western calendar," Kurosawa smiled, "Buddhist art has seen its greatest flowering outside the land of its founder."

"That is why the Cernushi would like to run a third exhibition. An exhibition that will show the changes in style made during that period when Buddhism came to Japan."

"Yes, statues of that period manifest numerous similarities with Chinese, Korean and Indian styles. Older works even show significant Persian and Greek influences that most people don't recognise. Is that what you are after?"

"I want to focus on Prince Shotoku and the time when, at the other end of the Silk Road, Muhammad was teaching in Mesopotamia. The years around 600."

Kannon Bosatsu and Mary Mother of Jesus

"Umm... there's that Christian calendar again. It has always interested me how the western calendar has come to dominate our political and economic world, and yet Japan did not adopt the western solar calendar until the fifth year of the Meiji era..."

"The year 1873," Françoise clarified.

"Yes," Grandfather Hiro smiled. "We even celebrated the start of the new millennium with fervour, but only one percent of Japanese profess a belief in Christianity."

"So the majority of Japanese people embrace the Buddhist religion?" Françoise asked.

Grandfather Hiro smiled. "Certainly Buddhism has a great influence, but I believe the true religion of Japanese people is simply being Japanese, which means being born to Japanese parents. I think the fact that everyone visits a Shinto shrine during the first few days of the new year, and almost everyone visits their family's ancestral grave at least once during the Spring or Autumn equinoxes, testifies to that."

"Do people still think in terms of nationalism, with so much global interaction?"

"Unfortunately yes, because when Japanese talk with people of other nationalities it reinforces their belief in being unique from all others. Of course, my colleagues and associates are highly educated, like my good friend Professor Kitamura, your old teacher, who understand how religion teaches the great beauties of life but, when mixed with nationalism, can be very dangerous. I fear Japan's racism is so deeply ingrained that most people are unaware that their questions can sometimes be so infuriating. My son fails to understand this, but I think my grandson feels the same as I do."

Grandfather Hiro paused deep in thought, and took a sip of water.

"But we have strayed a long way from the subject," grandfather Hiro continued, "That is not what you came to talk to me about, is it? What were we discussing?"

Françoise smiled, "I'm sorry, my mention of Japanese embracing the Buddhist religion distracted you. We were talking about statues of Prince Shotoku's era and I mentioned the western calendar."

"Ah, yes. I remember now. So, at that time we used a Chinese lunar solar calendar, and the people of what is today the Korean peninsula played a much more important role in the history of Japan than Japanese like to acknowledge. The Nara period tends to overshadow the legends of the Yamato era but most experts accept that the people of Paekche, or Kudara as we called it, brought Buddhism to our islands." Grandfather Hiro leaned forward, looked into her eyes and lowered his voice. "The emperor's line descends from that era, but our country chooses to ignore that fact. Thus the imperial household does not give permission for archeologists to open the great emperors' tombs."

"Findings could reveal a strong connection between ancient Koreans and Japanese?"

"Exactly! And they are the only known tombs in the world of such antiquity that have never been touched."

"Did Japanese not attempt to go to China before the people of Korea came here?"

"Oh, they did. There were four successful trips to the eastern end of the Silk Road, but Japanese did not bring back Buddhism at that time. That was introduced later from the area known as Paekche, and it was not until the end of the Asuka period that Shotoku Taishi established Buddhism in Japan. That would have been your 6th century." "Kudara then, was the Japanese name for Paekche that, along with the lands of Silla and Kaya to the south east, and Koguryo in the north were known as the three kingdoms, and that now make up the Korean peninsular of today?"

"That's right, although much of the land that was once Koguryo now belongs to China."

"Kurosawa-sama, may I ask a question that has long troubled me?" Françoise hesitated, "Do you believe that Shotoku Taishi was of Japanese origin or do you think he could have been a native of Paekche?"

"He could have been from Paekche certainly. I have heard it reasoned that he came from Kudara rather than going to Kudara and returning to Japan. It is certainly more logical. Most experts agree that he was probably of the Sogo clan that held great power. Personally I think he was probably born in Japan but of Paekche royalty. Whether he then ever went to Kudara is another question. Considering the skills accredited to him he may even have legends of more than one person attributed to him."

Grandfather Hiro reached for the water on the table, and Françoise remembered Shigehiro's words about not tiring him too much and changed the subject.

"What were your first sculptures?" she asked.

"The first complete statue I crafted was Miroku Bosatsu, the Maitreya or Buddha of the future. That one over there." He indicated an exquisite dark, shiny wooden sculpture that stood in the tokonoma on the opposite side of the room. "My last work, completed a few months ago, is a representation of the Buddha at birth. You probably know the style where his right hand is held above his head. That statuette however, is not here. My statues no longer remain on these premises. My son has leased them to other temples. If you want to see them you'll have to travel to Horyu-ji and some other temples a little north of there in the mountains. Excuse me. Let me call for my grandson," he reached for a small brass hand bell on his side table and gave it a short tinkle. "My grandson knows the details and can tell you exactly where to find them."

Françoise understood that the interview was over and stood to leave.

"Thank you. You have been most kind."

Grandfather Hiro eased himself out of the reclining chair and rose to his feet.

"I'd be delighted for you to put my statues in an exhibition but they may not impress people as much as works created by early masters. The Cernushi Museum already owns fine works of Asian origin, I believe."

"You have been there?"

"One does not need to travel in order to learn."

Shigehiro came quietly into the room.

"Ah, here's my grandson. He'll take care of you." Grandfather Hiro took Françoise's hand in his and they smiled warmly at each other.

"Now please excuse me. I must rest before the afternoon meditation session so I don't fall asleep during prayers. That would be a terrible example, wouldn't it?"

"You'll attend the taiko performance this afternoon, grandfather?" Shigehiro asked.

Grandfather Hiro nodded. "Yes, indeed. Why don't you take Madam René de Cotret here across to meet Miura? He can tell her about the taiko performance."

"I think he has already met her. He brought her to the house."

"Ah, trust old Miura-kun. Yes, he would have noticed her right away."

He chuckled to himself and walked back to his wicker chair as Shigehiro pushed the door to his grandfather's private quarters closed.

十 四

September 13th Kasanui

Shigehiro led Françoise back along the polished wooden corridor to the guest room near the front of the house. They entered and took seats facing each other; tea and sweets already set on the table between them.

"Forgive the inquisitiveness," Françoise began. "What is the taiko performance you mentioned to your grandfather just now?"

Shigehiro smiled, "When you arrived, I believe you went first to the Shinto shrine that adjoins this temple. At this time of the year, just before the rice is gathered in, they hold a performance of taiko drumming, so we can have a safe harvest. If you have time you are welcome to attend. It will start at 5 o'clock or so."

"I would love to see it, but I would inconvenience you."

"It is no trouble, and you have not yet eaten lunch? I will get something delivered."

"No! I can find a restaurant near here and return later," Françoise protested.

"There are no restaurants this side of the highway, and you don't want to return all the way to the station, and then come back again. I presume you can eat sushi?"

Françoise acknowledged that she could, and Shigehiro picked up the phone on the table next to his seat and ordered a dish of assorted sushi for two.

"May I ask what temples you plan to visit?"

"Tomorrow morning I want to visit Horyu-ji. I have an appointment at Nara Museum the day after, and I would like to visit both Yakushi-ji and Toshodai-ji."

"Horyu-ji is a good choice. Japanese revere it," Shigehiro approved her choice. "It was the first Japanese temple selected by UNESCO as a World Heritage Site. Saiin garan, the western precinct, holds the oldest wooden structures in the world. The museum has recently been renovated, and houses statues of Prince Shotoku. A special exhibition that would have included statues made by my grandfather was planned," Shigehiro's countenance dropped and a frown creased his forehead, "but it seems something went wrong and his statues cannot be displayed. If you don't mind," he continued, "I could accompany you. I want to find out more about grandfather's statues. Afterwards we could head for Yakushi-ji and Toshodai-ji, they are both located in the same area.

The sound of a nearby motorbike interrupted their conversation and announced the delivery of their lunch. A few moments later Shigehiro's mother brought the selection of fresh sushi to the guestroom. Along with two bowls of miso soup, seaweed and bite sized squares of tofu, the ample portions of fresh sushi: tuna, salmon, salmon eggs, squid, prawn and octopus, served in high-sided lacquered wooden trays, looked appetizing.

"Are you proposing to take me to those temples yourself?" Françoise asked, rather surprised. "I'm sure I would be able to find them myself."

"Unless you really want to travel on your own it would be silly to refuse my offer. My coming with you would make your visit relaxing and more time efficient. You wouldn't have to worry about finding your way around, and I could explain the history of the statues and their meanings. Hopefully I have enough knowledge to answer your questions. Your rejection would deny me the opportunity of practicing my English."

Shigehiro smiled warmly and Françoise conceded to his proposal. Shigehiro took a map from a drawer and spread it on the table.

"From here we take a train one station north to Tawaramoto, change lines and head for Oji. There we can transfer to the JR line, it is only one stop to Horyu-ji station, then a brisk walk to the temple. That will be our first destination."

The sound of slippers flip-flopped along the hallway outside and grandfather Hiro slid open the guestroom door.

"Let's go and see the drums!"

Françoise and Shigehiro followed grandfather Hiro outside. Across on the other side of the courtyard, near the vermilion shrine building, a huge oke-daiko drum, and two medium size nagado-daiko drums either side, were set up on trestles. A row of smaller drums placed on thin tatami matting, were set in a semi circle around them. The Shinto priest Miura saw them come out of the temple residence and came towards them.

"You are going to watch the drumming?" he queried.

"Yes." Françoise took in the weathered face and grubby off white gown.

"Where you are from?"

"Paris!"

"Not many westerners come to this Shrine."

"She came to see me about sculptures," grandfather Hiro cut in promptly and Miura responded with a grunt. Françoise noticed Miura used the word westerner rather than foreigner, which seemed to put them on a more equal footing, she remembered what Kouno told her when she met him in Nagoya and decided to ask Miura about it.

"I was told recently that Burakumin help to make these taiko drums, is that true?"

The priest's eyes opened wide as he looked around him, but no one else seemed to have heard Françoise mention the word Burakumin.

"Err… Yes… the people you mention cure and treat the leather used to make taiko drums, but… err… since you are aware of their existence you probably know that Japanese tend to treat them with contempt, better to not mention them in public."

Françoise respectfully lowered her voice as she asked; "I heard also that only Japanese were allowed to play the taiko drums at public performances. Is that true?"

Miura was taken aback and hesitated before he replied.

"Well… in some very rural areas maybe, but generally who plays the drums is not an issue these days. In fact two of the members you are about to watch are Korean." Miura also lowered his voice. "The problem is the association of the hides that cover the drums with the death of the animal. Anyone involved with slaughtering animals or even the tanning industry whether they run a meat shop, shoe shop or a drum workshop is looked down on." Miura cut a sideways glance at his old friend Kurosawa. "You see, Buddhism condemns killing animals and the eating of meat, and that has created this situation. Nowadays though most Japanese eat meat and don't …"

Grandfather Hiro overheard the comment and redirected the conversation.

"Let's stop that discussion for today, shall we? Let's just enjoy the festival. This troupe is from Tsuruhashi in Osaka and the members show remarkable talent."

The shrine ground was now packed with people that spilled over into the temple area. A crowd jammed the entrances. Others people, both men and women chatted together in the roadway outside, children spoke loudly and jostled to get nearer to the drums. Miura eased his way through the crowd with the others in tow bowing to people as they greeted him. The conspicuous Françoise raised a certain curiosity among the spectators, but since Miura and two Buddhist monks accompanied her, no one approached to talk with her. The crowd behind erupted into a noisy cheer as the men of the taiko troupe emerged from the changing rooms. Françoise turned to see the members heading her way. Fifteen young men clad in white loincloths tied around their waists and bright red happi coats emblazoned on the backs with the character *'Tamashi'*.

"Chulsoo! Kouno!" Françoise exclaimed suddenly as they passed by.

"You know those men?" Miura asked surprised.

"The one in front is my friend's fiancé."

"Ahh! And your friend is Japanese?"

"Yes."

"Now I understand why you know so much about this culture. Please tell your friend to think very carefully before marrying one of these men."

Françoise was about to ask Miura what he meant but a flurry of sound drowned out her thoughts. Members were at their places at various drums. Chulsoo and Kouno had climbed up to platforms erected at either end of the oke-daiko and in coordination with each other began to beat out a slow rhythm. The first strokes descended firmly and rhythmically then the tempo increased and in perfect synchronization other members created a flurry of motion and sound. Suddenly the boom from the two nagado-daiko drums filled the air. Françoise knew that Japanese first used the drums as battlefield instruments to intimidate and scare the enemy, she now knew why. The sound was overwhelming. The men pounded the drums with all their might. Each movement forced through their entire bodies to the drum batons. Vibrations so intense that Françoise could hardly hear herself think, she felt herself pushed back by the waves of sound that resonated inside her lungs, and she now understood why the drums had found a place in scaring away the demons of folklore. Spectators seemed hypnotized. Slowly the drumming lost its intensity until all of

the drummers stopped on a single beat. The performance ended
with a bow to the audience, and after a rousing cheer and a long
round of applause, the energized crowd gradually dispersed and
the drummers headed towards the changing rooms.

Françoise thanked grandfather Hiro and bade him and the
priest Miura goodnight. They in turn retired to their respective
homes, while she and Shigehiro strolled along the narrow lane
towards the station.

"What did you think of the performance?" he inquired.

"Most inspiring. I am lost for words. It all seems so quiet now."

"That's what it's for," he laughed, "All the demons have been
scared away."

"What happened to the drummers? I thought they would
stay around."

"There are shower facilities in the shrine. I expect a kimchi
nabe is waiting for them and after eating they will spend the night
here. We also provide bedding space."

At the main road a rendezvous for the next day was fixed.
Françoise was to board the first carriage of a local northbound
train from Yamato Yagi headed for Tawaramoto. Shigehiro would
get on at Kasanui station. Françoise wished him goodnight, trotted
briskly across the road and made her way back to the station. A
tumble of thoughts filled her mind. Why was it so bad to have
been raised in Tsuruhashi? What had Miura meant when he told
her; '... to think carefully before marrying one of these men?'
What other complications could there be on the horizon?

Part Three

Jizo - Protector of Children and Travellers

十五

September 14th Ikaruga

That evening at the Business Kanko Hotel Kawai, after so
many unexpected events, Françoise finally felt able to gather
her thoughts together. She made some green tea, and glanced
through the temple brochures she planned to visit. The first one
described Yakushi-ji, and Françoise smiled at the irony as she read
that although Emperor Temmu had originally commissioned the
temple for the recovery of Empress Jito from a serious illness, it
was the Empress herself who completed it after the Emperor's
death.

Françoise continued reading: One of the seven great temples
of Nara, Yakushi-ji is currently the head temple of the Hosso sect,
the second oldest Buddhist sect in Japan. The temple boasts two
pagodas. The western pagoda, reconstructed in 1981, houses relics
from Gandhara, India, while the eastern pagoda has survived
from the seventh century and is the only architecture of its period
preserved in natural wood. The other main edifice in the complex
unadorned with the vermilion paint of the other structures is the
Toin-do. First erected during the Yoro Period (717-724), it was
rebuilt in 1733.

Françoise turned to the other brochure, that of Toshodai-ji,
and read a little of its history. In the year 700 the Japanese Emperor
Shoumu invited the Chinese priest Ganjin to teach Buddhist

precepts in Japan. After twelve years and five unsuccessful attempts, Ganjin's perseverance made it possible for him to reach Japan. Sadly however, by that time he had lost his sight. Nevertheless he guided Japanese scholars in teachings of monastic discipline and had Toshodai-ji built. Thanks to the detailed pamphlet Françoise could feel the charisma of the devoted Ganjin. The picture that showed him seated with eyes closed gave her a sense of peace, and as she turned the page she pondered the haiku of Saint Ganjin penned by Basho so long ago.

> *Young leaves shining*
> *Ah, that I could wipe the drops*
> *From your sightless eyes.*

Françoise remembered a trip she had been on as a student, at that time she perceived Toshodai-ji as a site of impressive antiquity. Tomorrow she hoped to absorb some of its ambiance with more awareness.

The following morning, mouth dry from the air-conditioning left on all night, Françoise drew open the beige curtains of her hotel room to another bright day, she dressed quickly, breakfasted and walked up the road to Yamato-Yagi station. She bought a ticket to Tawaramoto and caught the 8:03 train as Shigehiro instructed. At Kasanui station Shigehiro joined her in the first carriage and Françoise frowned as her eyes travelled slowly up and down his faded blue samue. The loose jacket doubled over his stomach and baggy trousers tied at the ankles seemed rather worn. A short silence ensued before Françoise commented on his attire.

"I thought monks dressed more formally when they left their premises."

"Not all the time. A monk in formal robes is probably on his way to a private home to conduct a memorial service. Otherwise he wears his comfortable samue."

At Tawaramoto station Shigehiro led Françoise over the tracks at a nearby level crossing to Nishi-Tawaramoto station, the start of a spur line that connected the Kintetsu railway to the Japan rail network. Elevated for most of the way the track ran in a slow curve across open rice fields. At Shin-Oji they changed to a JR train headed for Horyu-ji station, their first destination of the day. They reached the temple as planned and walked through the grounds to the main hall. While Françoise looked around at the interior architecture of the ancient building, Shigehiro approached a middle-aged monk and spoke with him. A few minutes later Shigehiro rejoined Françoise.

"Well, grandfather's statues are not here. More to the point, they have never heard of an exhibition of statues from other temples. He said they haven't dealt with statue loans for at least..." Shigehiro's mobile phone vibrated and he retrieved it from the inside pocket of his samue. "Perhaps father knows where they are, but at the moment I have no idea where father is," Shigehiro said over his shoulder as he went down the steps of the hall to take the call.

Françoise walked over to the amiable monk and struck up a conversation. When she enquired about how to borrow statues the monk appeared perplexed. First Shigehiro asked if they had received any statues now this woman was asking to borrow some.

"Is this some kind of American joke?" He asked her.

Before she could reply, Shigehiro came back up the steps and walked across to join them. The brief phone call made him wonder if his grandfather's sculptures would ever be seen again.

"That was a fellow monk at Horin-ji near here," Shigehiro began. "He has been in touch with the other temples and could not locate any of the statues. Monks at Jiko-in and both Matsuo-dera and Yata-dera in the mountains say someone collected grandfather's statues two weeks ago, which can only mean that after..."

"This woman is your friend, Shigehiro-san?" The priest interrupted his thoughts.

"She is curator of the Cernushi Museum in Paris," Shigehiro replied.

"Shigehiro-san is kindly guiding me to various temples." Françoise clarified.

"Yes," Shigehiro rubbed his forehead as he came to terms with the situation, "I suppose the best thing for us to do now is to visit Yakushi-ji and Toshodai-ji as planned."

Françoise and Shigehiro took their leave of the amiable priest and once back on the main road Shigehiro hailed a taxi to go to the nearby Kintetsu Tsutsui station. There they caught a train for a short ride north to Nishi-No-Kyo station. With Shigehiro lost in thought, Françoise watched the farmers in the distance as they checked the ears of rice to decide when to start their harvest. Nearer to the tracks she saw the stagnant green quadrangle ponds she noticed on her way from Yamato-Yagi.

"Shigehiro. What are these horrible ponds full of slimy water?"

Shigehiro glanced out of the window. "Fish hatcheries," he said, "This area is famous for producing goldfish."

"Why don't they clean the water?"

"It probably is clean underneath. That green stuff is algae. Goldfish grow better in ponds full of algae. Like lotus flowers that symbolize the beauty that springs forth from the grime of this world, goldfish and lotus both grow best in murky water... Françoise," he began to change the subject. "Could you visit Yakushi-ji by yourself? Nara prefectural police headquarters is near here, and I would like to pay them a visit. Afterwards we can go to Toshodai-ji together."

"Yes. That's all right. I understand. Where shall I meet you?"

"The station at Nishi-No-Kyo is between the two temples. We could meet back at the station. Let's say in about an hour at the exit. We'll easily find each other."

They left the train, and while Shigehiro headed off on the short walk to the prefectural police building, Françoise crossed the road and entered the north gate of Yakushi-ji. As she looked around at the vast restorations undertaken during the last thirty years she pondered the exhaustive effort it must have been to bring the complex back to its original splendor. She stood in the central courtyard between the two pagodas and gazed up at the ringed ornaments on top of both. Composed of nine rings, symbolic of the nine levels of consciousness in a person's experience of life, Françoise noted they also served as excellent supports for the lightning conductors now attached to them.

The lecture hall still under reconstruction, Françoise walked instead to the eastern dormitories to study the artwork, then to the Grand Main Hall. No sooner had she entered than her eyes opened in amazement as she beheld the bronze Yakushi Triad. A seated Yakushi Nyorai, and, standing on either side, Nikko, the Bosatsu of the sun, and Gakko, the Bosatsu of the moon. In their current blackened, burnished condition after a fire in 1528, these imposing statues were magnificent and Françoise felt the need to put her hands together and pray for health and longevity. Her eyes then went to the medicine chest upon which Yakushi Nyorai was seated, for this was the Japanese cultural treasure that Françoise had come to see. The chest clearly displayed art from along the silk road of centuries ago. Françoise pulled out her notebook and jotted down the details: Chinese animal designs, Persian lotus designs, crouching Indian barbarians and decorative Greek grapevine scrolls. All figured on this unique pedestal.

Françoise then went to study the statues in the east hall. The first was Sho Kannon, considered by many to be the most beautiful reproduction of the merciful goddess in Japan, followed by the Shi Tenno, the four heavenly kings that clearly showed the evolution of Buddhism as it travelled from India to Japan. Ancient Indian Devas introduced into Buddhist doctrine as guardians of Shumisen, the inaccessible mountain at the center of the universe.

Chinese in turn integrated them with four Chinese gods who guarded the corners of the world and named them according to their respective colours, and Françoise noted with satisfaction that the red, green, black, and white still clearly showed on the faces of these four Tenno.

As Françoise exited through the south gate she discovered on the right side, near a small stream, a shrine to Benzai-ten or as Françoise knew her in Sanskrit, Sarasvati, the goddess of the river and patron of music. Françoise particularly appreciated this statue because it was a female figure and she had not yet resolved the puzzle of how a feminine form was displayed in a Buddhist temple. Benzai-ten's shrine however, was completely sealed with no way to peek through at the statue within. Since there was no picture of the statue in the brochure Françoise walked back to the office at the south entrance and asked the clerk if it were possible to view the statue.

"No!" was the immediate curt reply from the elderly woman. "Shrine cannot be opened! Cannot see Benzai-ten!"

Offended by the woman's attitude, Françoise knew from experience at the Cernushi that either there was no longer any statue inside or the keys lost. Françoise took leave of the woman and walked along the southern edge of the Yakushi-ji complex towards the railway line. In the distance she heard cheers and children's voices. A short walk down a side road revealed the reason for the commotion; a children's sumo competition. The September festival at Yasumi-ga-oka Hachiman-gu Shrine was in full swing, and Françoise watched, enthralled, as eight-to-twelve-year-old amateur sumo wrestlers pushed each other out of the ring.

Shigehiro entered Nara prefectural police headquarters second building and stood for a moment as he took in the scene. Behind a reception counter that extended the length of the room, metal desks were aligned in groups that formed several oblongs, and at the head of each, an inspector worked his way intently through piles of papers stacked in front of him. A heavyset sergeant with short-cropped hair took Shigehiro's name and asked the nature of his problem. Shigehiro gave him details of the lost statues and the disappearance of his father.

"Sir, if I may ask, why did you not report this before?"

"I reported the missing statues four days ago in Kashihara. My father has duties at other temples and sometimes stays overnight so there was no cause for concern at that time, but he calls when he stays for an extended period and we have not heard…"

"Have you not called his mobile phone?" The sergeant questioned.

"He doesn't have one." Shigehiro replied.

"Umm. And you think your father is in trouble with this man he was dealing with?"

"I think my father probably went to see him. I don't know what happened but I have the feeling something has gone…" Shigehiro was again interrupted.

"Do you know the name of the officer you reported this to at Kashihara police station?"

"An Inspector Sasaki."

The sergeant looked up at Shigehiro from under raised eyebrows. Placed his pen on the counter, excused himself, walked back between the rows to a desk at the further end and bent his head behind the files. Soon the upper half of an inspector's face appeared over the top of the files and peered in Shigehiro's direction. The inspector stood, stretched and, followed by the sergeant, came over to Shigehiro.

"Please tell me exactly what you told inspector Sasaki. As much as you can remember."

Shigehiro explained once more the details he reported to Inspector Sasaki; The theft of the Blue Buddha, and the details of the loaned statues that were never delivered.

"And you told Inspector Sasaki all this?" The sergeant asked.

"Yes."

"And you have not seen your father since the statue was taken from Honkomyo-ji?"

"That is correct," Shigehiro confirmed.

"Do you by chance have a photo of your father on you?"

"No I don't."

"Does he have a driving license?"

"Yes."

"Good. We can get that photo from our records."

The inspector turned to the sergeant. "You have all the other details?"

"Yes, I do," the sergeant replied.

The inspector turned back at Shigehiro. "We will put an alert out for your father and will contact you as soon as we have some news."

Shigehiro thanked the inspector, nodded to the sergeant and expressed his gratitude with a bow. Finally he felt reassured that something would be done. He descended the steps of the police station and beckoned a taxi to take him back to Nishi-no-kyo station.

Françoise crossed the railway tracks, turned right and walked the short distance to Nishi-no-kyo station. There she saw Shigehiro standing under a tree on the other side of the rail crossing, she crossed over, and together they walked along the narrow road to Toshodai-ji. As they entered the temple grounds Françoise took in the sight of countless bushes of stunning purple-pink blossoms that lined the many pathways, one of which cut through overhanging foliage led to priest Ganjin's grave. The previous evening she read in the brochure that during the month of September Toshodai-ji was famous for its bush clover, but she had not expected the sight to be so striking.

The Kon-do or Golden hall had a colonnade of eight pillars that emulated Greek design. Shigehiro approached the central bay, moved the small fence guarding the entrance and gestured for Françoise to enter. There, Shigehiro gestured towards three magnificent wooden images and explained what the statues represented.

"This is Yakushi Nyorai, the Buddha of healing. You would have seen him seated at Yakushi-ji. This is Senju Kannon, the same Bosatsu of compassion as the Sho Kannon at Honkomyo-ji but this time with an impressive thousand arms, and this is Birushana Nyorai, one of the earliest Buddhist deities to arrive in Japan during the 6th and 7th centuries. Birushana appears in the Flower Garland Sutra where the deity is described as encompassing everything in the cosmos. Birushana represents the spiritual body of Buddha-truth, akin to light pervading the entire universe. There are many words to explain it, cosmos, sun, light, for laymen it is usually translated simply as Dainichi, the Great Buddha. The famous Daibutsu at Nara is Birushana Nyorai."

"Interesting," Françoise said, "but not perfectly clear."

Shigehiro laughed. "Well, that's why they call it esoteric. Something of an easier nature to understand is that when Toshodai-ji was constructed the Ko-do or lecture hall was transported over from Heijo, the former imperial palace grounds, and reassembled here. How about a visit to the site where it used to stand?"

"Certainly," Françoise replied.

On the fifth floor of Nagoya Central Hospital Yoshihisa's eyes flickered open and took in the whitewashed hospital ceiling. As Yoshihisa gradually regained consciousness he recalled the spinning red lights of an ambulance, the voices, the local accents and the acute pain in his chest when paramedics lifted him to put him on a stretcher. Two days before he had undergone surgery for multiple fractures in his wrist and the removal of the remains of two broken lower front teeth. Now, as he stared at the ceiling of the semi-private ward, he slowly became acquainted with his surroundings.

"Thought you were never going to wake up," A voice nearby greeted him and he turned to see another man his own age sitting on the edge of a nearby bed.

"How long have I been here?" The pain as he opened his mouth to speak reminded him of the white gloves. The man grasped the pole that held a drip bag and leaned forward.

"Oh, I don't count days anymore. They are all the same here."

"Has anyone been to see me?"

"No identification on you. A policewoman came with a photograph, checked you against it and left. Heard they found you dressed in a black suit by the roadside. What you been doing? Go out and end up fighting."

"Umm," Yoshihisa looked back at the ceiling, "fighting with my conscience."

"They need your name and someone to contact."

"Name's Kurosawa. I'm a…"

The sound of their voices brought a nurse to the room. The nurse hushed the old man and bent over Yoshihisa. "How are you feeling?" she asked.

"You need to notify my family!"

"Don't worry, it's been taken care of. Get some rest. We will wake you as soon as someone comes to see you."

Yoshihisa remembered the black car and the door open beside him. Someone pushed against him. Was that what had happened?

Then he remembered the laugh and the words "…If you threaten me there can be no business between us."

His heavy eyelids began to close and with a grunt of pain he drifted off back to sleep.

~

十 六

September 14th Nara

Shigehiro and Françoise left Toshodai-ji and Shigehiro strode out ahead of Françoise. *Il peut être si discourtois parfois,* she thought to herself. *Qui doit marcher tellement rapidement dans cette chaleur?* The humidity was almost unbearable.

"Shigehiro, Why are you rushing?" she asked.

"I'd like to show you the ruins of the old city before it gets too late," Shigehiro replied.

"Just a minute. I am thirsty. I want to go to that store across the street." On the opposite side of the junction stood a 24-hour convenience store.

With Shigehiro in tow Françoise crossed the road and together they walked into the air-conditioned shop, she purchased two bottles of spring water and took a free photocopy of the local map. As soon as they stepped outside the humid atmosphere hit them once more, and Françoise handed one of the bottles of cool water to Shigehiro.

As they walked on Shigehiro again strode out in front, but at the next junction stood two open-fronted wooden structures set in the middle of the road.

"Shigehiro, those are Jizo over there," she called out. "Do we have time to take a peek?"

"If you'd like to," he answered as he walked back towards her.

Together they crossed to the knoll in the middle of the road.

"Tellement mignon," Françoise exclaimed as she gazed at the six roughly carved stone figurines with childlike faces. These particular Jizo Bosatsu, the protector of children, were older than living memory and not been moved for hundreds of years. Even twenty-first century road contractors had not touched them, instead they widened the road either side and created a small island where the figurines were safe. An appropriate gesture perhaps since Jizo also protected travellers.

After Françoise had taken a few pictures of the Jizo, she and Shigehiro walked on. Between the trees at the side of the road Françoise occasionally caught glimpses of open flatland. Ahead Shigehiro turned down a narrow pedestrian path and Françoise followed him. Suddenly she stopped dumbfounded at what lay before her. All that remained of the once great city of Heijo-kyo were a few circular stones that had served as building foundations, and an expanse of land that now served as a recreational facility for the people of Nara.

Designed according to the model of Changan, an ancient Chinese capital, Heijo-kyo had served as the Japanese capital from 710 to 784, a vital center from which Buddhism and culture blossomed profusely. Now the site where Heijo Palace once stood was a park where local residents came to relax. In the distance rose the distinctive mountain of Ikoma. Near at hand a young Japanese family spread a blanket on the grass. The mother read a magazine while the toddler played ball with his father. Further away two men in their mid-thirties flew model planes. An old man dressed simply in his long summer underwear swayed to-and-fro as he rode nonchalantly by on his bicycle, possibly on his way to the nearby stores of Saidai-ji.

"I didn't realise it was so vast," Françoise exclaimed.

"Yes, it is indeed very big," Shigehiro acknowledged as, in the distance, a maroon Kintestu train cut across the scene.

"Shigehiro, this is an archeological site. How is it that a railway company has been allowed to build tracks across it?"

"Permission was probably granted before the full extent of this site was known. Let's have a rest here and take in the atmosphere."

Seated on a grassy slope, Shigehiro began to explain what he knew of the area.

"You see, at first, archeologists only discovered remains of the ancient city north of that railway line. It wasn't until many years later that they regarded this southwestern area to have also been an integral part of the old city."

"It's regretful that no one realised it before the railway built their line, but I suppose progress takes priority over history," Françoise mused.

"Indeed," Shigehiro continued. "That's why you now see a great number of overhead cables. After the war, the need to modernise was given priority and the quickest and cheapest way for electric and telephone companies was to install the wires overhead."

"Why don't they put them underground now?" Françoise questioned.

"In many areas they have," Shigehiro replied. "Especially in the tourist areas and town centers but it is a long and expensive project."

Shigehiro turned and caught her pleasant smile.

"Would you stay in Nara tonight and join me for dinner?" he asked.

"But I have a reservation at the hotel in Kashihara. I have my luggage there, and papers spread all over the tatami."

"We can cancel the reservation. I can explain to the staff. They will take care of your luggage and papers and you can collect them tomorrow. We have service here in Japan."

"Well, all right."

"Let's walk back to the road and get a taxi."

Shigehiro once again strode out ahead of Françoise.

~~~~~

Nara Hotel, situated just outside the precincts of the deer park, was a supurb classic Meiji style edifice. Shigehiro and Françoise entered together and Shigehiro requested two adjoining single rooms and made a dinner reservation for two. Françoise did not understand how this Buddhist priest could spend money so freely but refrained from mentioning it to him. Françoise's spacious room was similar to that of any other countries' five star hotels, except perhaps for the electric kettle, teapot and tea bags on a table near the window. Françoise brushed her hair and freshened her makeup, without a change of clothes it was all she could do. A knock at the door, and Françoise smiled at her reflection in the mirror. *Ah! Le voici, si ponctuel,* she said to herself.

"Ready?" Shigehiro asked.

"Yes," Françoise replied.

In the first floor restaurant the waiter showed Shigehiro and Françoise to a corner table and handed each a heavy plastic bound four-page menu. They studied the selection of dishes for some time before Françoise finally peered at Shigehiro over the top of her menu with bewilderment showing on her face.

"Confusing, isn't it?" she said.

"Shall I order the shabu-shabu for two people? It's been a long day and we need some nutritious food." Shigehiro asked.

Françoise looked back at the menu and read the description: Select slices of hand massaged Kobe beef, fresh Chinese cabbage, Japanese shitake mushrooms, shallots and protein rich tofu will cook in a pot of boiling water at your table, then locally made Udon noodles will be warmed in the casserole to end your feast.

"Yes, that sounds wonderful. It makes my mouth water just reading the description."

"Shall I order a bottle of wine," Shigehiro asked. "What do you like?"

"I suppose we should have red since we will have beef." Françoise replied.

The waiter returned to their table and while Shigehiro ordered the meal Françoise realised she had not been out with her husband, Georges for many months. Fatigue or business always prevented him from wanting to go out in the evenings.

The waiter brought a bottle of house Beaujolais, opened it, poured two glasses, carefully wiped the neck, placed it on the table, bowed and left. Françoise and Shigehiro clinked glasses and took refreshing mouthfuls of the semi-sweet aperitif.

Françoise, hands together on the edge of the table, looked across at Shigehiro. "Tell me of your faith," she said.

"Do you want to know about Buddhism or my personal beliefs?"

"Your personal beliefs."

Shigehiro leaned back in his chair and studied her for a moment before he spoke.

"I believe we should try to help each other understand the things we have been taught since childhood, but at a deeper level, so we can mature and grow. In my role as a Buddhist priest I try to help others find a happier and more contented way of life by teaching them to let go of whatever it is that troubles them. When we are under stress or anxious over something that has happened, our power of reasoning is diminished and we are comforted by those who show compassion, but we also become vulnerable to others who would take advantage of us."

"Many then turn to religion for comfort," Françoise commented.

"Yes. When we are young we accept the teachings of our elders without question. Then as we grow older we come to believe that the religion of our ancestors, the religion into which we were born and raised, is the true faith. Dogmatically defending that belief is perhaps the greatest problem we have for achieving world harmony. In western cultures people are taught there is only one chance to achieve salvation. In eastern cultures people are taught there will be many incarnations until nirvana is reached. Which one of these ideas is true? They both cannot be… or can they?"

"Well, what is the truth for you?"

"There can be no absolute truth. It is only relevant in the context of each individual. What is true for some people is not true for others. All faiths seem to teach the truth to those tied up in the practices of its rituals day after day, but religion is tainted by money. It is the leaders of giant economic institutions that control events in this world and sizeable religious groups are entwined with them, as well as political and…"

"I understand you say that about the monotheistic religions, Judaism, Christianity and Islam," Françoise interrupted, "but surely Buddhism is different."

Shigehiro leaned forward and took another mouthful of wine.

"It's the same. There are many Buddhist schools of thought and a strict hierarchical system within all the different sects. Any religion that claims to have found the absolute truth deludes itself and deludes those who follow it, but what else can they do? Leaders of a faith cannot but believe in it themselves. Personally I think that belonging to any religion for an extended period of time may actually prevent people from accepting that other religions also teach the same basic values: responsibility, generosity, respect…" he shrugged, "even atheists come to the same conclusions. I think adults should study at least one other religion from the one they grew up with so they can be exposed to the ideas and guidelines on which other cultures are built. Hopefully they would then become aware their own culture does not hold the only version of an absolute truth and we may begin to see how all humans are interconnected. When we can develop compassion for members of other religions and, how can I say? Have an understanding of how others feel…"

"Empathy," Françoise prompted.

"Yes, that's the word," Shigehiro spread out his hands, "all of us could then live more peacefully and experience a life filled with goodness."

"That sounds incredibly philosophical."

"Like the western philosopher Karl Marx who said religion is the opium of the people, I think religious faith is a crutch. Once we have strength in our personal worth we should be able to throw away the crutch."

"Marx also said it is hard to live without opium," Françoise interjected.

"As it is to live without a crutch, or should I say without a church. It is extremely difficult to cast off one's childhood beliefs, because what remains is unknown. An understanding of this being all there is can be frightening. It takes humility, courage and a lot of personal conviction to overcome this challenge. A very long journey."

Françoise took a sip of wine. "Yet you are a Buddhist priest," she said.

"Not by choice," Shigehiro responded. "I would have preferred the life of an artist. My father thought differently however, so I did as I was told and became a monk. Now I try to follow the five key precepts that Siddhartha Gautama, the Buddha, taught us: refrain from taking life, refrain from stealing, refrain from sexual abuse, refrain from lying, and refrain from intoxicants that cloud the mind."

"Have you succeeded in those?" Françoise teased.

"Well," Shigehiro laughed, "Three out of five. I do enjoy a glass of wine, and I find an attractive lady like yourself difficult to resist, but that is perhaps a male thing."

As Françoise reached for her glass Shigehiro reached across the table and took her hand in his. Her eyes darted around the room then finally rested on Shigehiro's face. He smiled and released her hand. Shigehiro stood, signed the bill for the charge to be put with the room fee, and they left the restaurant.

Outside Françoise's room Shigehiro put his hand on her upper arm and, as she turned towards him, he pulled her near and kissed her full on the mouth. Françoise pressed her hand firmly on his chest and pushed him away.

"I thought monks did not get involved in such pleasures," she said.

"Japanese Buddhist monks are no more celibate than Protestant pastors."

"Even so. I think it would be best if we simply remained friends. Let's not complicate things," she said softly. "We have a busy day tomorrow, so let's get some rest. Thank you for the meal, it was wonderful. Goodnight."

Shigehiro nodded, and without further comment walked along the passage to his own room. Françoise turned and unlocked her door, inside, as she caught sight of her reflection in the mirror, she put a finger to her lips and smiled contentedly.

~

十七

September 15th Nagoya &
Sakakibara-Onsenguchi

Seated across from Chulsoo in the French restaurant of the Nagoya Hilton Hotel, Itsue listened without interruption as Chulsoo explained the circumstances that led to him being brought up by his uncle. His father long disapproved of the affairs his relatives engaged in and, while Chulsoo was still at elementary school, and wanting a better future for his son, his father decided to break away from the Osaka Korean community and take his wife and son to live in Nagoya. There he found employment in a car factory and, since it had been an era of affluence, the honest labour provided a good income to support his family.

Two years later his father disappeared. Chulsoo was told his father had died, but his body was never found and no police verdict ever issued. With no official death certificate the insurance held on his father's life was not paid out, and Chulsoo's mother had no alternative but to return with her son to Tsuruhashi. Uncle Cheong became their financial provider, and as an impetuous youth, Chulsoo obeyed him without question.

"Then it's true," Itsue's response was razor-sharp. "You are involved with a gang! Gambling, extortion, prostitution and who knows what else?"

"Yes, I am, but before you judge others, have an understanding of what we are. This is a business just like any other. There is a demand and someone supplies it. Customers are just as guilty as gangsters and customers include people like your own father."

Itsue's face flushed. "How dare you insinuate such a thing?"

"Face facts! Read the papers! Businessmen openly read porn on trains in trashy tabloids. Professors ruin their careers by taking high-school girls to hotels."

Itsue was incensed. "Chulsoo prostitution is wrong and you know it. It harms women physically and psychologically. It degrades women to prey and men to animals. Catering to prostitution is a symptom of a poor paternalistic society."

"What about wives who encourage their husbands to have affairs so they won't have to sleep with them anymore?" Chulsoo countered.

Itsue knew such wives existed, those who turned a blind eye to the infidelities of their husbands so they could keep a façade of respectability in front of neighbours. Women who, guilty of childish behaviour themselves, indulged their husband's immature fantasies. Itsue knew well that this attitude contributed to the deceit that was complicitly denied. One argument led to another and Itsue could see no solution.

"I'm sorry, Chulsoo." Itsue sighed deeply. "Our relationship cannot continue. I could never live with the threat of reprisals from your uncle hanging over us. You know my brother is set against us being together. If his employer ever found out his sister married into a Korean family, it would be bad enough, but to a family with your uncle's reputation it would ruin his chances of promotion forever. I'm sorry, Chulsoo. I simply cannot see you anymore."

Chulsoo was deeply hurt and took it badly. He needed a scapegoat and her brother was as good as any. "So your brother's success is more important than mine?" he stormed.

"I'm not saying that."

"Yes, you are!" he exclaimed. He sighed deeply. "You think we act shamefully even though we work hard. We may sometimes take the law into our own hands but we have our code of conduct. Everyone needs to survive one way or another."

"And your way, Chulsoo? Stealing from your own friends?"

Chulsoo frowned. "What do you mean?"

Itsue hammered her point home without sympathy.

"Kitamura-sensei phoned this morning to inform me his place had been burgled, and guess what they took? Fugen and Monju. What a coincidence that we were there just a few days ago! Don't tell me you and Kouno had nothing to do with it! You even helped get the statues out of the window!

Chulsoo pushed away from the table and his chair crashed to the floor behind him.

"And you just assume I am responsible?" Chulsoo's voice was just above a whisper. "We'll see about this!" He grabbed the bill from the table and strode off towards the exit.

Itsue buried her face in her hands. "I'm sorry, Chulsoo," she sighed. "I really am."

⁓

As Chulsoo neared the Sakakibara-Onsenguchi museum he exited the underpass, took a sharp right, swerved dangerously near to the attendants, roared across the parking area and screeched to a stop near two loud-speaker trucks parked on the further side. He then rushed up the steps of the outside iron staircase two at a time, pushed a thug stationed near the top out of the way, and burst into his uncle's office.

"Are you purposely making life difficult between me and Itsue?" Chulsoo stormed. "Is that your way of getting me to give her up?"

Cheong had heard the commotion from outside on the staircase and easily anticipated who was about to pay him a visit. He held his nephew in a hard gaze.

"Why did you have Kitamura's premises broken into?" Chulsoo shouted.

"Since when do you question how I run the business?" Cheong bellowed back.

Chulsoo leaned across the desk, grabbed his uncle's jacket and yanked him from his chair. Cheong brought his hands up between Chulsoo's arms, slammed the heels of his open palms against the sides of Chulsoo's face and in one swift motion pushed him forcefully backwards. Chulsoo dragged his uncle halfway across the desk before he lost his grip on the jacket and fell onto a low table in the center of the room. A glass ashtray flew into the air and crashed to the floor somewhere beyond his head. Chulsoo propped himself against the settee and stared across at his uncle who leaned heavily on his desk.

"Don't try that again! Don't ever disgrace me like that damn father of yours!"

Cheong flopped back down in the chair behind him and leaned back. He saw Chulsoo stiffen and the anger flare but continued to speak.

"Your father didn't die like you've been told. He may be dead now, he should be, but he was alive the last I heard. He deserted the organization. Ran away with my sister and you to another city where he thought no one would find him. But clerks at city hall can be bribed to reveal information and your father came to a bad end. Your mother brought you back here and I raised you. I paid your mother's debts, your schooling and everything else, so don't come charging in here questioning what I do."

Chulsoo got up from the floor and flopped down onto the settee.

"I will leave this organization." He said as calmly as he could but his voice trembled at the gravity of the statement.

Cheong's laugh echoed long and loud. "Ha, ha, ha, ha. Now you want to turn your back on us. Like father, like son! I knew it. You want to run off with the first Japanese bitch you have an affair with. Why should I allow you to do that? You'll end up the same as your father in one of those flea-ridden doss houses of Nishinari. I warn you, unless you leave the organization on its own terms, other members will suspect a possible turncoat in the community. They will look for you, like they did for your father, and when they find you, there will be nothing I can do for you."

Chulsoo was stunned, confused. So, as a boy his uncle had lied to him. The organization had been responsible for his father's disappearance. Perhaps Cheong himself ordered the reprisals, but something his uncle said echoed in Chulsoo's brain, '...flea-ridden doss houses of Nishinari...' His father had been tracked down, brought back to Osaka and forced to live as a homeless wretch. Now he probably collected old cardboard boxes and tin cans to survive, simply because he had tried to escape a life in the underworld.

"You know where he is, don't you?"

"I can have him found, if I need him," Cheong admitted, "and before you ask, no. I will not tell you where he is. Believe me you're better off without him."

"He is my father. I have a right to see him."

"I raised you. You'll do as I say!" Cheong responded sternly.

"I am tired of your ways, Uncle! You deceive others and smuggle anything you can get your hands on. You even help kidnap innocent citizens. I want out!"

"You are an impetuous fool. You assume things but you know nothing about the facts." Cheong moved to the edge of his seat. "You cannot imagine what it was like under Japanese occupation. People executed without trail. Thousands forced into the military to support the Japanese war effort. Others sent to Japan and coerced to work in the mines, your grandfather among them. Luckily he survived but many didn't. Korean language and history forbidden in schools, and Japanese names imposed on us, even your generation cannot escape that. You think I could ever forget those terrible times? Get out of here! Go try find your cowardly father!"

~

十 八

September 15th Nara to Kyoto

After a restful night Françoise showered, dressed and was eager to have breakfast. As Françoise appeared in the lounge, Shigehiro, already downstairs, put the morning paper back on the rack and accompanied her into the restaurant. They helped themselves to the buffet selection of western and Japanese dishes and took a table by a window whereupon Shigehiro suggested a visit to Todai-ji and some other sites in the area.

"I have an appointment at Nara Museum for twelve o'clock," Françoise reminded him. "I really can't afford time for a leisurely trip."

Shigehiro explained that the temples and museum were all within the boundaries of Nara Park and there would be sufficient time to see them before noon. He promised she would be on time for her appointment. So after breakfast, a short walk took them to the grounds of Nara Park.

"There are so many deer here," Françoise exclaimed as yet another stag came towards her searching for food. "I knew there were deer in Nara Park, but they are everywhere."

"More than twelve hundred, I am told," Shigehiro responded.

Soon they arrived at Nara's majestic eighth century Todai-ji. Renowned for its colossal bronze statue of Birushana Buddha seated inside the largest wooden structure in the world, the temple attracted millions of people yearly. Even at that early hour of the morning several people, along with Françoise and Shigehiro, had already purchased their tickets and entered the building.

Françoise looked down at the brochure she had been given at the entrance.

"Shigehiro, I'm confused. You said this is Birushana Nyorai but it says Rushanabutsu."

"Same thing," Shigehiro answered. "Maybe it helps if you understand that the name in Sanskrit is Vairocana the Cosmic Buddha. Birushana is the transliteration of Vairocana meaning coming from the sun. Butsu only means Buddha statue. Rushana-Butsu is just another way of saying Birushana Nyorai."

Shigehiro and Françoise walked around the base of the Great Buddha, then left the building and went on to the seventh century Kofuku-ji. Built by the political power of the Fujiwara family that ruled most of Japan until the fifteenth century. Eventually their walk brought them to the vermilion painted Kasuga Shrine famous for its good luck talismans, sandy paths, and for an endless array of literally hundreds of metal lanterns that hung under the eaves. Then Françoise spotted the western style Meiji period edifice of Nara Museum. It was just eleven thirty. Shigehiro had kept his word. They went to the coffee shop to rest before Françoise's appointment.

~

The curator and his assistant met Françoise with a formal bow and they exchanged business cards. The curator then explained that both he and his assistant were well aware of the Cernushi museum and its previous exhibitions and that they were quite willing to loan their pieces to such a reputable art museum. He added that his assistant would show her around and had authority to arrange the details of any loans. The curator then apologized for leaving, as he had to attend another meeting.

Françoise said she understood and thanked him for coming to meet her. The assistant then led her along underground passageways to the two modern extensions, constructed so as not to detract from the grandeur of the original distinctive structure. There he guided her along the displays. The two experts discussed several early sixth century sculptures, particularly one that showed Buddha holding his robe between thumb and forefinger, a feature of Indian art that represented a state of learning. The assistant curator then took her to a storeroom, not open to the public, and showed her statues they could lend to the Cernushi. He took notes of the ones she chose and they worked out the details. Françoise thanked him and rejoined Shigehiro in the coffee shop.

"Have you heard anything of your father yet," she enquired.

"Yes. Mother has just called me. He was found seriously injured by a roadside in Mie Prefecture and has been taken to a hospital in Nagoya. Police are at the temple with mother now, inquiring into what might have happened. It also seems that grandfather has been taken ill. I must return to the temple and see what is happening."

"I understand," Françoise commiserated and together they set off for the Kintetsu Nara station. In the station complex Shigehiro searched out a local travel agency and helped her make a reservation at a Japanese ryokan near Kyoto station. They went down the escalator to the underground platform where a train for Saidai-ji station was waiting. Alternate carriages of the train painted in light plum colors with scenes of Kyoto Gion Festival and in light green with scenes of Nara Deer Park.

Then, a short five minute ride to Saidai-ji where they transferred to two different trains; Françoise a semi-express to Yamato-Yagi, Shigehiro a local train to Kasanui. Françoise thanked Shigehiro for his help, boarded the train and stood by the door. As the train began to depart Shigehiro bowed to her from the platform, Françoise also inclined her head as they took leave of each other.

Françoise walked briskly to the Kanko Hotel Kawai where she had left her belongings, asked for the room key and went up to pack. Her brochures and documents were still laid out on the tatami just as she left them. She knelt on the floor, put everything back in their files, zipped up her case and went down to pay the bill. Once more at Yamato-Yagi station Françoise waited for an express to Kyoto. An autumn breeze filled the air and in a mood of sentimental dreaminess Françoise reflected on her day, her thoughts vacillating between her work, the Blue Buddha, and Shigehiro.

For Shigehiro the cooling afternoon air brought an ominous calmness. After he saw Françoise off on her way to Yamato Yagi he caught a local train back to Kasanui station. He walked pensively from the station and as he neared Honkomyo-ji he was overcome by a dreadful foreboding. He continued down the lane and saw ahead of him an undertakers van parked at the temple entrance. He rounded the van and saw the undertaker's assistants hanging wide black and white striped cloths around the temple gate. Shigehiro's pace quickened across the temple courtyard and he entered the private family quarters. His heart raced, for the inside walls had already been covered with the white cloth of Buddhist mourning.

With trepidation he removed his shoes and stepped onto the polished wooden floor. He started down the hallway when his mother stepped from the kitchen and stopped him. Dressed in formal black kimono her red tearful eyes needed no words to explain what had happened. Shigehiro nodded his understanding and continued quietly to his grandfather's quarters. Without his usual knock he slid open the door and took in the scene. Relatives knelt around a futon spread out on the floor began to move aside to make room for him. The barely discernable contour under the thin summer quilt came into view. He bowed to the family members in attendance, muttered thanks and followed by his mother walked across the room and knelt beside the futon.

"When?" he asked simply.

"At mid-day. Just after I called you," his mother replied. "I think the excitement of the taiko festival exerted him."

"And the loss of his last statue, and we know who's to blame for that!"

The words cut to his mother's heart, but she said nothing, just watched as her son fixated on the frail outline under the quilt. The undertakers had placed blocks of dry ice wrapped in white silk at the top and sides of grandfather Hiro's head. A square of thin white gauze covered his face. Shigehiro leaned forward and removed the cloth.

His mother saw the tears well up in her son's eyes, took a deep breath and watched grandfather and grandson together for the last time. Shigehiro gently replaced the gauze cloth on his grandfather's serene countenance. His mother kneeling, her lower legs tucked underneath, pushed herself forward to be next to him.

"Shigehiro you must go to see your father in Nagoya. The police said he suffered bruises and some missing teeth. They suspect he has been the victim of an assault."

The sight of his mother stricken with grief filled Shigehiro with angst. He stood, went to his grandfather's writing desk at the side of the room and searched through a drawer for a recent picture of his grandfather. He took a ring of juzu beads and two candles and returned to his mother's side.

"Don't worry, Mother," he whispered. "I'll go and see him, but right now there is something else I have to do."

Shigehiro bowed, took his leave of those in attendance, and went to the main hall. He knelt on the cushion next to his grandfather's and reached for his prayer beads. Regret caused by his sharp words to his mother weighed heavily on his chest. He gazed up at the statue of Kannon, the Bosatsu of compassion and,

148

accompanied by his steady beat on the wooden mokugyo, began to chant the sacred Buddhist sutras for the deceased.

While Françoise completely slipped away from Shigehiro's mind, he still featured prominently in Françoise's thoughts. On her arrival at Kyoto station she followed the directions he had given her and easily found the renovated Yuhara Ryokan. A thin frail woman welcomed her and showed her to a room on the second floor.

"Is it too early to visit the ofuro," Françoise enquired.

"Yes, okay. Bath open from three o'clock," The woman replied confusingly but Françoise understood, she placed her luggage on the floor of the room, took the perfectly pressed starched yukata, and followed the frail woman downstairs to enjoy a long hot bath.

Upon her return to her room Françoise found the air conditioner on and the table already set with an inviting dinner: grilled salmon, fresh tofu and soy sauce, slices of raw fish, a salad, a dish of soba, nori, pickles, slices of melon and peach. While Françoise dried her hair, a maid brought a covered bowl of hot miso soup and a wooden *ohitsu* with more than enough steamy rice for one person. A sip of the clear rice wine then Françoise put her hands together, whispered *"Itadakimasu,"* and eating slowly enjoyed the tasty meal. Later the young woman showed up again to clear away the dishes and prepare the futon for the night. Françoise gazed at the phone and wondered if she should call Shigehiro, thought better of it, and instead drank the last of the Nihon-shu and retired.

September 16th

The following morning Françoise joined other lodgers in a room downstairs where the owner supervised her maids as they served breakfast. Guests seated on square zabuton at a table of their choice, waited for their meals. Individual trays with various dishes were placed before them: grilled fish, fried rolled egg, clear bouillon with pieces tofu, a packet of dried seaweed, rice and a sour pickled plum. Françoise knew green tea would be served but wondered if she should dare ask for coffee. Fortunately, while the maids served pots of tea to other guests the owner offered a pot of coffee to Françoise.

"*Yasashii desu ne. Merci,*" Françoise said, as she accepted the offer.

While her guests ate, the ryokan owner squatted at a table near the entrance to read the paper. She quietly turned the pages, glanced over headlines and read one or two articles of interest. "Umm…" she muttered and looked across at Françoise who returned her quizzical gaze with raised eyebrows. The lady folded a page of the paper and slid on her zabuton across the tatami floor to talk with Françoise.

"Maybe this interesting for you." The woman indicated the page that showed a photo of a Buddhist monk standing in front of a collection of statues. Among them Françoise recognised carvings of Fudo-myoo and Kannon.

"What does it say?" Françoise asked.

The owner leaned forward and with her finger followed the Japanese characters as she translated. "It says statues taken from Omuro eighty-eight-temple mountain route at Ninna-ji," she paused. "Two men arrested for selling statues. Police think Japanese statues in Europe or California."

"Umm... makes sense," Françoise muttered.

"Why California?" The ryokan owner asked.

"A lot of ex-hippies live in California," Françoise explained. "They became interested in Zen and Buddhism back in the 1970's. Many of them are now quite wealthy so it would be easy to sell Buddhist statues there." Françoise wanted to hear more of the Omuro area. "How was it possible to take statues from these temples?" she indicated the photograph in the paper with her finger.

"You don't know Kyoto eighty-eight-temple route? It's nice. How you say... pilgrim route? It's in mountain near Ninna-ji. Like in Shikoku," she paused. "This one made in memory of Kobo-daishi. He came from Shikoku and this made by monk Sainin. All of the temples are just small wooden building. No one live in them. Not many tourist go there. You young, you should go there, get good exercise!"

"It sounds interesting," Françoise said, "but I'm afraid I don't have time. Thank you for showing me the article."

"Okay. Please, you finish breakfast." The ryokan owner slid on her zabuton back near the entrance, placed the refolded newspaper on the table, and went to the kitchen.

~

十 九

September 16th Uzamasa

Françoise left Yuhara Ryokan and walked north alongside the canal admiring the charm of the rustic homes on the narrow street. When she reached Shijo Street the town centre extended to her right but Françoise turned left towards the Keifuku electric railway line, a hundred-year-old local line built to connect the city with the outlying areas of Arashiyama. Since the trams traversed the most scenic spots of the area Françoise decided it would provide a pleasant way to travel to her destination at Uzumasa where she was to visit Koryu-ji.

Even as recently as the early 1900's this part of Kyoto had consisted of farmlands with few family homes. Rich in history, Koryu-ji was already established long before Kyoto became the capital of Japan, a period when people of Korean and Chinese heritage, people who engaged in textile and carving work, had already settled in the area. Although since developed beyond recognition, it still retained the appearance of early postwar Japan.

Françoise boarded a brown reproduction Meiji-era tram at Shijo Omiya and soon the old-fashioned carriage rattled along westwards behind the dwellings of Shijo Street. At Saiin station the line curved northwards and the tram crossed Shijo Street then passed service sheds hidden from the view of pedestrians behind a stretch of family stores. After leaving Sanjo Station the tram rocked from side to side as it continued west down the center of bustling Sanjo Street. Françoise enjoyed the experience of riding the tram through traffic but wondered how pedestrians and drivers could navigate around each other so skillfully. Yamanouchi Station was simply a raised concrete platform that measured little more than a meter wide. Trams rattled to a stop on one side while cars sped dangerously past on the other, so close in fact that Françoise marveled at people's apparent lack of concern.

Françoise's continued enjoyment of the ride however, was brought to an end when the tram arrived at Uzumasa. She left the station and crossed to the north side of the street then gave a startled cry as an acute blast on the horn signaled the tram was about to negotiate the major junction in front of Koryu-ji. Françoise watched the tram until it disappeared from view, then climbed the steps and entered the massive wooden gate of the expansive temple.

To her right the lecture hall erected in 1165 was known to be the oldest structure in Kyoto and Françoise walked across to inspect the image of Amida Nyorai seated within the building. An eight-foot tall masterpiece of Buddhist sculpture, hands held upright in front of the chest, delicate fingers spread apart with the middle finger of each hand curved down towards the thumb. The statue inspired respect.

Distracted by the open spaces of the temple Françoise walked slowly to the ticket booth located some way within the temple grounds, handed the woman her name card and said she was to meet the person in charge of the museum. The attendant made a brief call and minutes later a middle-aged monk came from the interior of the temple.

"Welcome to Koryu-ji," he said. "Please come this way."

He gestured for Françoise to enter and led her along the narrow flag-stoned pathway into the temple precincts. They passed by a pond filled with the withered leaves and stark brown seedpods of countless lotus plants. The thought of the lovely pink petals long since fallen into the water gave Françoise a certain sadness but she shook it away, hurried on over a small stone bridge, up a short flight of concrete steps and into a modern humidity controlled museum.

Miroku Bosatsu - Buddha of the Future

In the dimmed interior an impressive array of more than fifty notable Buddhist statues faced visitors. Life-size carvings of the twelve heavenly generals lined an entire wall. Along the further wall, Fudo and other venerated figures welcomed guests with a serene expression. In the centre, between a seated Buddha on the left and another Miroku Bosatsu of similar style on the right, was the famed Miroku Bosatsu statue. Françoise inspected it closely. *Alors ceci est Maitreya,* she murmured the Sanskrit name to herself. Maitreya, often referred to as a Bosatsu rather than a Nyorai, represented the Buddha of the future. Carved in wood, lacquered and treated with gold leaf it had emulated the gilt bronze statues first produced in Korea and China. Although only traces of gold lacquer remained in the folds of its torso, the slim fingers retained the mystical gesture that had enthralled millions of followers throughout the centuries.

"According to history Prince Shotoku Taishi himself carved this statue," the monk explained. Françoise knew this was doubtful but said nothing. Records show that Prince Shotoku had only presented the image of Miroku Bosatsu to Hata Kawakatsu, a respected official of the period. The temple had then been erected to house the work. Experts conclude it was probably sculpted by Korean craftsman and shipped over from Silla in 584. Prince Shotoku may have added a final touch but even that is unclear. The ceremony known as 'opening the eyes', where a monk paints in the pupils, may also be legendary since the eyelids were almost shut, a fact that Françoise now saw for herself.

"You own a statue of Prince Shotoku I believe?"

"Yes, two of them. Prince Shotoku here on the seat at the age of sixteen, and the one near the exit, the prince as a young boy."

Guided by feminine instincts Françoise walked over to the statue of the boy Shotoku and was attracted to it immediately. Bare-chested to the waist the contrast between the smooth round boyish belly and the cloth draped over the lower half exhibited excellent sculpting skills. *Je me demande si la statue du Bouddha à la naissance faite par le grand-père ressemblait à cette oeuvre,* Françoise thought to herself as she wondered if the statue of the blue Buddha made by Shigehiro's grandfather resembled this one. If it were so, it would surely appeal to everyone whether they appreciated Buddhism or not. A thief who took such a work would surely hope for a significant reward.

Roused from such thoughts Françoise moved back to the other sculptures. Four images of Kisshoten showed the influence of Silla artists that was particularly apparent in the style of the pointed shoes. Four Shitenno, heavenly kings that, since they guarded the four corners of the world, had been appropriately placed in the four corners of the hall. Françoise then stood in awe in front of three two-metre high reproductions of the thousand-armed Kannon that, despite the hands having been severely damaged, from their size alone still exuded an aura of importance.

Françoise turned to the monk beside her. "Forgive a rather intricate question," she began, "but I was not aware of the number of Buddhist statues that do not have the hands held together in their laps. Instead, like the statue of Amida Nyorai you have near the entrance, the hands are held in front of the chest or like the statue at Todai-ji in Nara held apart and open. Can you tell me the reasoning behind this?"

The monk smiled. "As you are well aware the style of Buddhist statues changed to suit local sensibilities as it proliferated from country to country. Over the centuries fourteen varying sects of Buddhism were established in Japan. A veritable treasure house of ideas I might add. Each sect established major head temples and affiliated temples throughout the country that gave support and credibility to their principles.

"Over time artists created countless representations of Nyorai and Bosatsu for these temples and each is associated with a particular hand position or mudra which symbolizes the statues' meditative, contemplative, or compassionate level. Nyorai and Bosatsu however, are multi-faceted and sculptors used their artistic license to create their own variations, thus lay people remain puzzled when they try to identify statues from the hand and finger positions alone. The esoteric sects, notably Tendai-shu and Shingon-shu, clarify this situation by maintaining nine positions of related mudra."

"This is getting complicated," Françoise murmured.

"Not so complex," the monk took a leaflet from a table and handed it to Françoise.

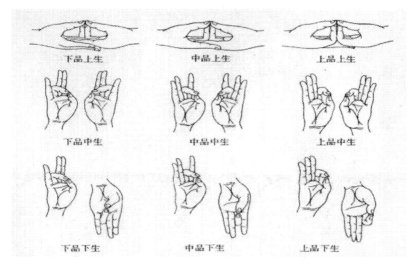

"Notice the three levels of hand positions. Within each level different fingers touching the thumbs denote lower, middle and upper rank. These are the same fingers in each of the levels. Thus the third finger denotes the lower rank, the middle finger the middle rank, and the forefinger the upper rank.

"At the meditative level both hands lay together in the lap. This is the style of the great Buddha at Kamakura, first finger to the thumbs indicates the highest rank. At the contemplative level both hands are raised to chest height with palms slightly outward. This is the style of the Amida Nyorai you saw near the entrance, ring fingers to the thumbs represents the lowest rank. At the compassionate level the palm of the right hand faces outwards at chest height, while the left hand rests palm upwards on the knee. This is the style of the great Buddha at Todai-ji in Nara, middle fingers slightly forward appropriate for the middle rank."

Françoise studied the sketches on the leaflet and nodded her comprehension.

"Now to business!" The monk abruptly changed the subject. "The abbot and I have already discussed the possibility of loaning you statues. He agrees to share our riches but having never dealt with an overseas museum makes us feel rather anxious."

"Be assured the Cernushi Museum enjoys an excellent safety record and we would deal with a reputable Japanese shipping company."

"Our concern is theft such as occurred at the Tokyo National Museum recently. We heard that the police suspect those pieces may be offered for sale in Europe or America."

Françoise was surprised at how quickly the news spread and thoughts and images crossed her mind, including those of Georges' antique shop.

"Yes, that was unfortunate but I promise we will take the utmost precautions to make sure the statues remain safe and intact."

"Well, that seems the most we can do. Of course we cannot part with the Maitreya but you can select any of the heavenly generals or these Kisshoten. They are all of the same period. May I suggest the statue known as Bishamonten, holding aloft the small pagoda? He is an incarnation of Tamonten, one of the four heavenly kings, but as Bishimonten he's not part of a set. He should be up to travelling."

"Prince Shotoku as a boy is out of the question I suppose."

"Yes. He's too precious. Besides he is too young," the monk smiled.

"In that case..." Françoise moved to the line of Kisshoten statues and selected one that clearly showed Korean influence in spite of its more recent creation."

"A good choice," the monk reacted.

"And I will follow your advice and take the Bishamonten. I hate to deprive eleven generals of one of their colleagues so I will leave the heavenly generals. Besides they look as though they might be quite a challenge to have them packed and sent abroad."

"Actually each statue has enough hollow space inside to store the attachments when they are moved. If you are interested such things, you should you pay a visit to the Matsuhisa Sohrin Buddhist Art Institute at Sanjo Gokomachi where experts can show you the latest techniques used for transporting statues properly."

"Thank you. Yes, in fact I have an appointment with them and I am already late. I really should get there soon. I am getting very behind in my schedule."

Françoise withdrew a packet of documents required for the release and shipping of statues from her bag and handed it to the monk. "If you could complete these forms and send them to the Cernushi, that would be most appreciated. There's an addressed envelope inside and the shipping agents will contact you to confirm dates and other details probably around the middle of next month."

Françoise thanked the monk for his help, and for the leaflet of mudra, then took her leave. As she walked back through the temple grounds to the exit thoughts of Shigehiro came to mind and she wondered how things were back at Honkomyo-ji.

In Nagoya Central Hospital in the bed next to Yoshihisa, the old man looked up from his newspaper over at the doorway of the four-bed room.

"Huh! They've sent a priest to see you," he said.

Laid on his back staring at the ceiling, Yoshihisa thought it was an hallucination when he saw his son's face loom into view above him.

"Father, I have bad news," Shigehiro said quietly. He wondered if his father was too drugged to comprehend. He saw a faint nod and he continued.

"Grandfather passed away at midday two days ago."

Yoshihisa's eyelids closed and a long sigh emitted from the bandaged jaw.

"The funeral will take place in two or three day's time?" he queried. "I will be well enough by then."

"No, Father. The wake was last night and the funeral will be tomorrow. You cannot be discharged from the hospital for three or four more days. I have already checked."

"I just wanted to expand the temple. All ego. I can see that now. I just wanted to achieve more than your grandfather. Even told the other temples to lend their statues to Yamamoto. It was only after we found out they'd taken that Buddha statue from the workshop that I realised how wrong a path I had taken. I promised I would get it back. Even went to Yamamoto to…" He coughed painfully. "and learnt the hard way not to…" He coughed again. There was anguish in his father's face but Shigehiro was low on compassion.

"What you don't appreciate is the life that grandfather breathed into those statues. Carving was his sustenance. He could not have lived without sculpting. His carvings were venerable figures that few people can emulate."

Shigehiro stood the picture of his grandfather he had taken from the writing desk on the table beside his father's bed, placed the ring of juzu prayer beads and the two candles beside it, and with a nod to the old man that shared the room, turned and left.

～

As Françoise descended the steps of Koryu-ji a blast of horn warned of an oncoming tram, she ran to the nearby station, boarded a traditional green one-man streetcar and returned to Omiya. On her walk back to Ryokan Yuhara she tried to photograph the rustic canal scene she had passed earlier that day but, annoyed with the mess of utility poles, telephone wires and electric cables, she gave up. *C'est terriblement disgracieux, pourquoi ne pas les dissimuleler sous la terre?* she asked herself. However, a few meters further a splendid growth of ivy that climbed a support cable provided an opportunity for reflection on a different kind of aestheticism.

Back at the Ryokan the frail owner greeted Françoise and asked about her day.

"Thank you. Yes, a fine day," Françoise replied. Return to Paris was approaching and Françoise wondered what Georges or any of his associates knew about a black market for Buddhist statues in Europe, she asked the ryokan's owner if she might send a fax and upon being assured that she could, wrote out a note to her husband.

Georges, demande à tes connaissances dans le domaine des antiques s'ils sont au courant d'un certain marché de statues Bouddhistes Japonaises vendues en Europe. Ce sont peut-être des pièces volées au Japon. Envoie-moi une télécopie chez Itsue. Je quitte cet hôtel demain. Je t'embrasse.

Françoise sent the fax and went upstairs to her room, grabbed the fresh starched blue yukata and skipped back downstairs to enjoy a well-deserved long hot bath. Afterwards, feeling refreshed and relaxed, she put four 100-yen coins in the green public phone by the hotel entrance and called Itsue's number.

"Hello. ... I'm in Kyoto. It's marvelous. I just wish I had more time. ... I was with him yesterday. He has returned to his temple. ... Grandfather Hiro? ... Oh, No! ... Kitamura-sensei has gone to the funeral? ... There's a woodcarving center I must visit tomorrow. Would it be too late to pay my respects in the evening? ... Should I take flowers? ... Okay. I understand. ... Probably the day after tomorrow. May I stay one more night? ... That's great Itsue. Thanks. ... You too. Bye."

Françoise put the handset back in its rest. Distractedly slid open the entrance door of the ryokan and stepped across the narrow road to the canal.

Ainsi, le grand-père Hiro est parti, Françoise thought as tears came to her eyes. *La police avait-elle trouvé son fils, le père de Shigehiro?*

The thin frail owner of the ryokan, always alert to the click of the door, came to the entrance, saw Françoise standing on the other side and went across to her.

"You okay?" she asked.

"Uh! Oh, yes. I'm okay. Thanks."

"You shouldn't leave door open. Mosquitoes get in."

"Oh! I'm so sorry, I wasn't thinking."

"You want dinner?" she asked.

"Yes. Yes, please."

"Okay. I tell them to bring your room."

二十

September 17th Kasanui

The austere dinner that preceded the Buddhist funeral service at Honkomyo-ji took place in a sombre yet relaxed atmosphere. Fellow monks from nearby temples of the same sect had arrived earlier to help in the kitchen and assist with preparations for the ceremony to be held the following day. Shigehiro and his mother joined their family in the main room while other relatives formed small groups in adjoining rooms of the temple residence. In the narrow street outside the temple, more than a hundred people from the neighbourhood waited quietly to pay their last respects to the beloved wood carver who had been such a well-respected member of the community. Others who lived further away would come early the next morning.

As soon as meal dishes were cleared away, monks opened the main gate and visitors filed respectfully through the temple grounds. They headed directly for the main hall where grandfather Hiro lay reposed before the Bosatsu of compassion. Slowly, in turn, people took a pinch of granulated incense between the tips of their fingers, lifted it reverently to their foreheads and then sprinkled it onto the glowing charcoal embers in the incense burner placed in front of the open coffin. With prayer beads wrapped around their hands, each mourner put their palms together for a personal prayer, before they moved aside for the next person to do the same and whisper goodbye.

By the time the last visitors departed it was well after midnight. The undertakers formally reminded Shigehiro that someone should be in attendance throughout the night to maintain the lit candle that would guide the deceased into the next world, several relatives nodded in agreement, and the undertakers, reassured that everyone understood, bowed and discreetly left. Some relatives did indeed stay awake the whole night. Others, squatted on the tatami floor or seated on grey metal folding chairs, to ease their legs, gradually tired and became drowsy. A few left for an hour sleep and came back when a bit rested, but most quietly chatted to keep each other awake, and around the nether hours conversations turned to lesser known memories and family secrets. In spite of the circumstances some kinfolk were happy to have the opportunity to meet again and several stagnant relationships experienced an awkward renewal. Suddenly a younger sister of Shigehiro's mother awoke from her drowsiness, glanced in the direction of the coffin and screamed. Everyone's head turned towards her, then to where she pointed. The candle to show the deceased the way in the new world had burnt out. Calmly Shigehiro took another candle from a box, lit it and placed it in the holder.

At sunrise Shigehiro stood, stretched his limbs, stepped down from the main hall and walked across to the main gate. A stray cat meowed. Shigehiro lifted the wooden beam from the brackets that held the temple gates closed and pulled open one of the heavy doors. The cat scurried off and Shigehiro noticed further down the lane a young man conversing with Miura from the shrine. Perhaps an opportunist who pretended to know the deceased in order to receive the token of thanks presented to all mourners. His face however, seemed familiar and Shigehiro studied him for some moments. He then remembered him as one of the drummers that performed at the autumn festival. Françoise had called out to him. What was his name? Chulsoo? What was he doing here so early in the morning? Shigehiro pondered as he headed back into the temple, and across to the private quarters for a wash and an appropriate change of clothes before the funeral prayers.

At ten o'clock the oldest follower of grandfather Hiro who led the rituals rose and folded his wooden-framed seat. This signaled the end of the initial prayers. Family members left and the undertakers hurried to stack the chairs against the walls. Two trestles were opened in the center of the room and the straight-sided coffin was placed on top of them. The lid was lifted and brought down beside the trestles. Shigehiro, in the absence of his father, led the line of relatives towards the pearl gray wooden coffin and each in turn surrounded the body with flowers and small gifts. Friends and neighbors followed; added a single white chrysanthemum to the coffin and paused for a prayer or a gentle stroke of the weathered face. Outside Shigehiro was handed the urn that would contain his grandfather's cremains. Shigehiro's mother, the eldest woman in the family, held the wooden tablet that would be inscribed with Hiro's posthumous Buddhist name. Another female relative carried in a frame, the upper corners draped across with black ribbons, a portrait of grandfather Hiro.

Near the women a hearse stood ready to receive its sorrowful load. Its front section, like any other hearse, was a highly polished black limousine, but the rear two thirds built of light beige cedar wood, was uniquely Japanese. The elegant calligraphic lines of the curved roof, reminiscent of a Buddhist temple, overhung either side of the vehicle. Underneath, on both sides, a small glass window was surrounded with intricate carvings of flowers and birds embellished with gold leaf. At the back, skillfully carved twin doors stood open.

After everyone stepped outside, the undertakers closed the coffin. Then, preceded by a senior monk chanting and tinkling a bell, six other monks lifted the coffin, carried it out and slid it smoothly into the waiting hearse, at which point the chanting ended. An undertaker placed a microphone into Shigehiro's hand

and urged him to say a few words. Shigehiro took a step forward and spoke of his feelings for his grandfather, and expressed regret that he had been absent when his grandfather passed away. Thanked those in attendance for attending the funeral in spite of their busy schedule and entreated them to continue their support of the temple to prolong the memory of his grandfather's work. Shigehiro then looked across at the coffin through the still open doors of the hearse and remembered his father on his own in the hospital in Nagoya. He then choked back tears as he appealed to neighbors to forego the troubled circumstances that kept Yoshihisa away from his father's funeral. The doors of the hearse were then closed and family mourners directed to two black limousines that would take them to the crematorium. Other mourners stood with their heads bowed and the limousines' horns blared a full fifteen seconds to signal departure before they drove off. At the side of the road outside the temple, a female undertaker's assistant knelt, lifted a rice bowl, smashed it on the ground beside the gate then put her hands together in prayer over the broken remains. It was the sweetest of the complex gestures carried out that day, for although members of a household share most of the dining ware, each person has their own rice bowl, and grandfather Hiro would not need his anymore.

Upon arrival at the crematorium the hearse continued along the side of the building passed the main entrance and stopped in front of another entrance further down. Other private cars of relatives and friends had followed the three black limousines to attend the last moments of the funeral ritual in the mountains of Ikoma and the passengers now joined the other family members. The plain wooden coffin was unloaded onto a chrome electric powered transporter and the operator steered it into the interior. Everyone followed into the marble hall and the senior monk once more took up chanting. The last minutes of farewell had come, the coffin was opened once more and mourners of the immediate family gave a last offering of incense, clasped hands in prayer and murmured words of goodbye. In the presence of the grim reaper's scythe a rush of questions surfaced in the minds of many. Faced with life's inevitable cruelty the wise amongst them recognised their own mortality and viewed their own future with a little more foreboding.

The further wall was set with what appeared to be three miniature sets of steel elevator doors. The trolley was wheeled to the left-hand side and a button pushed. The doors opened, the powered rollers eased the coffin forward and the doors closed. A female crematorium assistant led the mourners outside, across a courtyard and up to the second floor of an adjacent building where large brown leather settees and armchairs offered them rest. Other family groups were already present. Nothing seemed to happen and no refreshment was served. Shigehiro, his mother and two older close relations were seated together conversing quietly. One man held council, two others light-heartedly discussed various matters and others visited the restrooms. One man stood at the plate glass window and waited for smoke to come from the roof vents of the opposite building but with a temperature inside the furnaces that would reach five hundred degrees Celsius there would be little to be observed in the way of fumes.

Twenty minutes later the same female assistant came and spoke to Shigehiro. Family members then followed him down the stairs and along the side of the crematorium to a small bare concrete room. The assistant warned them not to touch the sides of the still hot metal trolley as they entered and gathered around the scorched white bones that lay before them. Whispers and nervous coughs stopped. The stark reality of death hit everyone. The skeleton, both holy and monstrous, demanded reverence, for many it felt somehow obscene to gaze upon the bones of a man whom one had known in the flesh.

In a matter of fact tone the woman explained how the unblemished appearance of the bones meant an absence of disease, and that a good wholesome life had been lived. The woman then handed each guest in turn a set of steel chopsticks designated for the situation and guided everyone to pick a piece of bone from a different part of the skeleton and place it in the ceramic urn that she held. The woman herself then singled out a piece of bone from the neck and explained how its shape resembled a Buddha with legs crossed in meditation, she wrapped it in cotton, positioned it on top of the other pieces, sealed the urn, set it into a white silk-covered box and handed it to Shigehiro.

Followed by his mother and the others, Shigehiro carried the urn out to the designated car. Once passengers entered the limousine they were alone with their private thoughts and Shigehiro began to reflect on his life as a youth. A boy who would slip into the main hall, creep under the barrier that separated the monks from the abbot and sit at his grandfather's side. The same boy who would hear the irregular rhythm of the sculptor's mallet, ease the door of the storehouse open, and watch his grandfather at work. Shigehiro can you keep a secret? Shigehiro remembered those sacred words. I'm going to give this statue to you, grandfather had said, but not a word to anyone. Do you promise? Shigehiro had promised.

The cars returned to Honkomyo-ji, Shigehiro took hold of the silk covered box on his lap and carried it to the main hall. He placed it on a white table between a photograph of his grandfather and the posthumous nameplate, already engraved. In such a short time the long life of his grandfather had been reduced to pieces of bone, but what happened to his distilled wisdom and his years of diligent work? Did all that disappear in those few short hours, and at a time of such humiliation? Shigehiro glanced up at the benevolent countenance of Kannon Bosatsu, then back at his grandfather's photograph and the urn before him, as he pondered again the missing statues and the theft of the Blue Buddha.

二十一

September 17th Nagoya & Mie

In the back room of Kitamura's antique shop in Nagoya the Professor greeted his guest respectfully. Chulsoo in turn, seated in the formal seiza position, slid a thick unmarked envelope across the tatami towards his host. Kitamura already suspected a connection between either Chulsoo or Kouno and the theft of the stolen statues. This confirmed that it had been Kouno who supplied the information to whoever had broken into his premises and committed the theft.

"You don't have to do this," Kitamura said. "The insurance will cover the loss."

"You will still have to pay for other damages. Meanwhile, I will do what I can to get them returned to you. You have my word."

"Do you know where to find them?"

"In Mie prefecture. I can't say more, but if I have a chance, I will get them."

"That might put you in serious trouble. Don't risk it. This and the insurance will see me through. Make it up with Itsue-chan instead."

"I don't think it will work, Kitamura-san. There is too much about me she cannot accept. I should have known better and never gotten involved with her in the first place."

"Unfortunately we have not much control over affairs of the heart and when we ignore them we get depressed, angry, miserable. You must be honest with yourself, Chulsoo. Korean or not you must decide what you want and act accordingly. Complying with other's wishes may avoid unpleasant confrontations, but you must do what you feel is right for you otherwise you will regret it. Believe me. I know it to be true."

Chulsoo frowned. It was the first time Kitamura had ever hinted at a woman he wished to marry.

"I want to, Kitamura-san, but there are too many social pressures in Korean families, even among the younger generation born here in Japan."

"In the old days Japanese families were the same. Sadly we could not always marry the person we fell in love with. Personal feelings too often sacrificed for the good of others, but these days' people are more assertive and can marry whomever they want. There should be nothing or no one to stop you marrying Itsue."

While Kitamura spoke Chulsoo looked down at the tatami flooring before him, the tightly compacted woven reeds seemed to epitomize the situation he was in, with no room to move one way or the other and no way to get out of it.

"Chulsoo, I haven't spent the better part of my life in the classroom not to become a pretty good judge of character. I don't know your uncle, but you are a good man and Itsue knows it. I can see enchantment in her eyes when you are together, but she is desperately worried about making the same mistake again."

"You mean what you told me at Kasanui? That she was married before?"

"Well, it was a short affair." The old professor realised he had said too much. "Anyway, stop listening to me. Go and see her."

170

Once again in the French restaurant of the Nagoya Hilton Hotel, at a table too near for Chulsoo's liking to the table where they dined before, Chulsoo faced Itsue once again. The waiter remembered all too well the previous time they were there and eyed them apprehensively as he handed over the menus. The night before Chulsoo wide-awake with anxiety had envisaged life with the misery of losing Itsue. Finally he decided to follow Kitamura's advice, called Itsue and implored her to meet him. Grudgingly she agreed and was now seated before him.

Chulsoo ordered a bottle of wine to ease the situation but Itsue seldom brought her glass to her lips to take a tiny sip as Chulsoo tried again to regain her trust. He told her he would try to get his uncle to return the stolen statues. It was against the underworld's principals to make trouble with ordinary citizens.

"Even if you don't respect the people I associate with, at least make an effort to understand the hardships they have lived through in order to just to survive. Yes, some men who work for my uncle are thugs and others uneducated, but that doesn't make them evil. Most of them would rather have respectable jobs and responsibilities they could be proud of, but because of social traumas and discriminations they have not had the same opportunities as other members of society, thus they have turned to other ways to support themselves. Their ethics may be unacceptable to you but they have helped me and taught me certain values to live by."

"And what values are those?" Itsue retorted sarcastically. "Theft, rape?"

"No. Itsue. We have a very strict code of conduct, and most of us stick to it. Street crime is forbidden. We have even helped police track down that kind of offender. They do not represent us. They are simply punks. We work within the law and contrary to popular belief the majority of us do not have anything to do with drugs."

Chulsoo paused, then asked Itsue again to marry him. If she would, he swore he would seek permission to part from his uncle and work hard to create a new life for them both. For Itsue the image of a future life with Chulsoo alternately cleared and misted. It was obvious that as a youth Chulsoo had been obliged to comply with his uncle's requests, but his duties were now more consequential and he questioned his future. Itsue knew he loved her, and she wanted to be with him, to help him make a new life, but there was so much to consider.

"Chulsoo there is something you don't know."

"About what?"

"About my past. – I was once married before."

"It's not important, but thanks for telling me."

"My husband was abusive and… You are not surprised! Who told you?"

Chulsoo remained silent.

"Kitamura..? It must have been! He is the only one who knows both you and my past."

Chulsoo hesitated but it was too late. Itsue easily realised the truth.

"He said if I were to leave the organization, you would see things differently."

Itsue's eyebrows rose.

"And just when did you talk with him about this?"

"In Kasanui when we went for his friend's funeral."

"You took Kitamura-sensei to Kasanui?"

"He asked me to drive him. He didn't want to face the crowded train. We went down early so he could attend the wake. We stayed in a Ryokan. I woke early and went out for a walk. I passed the temple and met Miura. We chatted for a bit then…"

"Who is Miura?"

Chulsoo sighed. "You are worse than the police. He is the priest at the shrine next to Honkomyo-ji. Our troupe has performed there several times."

"Why didn't you mention this to me?"

"No reason to tell you. It was between him and me."

Itsue's mind was turned upside down. He was right, there was no reason to tell her, but she had done nothing but think about him for the last forty-eight hours. She respected Kitamura, and his obvious faith and confidence in Chulsoo brought severe doubts into her mind about her mother's judgment. Her father said nothing and she wondered which side of the fence he would come down on, but either way she would have to be certain that this man loved her unconditionally, without that she would have no choice but to adhere to her mother's demands.

"Chulsoo do you seriously expect to be able to leave your uncle's organization, for me to walk away from my family, and for us to get married, just like that?"

"Why not?"

"How can I be sure that your leaving would be final? That they would have nothing more to do with you."

Chulsoo hesitated. "Okay, I can give you proof, if that is what you want," he said.

Itsue had no idea what she asked for. What she had set in motion. What leaving the underworld entailed.

~

After sitting in his car on the outskirts of Sakakibara-Onsenguchi for more than an hour, Chulsoo decided the time had come for him to act and drove off in the direction of the museum. The scattered cigarette butts left on the verge of the lay-by testified as to how long he had been there.

Chulsoo drove past the car park attendant and parked his dented Cima near the iron staircase that led to a back door of his uncle's office. Instead of climbing the staircase however, he walked to the main entrance, through the museum and approached his uncle's office from the inside door. Cheong turned from the window as Chulsoo entered.

"Well? Did you find your father? Ha, ha, ha, ha. And don't tell me you haven't been searching for him, because I have reports of your activities."

Cheong knew that Chulsoo had exhausted himself trying to track down his father in the maze of unfamiliar streets of south Osaka. Cheong thought he held the cards; he was not going to tell Chulsoo where his father was, but his eyebrows rose as his nephew strode across the room and stood before him.

"Uncle Cheong," Chulsoo bowed formally. "I want to make a new life for myself outside the confines of Tsuruhashi, but I cannot do so without your consent. Please grant me your permission to part from the organization. Without it I cannot leave."

"You treacherous bastard! After all I've done for you."

"Uncle. This decision is not easy for me. It's true you have raised me well, but you wronged father because he would not bow to you and in doing so you deprived mother of her husband. For me it is different. I will forever hold you in my heart. You taught me never to be afraid of any man, and so I can ask you to grant me this one last request."

Cheong walked around his desk, slumped into the seat and held his nephew in his gaze for an interminable time. Chulsoo in turn kept his eyes steadfastly on his uncle.

"You are serious about this?" Cheong reluctantly asked.

"Yes I am," Chulsoo nodded.

"You know what a decision like this entails?"

"I will accept whatever the oyabun demands."

Cheong studied his nephew carefully and acknowledged the younger man's courage in choosing to go it alone. Everything he had taught him now come back upon him. The boy had character and determination. Bitter memories of how he treated Chulsoo's father came to mind. He would have to let the boy go.

"Go down and tell Kouno to get my car ready and both of you wait for me downstairs."

After Chulsoo left the office Cheong picked up the phone and tapped in a number. A brief conversation and he hung up, grabbed his coat and locked the office door.

Downstairs Kouno drove Cheong's immaculate limousine up to the side entrance where Chulsoo waited.

"What's going on?"

"I'm leaving the organization."

"You're crazy! For that woman?"

"Kouno. I have a chance to make a respectable life for myself. I have to take it."

"You never did take the easy way, did you?"

"I'm sorry, Kouno. I have to do this."

"Well, if you ever need…"

They were interrupted by Cheong's arrival. He indicated for Chulsoo to get into the front passenger seat. Cheong himself then climbed in behind the rear black tinted windows. Kouno waited for instructions, then drove off down the narrow country lane and out onto the highway. If this request were rejected, Cheong knew he would be chastised for giving his own tacit permission. If it were granted, the organization would lose a valuable and trusted man. Either way the senior advisor would not be pleased.

The three men reached the country home of the syndicate's senior advisor in less than an hour. Kouno leapt from the drivers seat to open the rear door. As Cheong stepped from his Sovereign President he swallowed heavily when he saw the majestic lines of a classic cream Mercedes-Benz S170 parked in the front courtyard of the farmhouse. He knew the owner of that particular vehicle to be none other than the oyabun Hyuun Pak. The main door of the building opened, Chulsoo and Kouno were shown to a side room and asked to wait. Cheong was directed along his usual route to the guestroom. As he progressed down the hallway two familiar voices became clear. Those of the senior advisor and the man he both respected and feared, Hyuun Pak himself. The door slid open and Cheong stepped apprehensively into the room.

"How is it that we get these problems from you?" The advisor asked immediately.

"Calm down, Lee. We have enough problems," the oyabun said as he strode across the room to embrace Cheong as an old friend.

"This is most irregular," the advisor protested but the oyabun cut him short.

"Leave us," he said firmly. His arm around Cheong's shoulder, Hyuun Pak walked him across the room to the full-length glass doors that overlooked the garden.

"I know how it is," he said quietly. "The old days are over my friend. We can no longer expect devoted loyalty anymore. The world has changed and we must accept these facts. You see how I abuse my advisor and he still does not question my decisions. Remember it was he that invited you to bring Chulsoo into the organization. However, the young blood is different. They work for us as long as we pay them, but loyalty like you have given me, my friend, is no longer part of their contract."

"Thank you most sincerely," Cheong muttered. "I have absolutely no excuse."

"The young think they can handle life by themselves," Hyuun Pak continued as though he hadn't heard Cheong speak, "until something unfortunate happens, then they come running to us for help. We older ones know the ways of the world," the oyabun chuckled, "I don't suppose it will be the last time you will see young Chulsoo at your door."

"We have become weak," Cheong protested. "Our parents would not believe how much we give in to this younger generation."

"To survive we have to change with the times. We learnt from our parents, now we learn from our children. We have to bend like the bamboo or get broken like the oak."

Hyuun Pak and Cheong looked out over the Garden.

"Does Chulsoo understand the cost of his decision?" the oyabun asked.

"I think so."

"And he is prepared for that?"

"It seems so."

"Then we must let him go. I know he has been a son to you and you want him to show his loyalty to me just as you have done but that is not important anymore. Come, let's get this over with."

They turned and crossed the room together. Hyuun Pak called for the advisor who arrived within seconds with two other men. They moved the rectangular lacquered wooden table and zabuton to one end of the room and at the other end a block of wood on four short carved legs was set out. It was a board used for the game of Go. It could have been that a game was being prepared except that the board had been set upon a white sheet and the two bowls of Go pieces remained in a corner of the tokonoma.

The oyabun and Cheong were seated cross-legged on *zabuton* at the far end of the room. Chulsoo was summoned and they soon heard the sound of his approaching footsteps. He slid open the door, bowed and entered. Two other men in their early forties accompanied him. One man carried a bundle of white towels, the other man a natural wood chopping board and a long thin bladed knife, much like the ones sushi chefs use for preparing raw fish. Everything was placed near the Go board and Chulsoo sank to his knees on the tatami floor.

The advisor, HaJoon Lee addressed Chulsoo from the far side of the Go board.

"Are you sure you want to go through with this?"

"Yes," Chulsoo replied.

"You will pay 5,000,000 yen into Cheong's bank. You have such money?"

"That will not be necessary," Cheong interrupted.

"That will be necessary," HaJoon insisted.

Cheong knew better than to protest. Chulsoo acknowledged the demand.

"Well then," the advisor said and nodded to the two men near the wall. One of the men motioned for Chulsoo to sit opposite him on the other side of the Go board. The man reached out, took Chulsoo's left hand and pulled it sharply towards him forcing Chulsoo to grab the edge of the Go board with his other hand. The man took a short piece of thin string from the top of the pile of towels, wound it twice around the base of Chulsoo's little finger, pulled it tight and tied it. He placed the chopping board on top of the Go board, took a long strip of white cloth and bound it around Chulsoo's hand to hold the other fingers curled under. He pushed Chulsoo's hand back across the board and pulled the ends of the cloth underneath so that Chulsoo's hand was pulled against the edge of the chopping board with his little finger protruding over the top. Chulsoo's fingers jammed tight against the board, the man pulled the cloth sharply and tied it. He took the knife, placed it in front of him on the board and leaned back on his heels. The other man knelt in front of the tokonoma, lit a small white candle and placed two sticks of incense in the burner. He now knelt next to Chulsoo and gave him a small glass. The man poured cold Nihonshu to the brim. Chulsoo downed it in one gulp and placed the empty glass on the board. The man removed it. Sweat beaded on Chulsoo's forehead.

Hyuun Pak leaned towards Cheong with an interrogative look. Cheong nodded and the oyabun in turn nodded to the advisor. The man took the knife, stabbed the point lightly into the board some distance from Chulsoo's unprotected finger, held on to the point and brought the handle expertly down across the finger. HaJoon grunted and shook his head from side to side. Chulsoo felt a sudden sting and immediate numbness. The end joint shot out across the board. The man removed the knife and the other man threw one of the white towels down on the stub. Chulsoo grabbed the towel with his other hand and clamped it to the wound. The numbness began to turn to pain and blood seeped through. The long strip of cloth was untied and Chulsoo was handed other towels. The man who had welded the knife picked up the end of the finger, placed it on a square of white cloth and put it between the candle and incense in the tokonoma. As the flow of blood slowly abated one of the men expertly applied a dressing to the base of Chulsoo's finger. The pile of bloodied towels and cloth were gathered on top of the cutting board, the knife wiped and the other man took them from the room. The stub of Chulsoo's finger began to throb and the pain intensified. Chulsoo was offered another glass of Nihonshu and told to remove the piece of string around the finger in about an hour, but to keep the dressing on for two or three days. Chulsoo was no longer Cheong's nephew. He had been literally cut off from the organization. The advisor moved forward until his face was inches from Chulsoo's ear.

"You have significant knowledge about the operations of this organization," HaJoon Lee intoned, his voice no more than a whisper. "If you ever leak the slightest information to any member of the police, you will lose far more than a finger."

Chulsoo nodded, leaned heavily on the Go board and started to rise. Cheong also started to rise but the oyabun gestured for him to remain seated and called for Kouno.

"Kouno, take Chulsoo back to the office in Cheong's car. Help him gather whatever possessions he has there and get the hell out," he ordered. "I will bring Cheong back in the morning."

The tension was immense. Hyuun Pak, Cheong, HaJoon, all remained silent while the men cleared the room and Chulsoo and Kouno were shown out. Even after the sound of Cheong's Sovereign faded in the distance neither of them spoke. Finally HaJoon called out loudly and an aide slid the door open.

"Let's have some Nihonshu in here, and some food," he ordered.

After a few drinks the oyabun opened one of the glass doors that overlooked the garden, lit a fat cigar, and inquired about current business matters.

"Sasaki has been stripped of his rank and faces dismissal from the police," the advisor said. "That however, is not our problem, but it means that we no longer have a local inspector in our pocket. Until we find someone else, we will have to use more caution."

"Anything else," the oyabun asked.

"Yes. There have been arrests in France, including Cheong's contact in Paris."

"Ha, ha, ha, ha. Old Georges René de Cotret?" Cheong laughed. "I knew he would be in trouble one day."

"The point is," the advisor continued. "We don't want any ramifications so I suggest we suspend the export business for a while."

"In that case, Cheong." The oyabun looked across at his slightly younger cousin. "You'd better think of a new scheme for getting money out of the country."

Cheong sighed. This had not been a good day.

⌇⌇⌇

Part Four

Louvre Sculpture Museum at Sakakibara-Onsenguchi

二 十 二

September 17th Kyoto

At Yuhara ryokan after another Japanese breakfast with a double helping of rice and complimentary coffee Françoise enquired of the owner if she could leave her bag at the ryokan until the evening. Assured that she could, she returned to her room, packed and took her case down the narrow stairway to the entrance where the frail host asked her to place it behind the reception desk. Françoise thanked her, left the ryokan and turned south alongside the canal for a short walk to the Keihan Railway Station. At Shichijo she turned east, crossed the bridge over the Kamo River, descended the stairs to the platform and boarded a train going north.

Three stations later Françoise alighted at Sanjo Station, climbed the stairs to street level, and walked back across the River. At the apex of the bridge stood a middle-aged Buddhist monk dressed in a traditional black robe and rough rope sandals. His back against the parapet, ringing a tiny brass hand bell he quietly chanted Buddhist sutras. An old lady shuffled towards him, dropped a few coins into the bowl at his feet and stood with head bowed while the monk, oblivious to the noise of traffic and bustle of pedestrians, recited the prayers dedicated to the wellbeing of her soul. Minutes later the lady went on her way and the monk resumed his melodious chant, but Françoise gazed a while longer captivated by the traditional and contemporary worlds.

At the junction of Kawaramachi and Sanjo streets, Françoise crossed over and continued west along Sanjo, inside a covered shopping arcade with countless shops that sold everything imaginable from fashion goods to musical instruments from pizza to French cuisine. At the further end of the arcade, once more out in the open, Françoise looked up at the moving legs of a gigantic mechanical red crab mounted above the entrance to a restaurant. She then walked on to the next junction and turned left to the Matsuhisa Institute of Buddhist Art.

Wedged between a Christian wedding chapel and a traditional timber-framed Kyoto town house, the institute displayed in their windows two recently completed Nio kings that faced the interior of the gallery. Eager to examine their visages Françoise entered the institute where two other resplendent statues in a glass showcase distracted her. After years of working with antiques Françoise was overjoyed to see recently made works. The difference between the weathered statues encrusted with grime and these fresh clean works of art was striking. These gods exhibited such a different allure. As Françoise closely examined the lifelike hands, muscular arms, and the delicate application of gold leaf, she became aware of a Japanese woman her own age, dressed in a dark blue smock, on the opposite side of the showcase. The woman smiled and Françoise walked around the showcase to meet her.

"Allow me to introduce myself. I am from the Cernushi Museum in Paris." Françoise took a card from her lacquered card case and handed it to the lady.

"I am Kayu Matsuhisa," she gave Françoise one of her own cards. "We have been expecting you. Your secretary said you would be in Kyoto sometime this week."

"I am running late, Japan is such a fascinating country."

"Have you found what you are looking for? I noticed you studying these two statues quite intently."

"They are magnificent," Françoise said. "As a museum curator I only deal with antique works and it's so refreshing to see contemporary works. I can't get over the difference between these statues and the ones I deal with. These gods seem young and virile."

"An appropriate comment," Kayu responded, "They are Fujin and Raijin, the gods of wind, thunder and storms. The Japanese archipelago is vulnerable to all types of natural disasters: earthquakes, typhoons, floods and we feel the need to pacify these gods who threaten our homes with the perils of our unstable and challenging climate."

Kayu's card stated that she was Curator of the Matsuhisa Buddhist Image Engraving Hall and President of Matsuhisa Sohrin Buddhist Institute and Religious Arts Institute.

"You hold quite a position," Françoise said.

"I'm the youngest daughter of Matsuhisa Sohrin. I became president of the Matsuhisa Buddhist Institute and the Religious Art Institute after my father died in 1992."

"Are there still sculptors here at this institute," Françoise queried.

"Yes, several work here daily. However, more than a hundred sculptors have completed apprenticeships, become masters and moved on. We keep some of their statues at the institute while others are displayed at temples throughout Japan. We firmly believe that culture should be passed on to future generations and we endeavor to work to the highest standards. Just as sculptors in India, China and Korea gave their images a national sensibility, we strive to transmit a sense of the Japaneseque."

"Are you a sculptor yourself?" Françoise asked.

"I'm a painter. I specialize in restoring traditional Buddhist paintings.

"Your roots obviously led you to this artistic life?"

"Yes, my grandfather, Matsuhisa Hohrin, started to engrave figures at the age of ten, and after a career of seventy years it is said he created seven thousand Buddhist images. He believed the Buddhist principle that the soul of Buddha exists within each of us. He wanted his students to find their Buddha soul and bring it to life through sculpture. They could then be reminded of the Buddha they ought to follow and keep him in sight. Matsuhisa Hohrin taught that a Buddha skillfully crafted need not be the best sculpture of all, instead it should represent the individual's desire to welcome the Buddha into their lives."

"Interesting thought," Françoise acknowledged. "And your father was also a sculptor?"

"Yes, my father, Sohrin, devoted his life to Buddhism and education. He imparted his knowledge of carving and engraving techniques to professional artisans and amateurs alike. He kept his works close at hand for others to study. We continue to respect his principles and use many of his works at the institute to inspire others."

"I am curious about statues decorated with gold leaf. Is gold still used today?"

"Well, the art has lost much of its popularity, but my elder sister Maya has adapted her skills to the ancient technique. In fact in 1979 she published a book about it. Let me take you upstairs to meet her, she always enjoys the chance for a break."

Françoise followed Kayu to the second floor where a vast open workspace was packed with statues in all stages of completion. Maya came across and Kayu introduced her. After formalities Françoise asked Maya about her work.

"Decorating statues with gold leaf was a tradition brought from China during the Tang Dynasty but few people practiced it and the techniques of this art remained almost unknown until recent research was initiated."

"Is there more than one method?"

"Yes. The Kirikane technique as it is commonly known comprises three categories. The first involves decorations of Buddha's clothing and accessories. Another focus concerns ornamentations of Buddhist paintings and frames of the illuminated images. The last type includes embellishments of lacquer or glass work done with a brush; an attractive modern form that provides an opportunity for artists to express their individuality."

"Could a statue be completely covered in gold leaf?"

Maya laughed, "Yes, it could, but it would hardly be worth producing. Although gold leaf is purchased at the market rate it is only 0.1 micrometer thick. It is difficult to work with and tedious. It takes weeks and significant funds to highlight even a small part of a statue. One must also take into account the quality of the work because if an entire statue were covered with gold leaf, the fine details of the sculpture would be compromised. The artisanship alone would take too long. If someone had that amount of money and time, they would be better off having a smaller statue cast in pure gold."

Francoise thought about the life size statues taken from the temples, and whether, rather than being covered in gold leaf, they were perhaps used for something else.

"*Umm,*" she wondered aloud, "*Etant donné qu'il semble que d'énormes statues de grandeur nature aient été volées, peut-être l'intérieur a été utilisé pour un cause profitable.*"

"I'm sorry I don't understand," Maya said with raised eyebrows.

"Why are you so interested in the Kirikane technique," Kayu asked.

"Forgive me, just an idea. Thank you both very much for your help. I'm sorry to have taken so much of your time. I really must get to my next appointment."

The two sisters looked at each other incredulously as Françoise turned and scampered down the stairs. Outside amid the bustle of Kyoto housewives and tourists, Françoise walked briskly through the covered shopping arcade to Shijo Street where she boarded a bus headed for east Kyoto. There was one more temple she wanted to visit. A temple with a renowned Buddha she longed to see firsthand.

Françoise left the bus near Nanzen-ji and walked the short distance to Zenrin-ji. She paused at several halls as she made her way around the temple complex until she came to the room with the statue she specifically wanted to see, the Mikaeri-no-Amida, the famed 'Buddha looking over his shoulder'. Françoise seated herself on the tatami floor and read the pamphlet the attendant gave her at the entrance.

The temple Eikan-do, another name for Zenrin-ji, is derived from the seventh head monk Eikan (1032-1111). According to history, on February 15th 1082 the monk Eikan spent time walking inside the main hall chanting the name of Amida when the Amida Buddha descended from the altar and walked ahead of Eikan. In shock, the monk stopped in his tracks whereupon Amida looked back over his shoulder and said, "Eikan you are dawdling." Monk Eikan later commissioned a statue to commemorate the event.

Amida Buddha at Zenrin-ji

Françoise walked around the side of this mysterious Buddha statue that, locked behind fine meshed wire netting, could not be seen clearly from the front. As she peered through various parts of the enclosure, she finally got a clear view of its face and, in the shadows of the dim light, it seemed to Françoise that the Buddha was staring at something behind her. She turned instinctively but all she saw was an open window. Compelled, she walked over and looked out. There on the ground, an old fallen tree, split in half lengthways, lay in the dirt with the insides facing up. Stretched out in one of the hollows a large tabby cat blinked in the sunlight as it saw Françoise appear in the window above. Its orange fur glistened like gold and the sight captured Françoise's imagination. Her mind filled with a series of images that flashed by like frames on a roll of film as she remembered what the middle-aged monk at Koryu-ji had said, '...each statue had enough hollow space inside to store attachments...'. Now she understood why the statues had been stolen and what they were to be used for. She blew a kiss down to the overweight tabby, turned and walked out of the room. Suddenly she stopped, went back and faced Amida Buddha again. She clapped her hands together and bowed in gratitude. *"Merci,"* she whispered, took a deep breath to calm down, then retraced her steps past the many halls of the temple complex to the exit and took a taxi to Yuhara. At the Ryokan she collected her case from behind the reception desk, thanked her host for her kindness then headed for the not too distant Kyoto JR railway station.

二 十 三

September 17th Kashihara

As the 16:23 train from Kyoto travelled south towards Kashihara the glow of the sun, reflected from beneath the wispy clouds, spread throughout the carriage. Harvest time was imminent and the evening sun cast rich orange rays over the ripened rice paddies. Françoise turned slightly to the window and watched the warm panorama. Eventually the digital screen at the end of the carriage displayed information for her stop: *We will soon make a short stop at Saidai-ji station. Change here for Nara. Thank you for riding with us today.* As Françoise exited the station she asked the staff if there was a florist nearby and was directed to a shopping arcade a short walk away. A few moments later she returned to the station with her purchase and took a local train to Kasanui.

At Honkomyo-ji, the black and white cloths hung up at the time of grandfather Hiro's funeral had been taken down, and everything appeared to Françoise the same as it had during her previous visit. The temple and the adjoining Shinto shrine were quiet and the gravel crunched loudly under Françoise's shoes as she walked through the deserted grounds to the private quarters. Shigehiro's mother answered her knock, acknowledged Françoise with a bow and informed her that Shigehiro was in the main hall. Françoise thanked her, crossed the courtyard and stepped quietly up the outside steps.

Shigehiro, his back to the open entrance, was kneeling at a low white table in front of the Bosatsu of Mercy. On the table rested a metal bowl, from which the smoke of bundled incense sticks curled upwards, beside it a photograph of the old priest in a black and brown frame draped with black ribbons across its upper corners, and a black lacquered plate with grandfather's posthumous name inscribed in gold. Along with these items rested a simple white silk covered box tied with cord, the tasseled ends of which hung down in front, which contained the mortal cremains of the beloved Buddhist sculptor. Françoise knelt next to Shigehiro and placed the dozen white chrysanthemums on the tatami floor in front of her. Shigehiro paused his chant and turned towards her. "Thank you," he said quietly and resumed chanting.

While Shigehiro recited Buddhist sutras in a steady monotonous rhythm, Françoise prayed silently. Finally the chanting ended and Françoise struggled to her feet, her legs numb from kneeling too long.

"You are staying in Kashihara?" Shigehiro asked.

"I haven't booked a hotel yet. I'm going to ask at the station information centre."

"In that case let me drive you to Kashihara Royal Hotel. I'm sure you can get a room there and if you agree we can have dinner together."

"No, Shigehiro, it's all right. You've already been too kind.

"But, there is nothing more for me to do here."

"Well, all right. Dinner would be nice." Françoise gave in easily. She had a lot of paperwork to do but, after two lonely evenings, company for dinner was welcomed.

Shigehiro fetched the temple's comfortable Nissan Cedric from the parking lot, and while he drove Françoise studied him from the corner of her eye. A stubborn, sometimes insensitive man, yet she felt an unexpected fondness for him. His unconstrained consideration enabled her to see a lot more of Nara than she had planned. Yet in the midst of helping her, his grandfather's life ended, and he lost a man so very dear to him. He bore stoically the sadness it caused him, but Françoise knew he was hurting inside.

They arrived at Kashihara in less than thirty minutes. Shigehiro parked in the Hotel's spacious car park and accompanied Françoise into the four star hotel. Françoise went to the front desk where she was told that all the single rooms were occupied. Her mind went blank, her eyes went from left to right and back again as she wondered what to do. With the attractive French woman standing in front of him, the desk clerk checked the reservations again then quietly told her she could have a twin room at a reduced rate. Relieved, she smiled warmly at the clerk, thanked him, then turned to Shigehiro.

"I must freshen up before dinner. Please wait for me here."

The bellboy took Françoise to the room, showed her how to use the card key to unlock the door and then gave her the card. She thanked him and entered the room. Furnished with two single beds, one slightly larger than the other, that reflected the Japanese fondness for male and female versions of different sizes, often represented in paired cups and paired chopsticks. Some believed the larger bed was for the male, others thought it was for the woman and their child, whichever it was, the extra space was welcomed. Françoise hoisted her case onto the smaller bed, and changed into a black dress that had become a little too tight for her. *"Eh bien, ça va m'empêcher de trop manger,"* she whispered to herself as she looked at her reflection in the mirror. With one last pat on her hair, she slipped the card key into her bag and walked down the hallway to the elevators.

Françoise and Shigehiro entered the European style restaurant and a waiter guided them to a secluded table near the windows. The menu presented a wide range of dishes with small photographs to help customers decide. La table d'hôte composed primarily of grilled fish accompanied with sautéed autumn vegetables seemed to be the best choice, but first a bottle of Sauternes.

Kashihara did not have much in the way of famous landmarks, nevertheless the restaurant, located on the top floor of the hotel, offered a pleasant view and the night scene provided an aura of inspiration and relaxation. While Françoise looked at the lights, Shigehiro watched her across the table. She was an attractive woman and, with her hair brushed away from her sharp jaw line, she exuded a mesmerizing allure of which she was not unaware. Minutes passed before she turned back to Shigehiro.

"It may be the wrong time to ask," she began, "but when I studied in India I learned Buddha laughed at the ceremonies that surrounded funerals. He taught entry into nirvana depended on a person's life, not on the funeral, yet Japanese Buddhists conduct such elaborate services. Why is this?"

"First, remember a funeral service is a way for us to send our prayers to the deceased. We can perform this ceremony any way we choose. However, when it comes to Buddhist ceremonies, don't confuse liberal Mahasanghika Buddhism followed in China and North Asian countries, including Japan, with traditional Theravada Buddhism taught in south Asian countries like Myanmar and Thailand."

"You mean Mahayana and Hinayana?" Françoise queried.

"Yes, but Hinayana is actually a derogatory term for Theravada Buddhism. It comes from a rigid teaching style. One of the scriptures compares the world to a house on fire. To escape disaster inhabitants send for a cart, but there is only room for a few devout believers. Thus Theravada Buddhism is known for teachings of the small vehicle while Mahasanghika, Mahayana if you like, for teachings of the great vehicle, where everyone can be saved."

Shigehiro paused while the waiter came to the table with the wine. He carefully poured two glasses and wriggled the bottle into the ice of the wine cooler.

"It was the more liberal Mahasanghika Buddhism," Shigehiro continued, "especially Shingon Buddhism, that was brought from China by Kukai, that gained popularity in Japan. This Buddhism adapted its principles to the needs of Japanese society, allowed traditional shamanistic customs to continue, and Shinto deities were incorporated as manifestations of Buddhist saints. It recognised that ceremonies for the dead played an important role in the lives of Japanese people and, except for a few temples in the Nara area that still refuse to conduct them, took over the responsibility of organising funerals. Indeed the tradition has been so completely incorporated into Japanese Buddhism, regardless of the sect, that most people now regard funerals as an integral part of Buddhism, and Buddhism itself as a purely Japanese religion."

Françoise nodded. "The same occurs with Europeans who ignore the Middle Eastern origins of Christianity. Italians, Spanish, English, Germans all see Christianity as their national religion."

"Of course, religion takes on national characteristics and the iconography of Shingon Buddhism has certainly reached a peak of complexity in Japan."

"And the religious art of the renaissance period, paintings of people with Anglo-Saxon features in European settings, has influenced each nations view of Christianity."

Shigehiro took the nearly empty bottle out of the cooler and refilled their glasses. The waiter approached and Shigehiro ordered another.

"What then are your views on the different religions of the world?" Françoise asked.

"To me religions are like the spokes of a wheel, at the centre of which rests god. Just as spokes radiate from the centre of a wheel, different religions give us other ways to learn about various civilizations' interpretation of god. Each spoke is equally important for the wheel to function, each religion equally important for humanity to live in diversity. Many spokes, many folks, the wheel goes round, life goes on. *'Vive la Difference,'* as you French people say."

"Why then so many conflicts between religions?"

"The historical search for truth has always caused pain to us all. Just as businesses vie for customers, universities vie for students and religions vie for members. People buy the latest products, compete for prestigious universities and are willing to sacrifice critical thought in order to feel comforted in times of trouble. All religions are internally diverse. They constantly change and evolve over time; some advocate a universal teaching while others believe in an elitist body. There can be no universal path. Religions claim to seek the truth, but impose dogmatic beliefs. Then hypocrisy becomes paramount. Instead of nurturing wisdom and learning from each other, religious leaders try to convert others to their way, and seek the destruction of those who oppose their views. Hence we still experience a number of severe religious conflicts. You studied in India so perhaps you will recall that the historical Buddha, Siddhartha Gautama, said little about god and even refused to discuss the idea of a divine being."

"Are you saying that you don't believe in god?"

"Like the spokes of a wheel at the centre of which is god.'

"Simply an empty space?"

"Incomprehensible I know, but without the hole at the centre, the wheel is useless. Likewise, for many people, without god at the centre, human life is pointless. The hole gives meaning to the wheel. God gives meaning to many people. We create the wheel and the hole is present, we create the religion and god is present. Take away the wheel and there is no hole. Take away religion and god disappears, like the religions of ancient Egypt and the gods that no longer exist."

"Like Isis and Horus? And Ra, the god of the sun," Françoise said, "believed by many to have been the first Pharaoh of the world."

"Yes, that interests me," Shigehiro continued. "How the gods have constantly moved further away from us mortals, always just a little more out of reach. First, the gods were in the woods around the hamlets, places that one would not visit alone. Then as villages expanded the gods moved to the mountains or under the sea, abodes difficult to get to. Then, when Greek gods were taken over by the Roman Empire, the gods moved to the planets. The Greek god Zeus became the Roman god Jupiter, and Hades became Pluto, the god of the underworld. Aphrodite became Venus, and Hermes became Mercury, all of them the same gods with two different names. Then as we began to explore the universe the gods moved to the heavens. Safe there, I think, for the moment."

"Perhaps," Françoise laughed.

Shigehiro smiled as he poured the last of the wine.

"That saying; 'Can't see the wood for the trees.' What do you think it means?"

Françoise pondered the seemingly simple question.

"When I walk in the woods I can't see its size because the trees surround me. That means I can't see the larger and dominant matters when insignificant issues keep me occupied."

"All right, but the word 'wood' may also mean prepared timber. Carpenters may think of wood as material for homes and furniture. That saying could suggest you can't see the uses for wood if you focus only on living trees. A fixed mindset can prevent you from considering other views, other ways."

"I am completely confused."

"Confusion is the first step to enlightenment."

Françoise glanced at the two empty bottles of Sauternes that stood on the table.

"I think we need a breath of fresh air," she said.

"Good idea," Shigehiro responded and pushed back from the table. "An evening walk."

Françoise signed the bill and walked with Shigehiro to the elevator. Outside in the still, humid evening air Françoise slipped her arm under Shigehiro's. He looked at her and they continued on in comfortable silence. When they came to a twenty-four hour convenience store, Françoise pulled Shigehiro inside to look around.

"Oh! Drip coffee," she exclaimed. "Let's take some back to the hotel."

Shigehiro nodded in approval, selected a pack of soft American cookies from another shelf and handed the packet to Françoise.

They returned to the hotel, took the elevator and walked along the corridor to Françoise's room. Shigehiro stood facing her as she searched for the card key in her bag. When she found it she looked up into his eyes, paused, slid her hand around the back of his neck and pulled him towards her. A minute passed before she broke away, turned and touched the card to the lock. Without a word Françoise took Shigehiro's hand and led him into the room. The automatic door lock clicked into place behind them. The air conditioner had been left on a high setting and Shigehiro adjusted the temperature. Françoise placed her bag and the white vinyl carrier from the convenience store onto the counter near the television and turned to face him. He took her into his arms, his hands spread firm against her back, and excitement spread throughout her body as his fingers eased down the fastener of her dress. Shigehiro seated himself on the edge of the bed with Françoise in front of him.

"Are you sure about this?" he asked.

Françoise tapped him on the top of his closely cropped head and pushed him backwards. For the briefest moment she hesitated, then reached out to the light switch, flicked it off and in the glow from the neon signs outside the window scrambled on top of him. The white vinyl carrier collapsed onto its side and the packets of coffee and cookies spilt out onto the floor.

二 十 四

September 18th Nagoya

Resting in the crook of Shigehiro's arm, Françoise awoke to the morning sunlight that shone through the undrawn curtains. She smiled at the sleeping face next to her, slipped from the bed and went to the bathroom.

In the confined space of the hotel suite the sound of splashing water from the shower soon woke Shigehiro. He slid his legs over the side of the bed, walked across the room and turned on the television. He picked up the vinyl bag and its contents from the floor and placed them on the counter top. He switched on the electric pot already filled with water, tore open the packets, assembled the drip coffee feeds on the two hotel mugs and poured the hot water onto the grinds. The aroma of fresh brewed coffee filled the room.

"Umm… Better late than never," Françoise exclaimed as she emerged from the shower.

Shigehiro took a sip of coffee, handed Françoise the other cup and went into the shower. Several minutes later as he dried himself, his voice came from behind the door.

"Are you going back to Nagoya today?"

"Yes. I have to," Françoise replied. "I have been in Japan for ten days already. My superior probably thinks I have taken up residence here."

Shigehiro put his head around the edge of the bathroom door.

"Do you mind if I go with you? I have to pick up my father from Nagoya Hospital."

"Oh, of course not, but what about your car? It's still in the hotel parking lot."

"I'll pick it up when I return. It will save me waiting for the local train."

Françoise and Shigehiro left the hotel and took a taxi to Kintetsu Nara station. They returned to Yamato Yagi, bought tickets for reserved seats on an express to Nagoya, then relaxed in the reclining seats of a yellow and white Kintetsu Urban Liner as it sped eastwards across the Yamato plain. Françoise stared out of the window. During the last ten days the scenery had changed tremendously. Many of the rice fields had already been harvested and the stems, stripped of their treasured grain, hung over bamboo poles at the edges of the fields to dry. Tufts of brown stubble covered the dry paddies, and bright red flowers sprouted between the harvested rice fields.

"I don't remember these beautiful plants," Françoise commented. "What are they?"

"A variety of amaryllis. Cluster amaryllis to be precise," Shigehiro explained. "In Japanese they are called *Higanbana*. Higan means equinox and hana means flower, so perhaps equinox flower is a good name for them. They shoot up at this time of year but don't last long. They'll soon be gone," he paused. "Just like you!"

Françoise turned and smiled at him. "There are so many of them," she said.

"People say that if you take them home a calamity will befall your family."

"An old wives tale surely?"

"Well, the roots of the plant do contain a mild poison and they grow in close proximity to the rice paddies. If the plants were to be cut carelessly, the poison may well leak into the rice fields. That probably explains the reasoning behind the belief, and, as you can see, nobody cuts them."

As the train wound its way around the foot of the mountain range, passing village after village, similarities began to blur, then Françoise spotted workers on the other side of the valley who were zealously fixing wire to an almost vertical hillside.

"What are these men doing over there?" she asked Shigehiro.

"They are fixing wire mesh to the side of the mountain, when they have secured it they will spray concrete over it, the concrete will set around the wire and prevent further rock falls onto the road. Those grayish areas without trees have already been finished."

"You mean they spray concrete straight onto the mountain?"

"Yes. It's not very economical or environmentally friendly but it protects the contours of the mountain, and from a distance it looks quite natural."

Françoise stared at the back of the seat in front of her. The idea reminded her of the hollow wooden statues, the Buddha of Eikan-do that glanced over his shoulder, and the tabby cat in the fallen log ...and from a distance it looks quite natural... but was it?

The digital panel at the end of the carriage changed to the name of the next stop: Sakakibara-Onsenguchi. *La station avec un long nom et les statues si horribles*, Françoise thought to herself as she searched for black limousines and men in dark suits, but only the disgraceful replicas stood as sentinels over the still valley. As the train pulled away from the station she turned from the window to face Shigehiro.

"Just why are those incredible reproductions there?"

"It's a museum that owns replicas of works of art from the Louvre in Paris. Further up the valley is a temple with a collection of Buddhist art."

"Why didn't you say so before? They may have something I'm searching for."

Shigehiro smiled, "I don't think so. They are of a dreadfully curious nature. Things like oversized representations of Buddha's footwear, an orchestra of cats, and such things."

"Who puts such works out here in the countryside?"

"I suppose it does seem strange but it was probably built to avoid a higher income tax bracket. Religious groups in Japan are exempt from paying taxes. Once it may have been no more than a local temple that took advantage of this benefit, then someone from the area became president of a successful company and decided to invest money in art rather than pay excessive taxes."

"But way out here in the country, no one would come to see it."

"That wouldn't be important, would it? Actually it used to be a popular resort. You can tell from the station name there is a hot spring here. Perhaps local businessmen, either with their own money or with money donated to the temple, attempted to make the area a place of pilgrimage. Then a wealthy entrepreneur likely decided to build the museum as a distraction for tourists."

"It still seems a long way to come," Françoise persisted stubbornly.

"The express trains that run between Osaka and Nagoya stop there, as we have just done, as well trains going to the Ise peninsula. Kintetsu railways may have sponsored it for people on their way to and from Ise-jingu. There are several possible explanations. Either way, bad taste or not, there is nothing criminally wrong with the legal avoidance of heavy taxes."

Françoise frowned. She had other ideas. She was sure there was something more. A secluded area, with few visitors, private enough for any activity, and with a seemingly genuine reason for existence. Could there really be nothing else going on there?

~

In the back room of Kitamura's antique shop in Nagoya, the Professor and his wife Kyoko were seated across from Kyoko's younger sister, as they tried to explain why, in their opinion, Itsue should feel free to marry Chulsoo. Sadly the therapeutic cups of sencha before them had no effect on the heated discussion. Concerned about her daughter's welfare and the family status, Itsue's mother could not accept this union. She had paid an impromptu visit to Kitamura and her sister purposely to get the support of her learned brother-in-law, but now she could hardly believe her ears, her own sister advocating Itsue and Chulsoo's marriage.

"You don't need to worry so much," Kyoko had said, "there have been many marriages between Japanese and Koreans."

"That may well be true, but this is my daughter we are talking about."

Professor Kitamura, hands in his lap, leaned forward and spoke softly.

"Nomura-san, You must realise that Korean descendants of Chulsoo's age are now the third generation born in Japan. They have grown up here, it is their home and they know no other. I feel we owe them the respect they deserve and learn to treat them as equals. I doubt Chulsoo has ever been to Korea and I know for a fact his Korean language ability is not as good as his Japanese."

"But how can she pass on her Japanese bloodline if she marries into a Korean family?"

"You still believe your bloodline to be purely Japanese?" Professor Kitamura asked.

"Are you insinuating the Nomura family is not Japanese?"

Kitamura knew what he was about to say would be hard for her to accept.

"We are taught at school that Japan is one of the few countries not to have been invaded and that Japanese are a race apart from others. In the sense of the more recent past that is true, violent invasion has been held off by divine winds, but how can we not have mixed roots? Long before the Meiji restoration unknown numbers of Mongolians and peoples from the ancient Korean peninsula came to this archipelago on peaceful missions. There must have been relationships between them and the Japanese of those times. Even in more recent times, countless Europeans have lived in Japan who surely had love affairs. The Taisho era was not called romantic without a reason, and offspring of those liaisons would have been registered as Japanese nationals. You only have to examine Japanese people's physical characteristics to realise that our features don't have a single set pattern."

"You're telling me that... that many Japanese are not... well... not pure Japanese?"

"It is a fact that cannot be changed. A fact that too few people are, regretfully in my opinion, prepared to admit. For example, at the end of the occupation after the Pacific war, many American soldiers returned home leaving behind pregnant Japanese girls, consequently the authorities had to accept registration of those children as Japanese."

"I don't believe this." Nomura retorted.

"Because you don't want to. It goes against everything you were taught, but look at facts without prejudice and you'll discover that many elements of our culture have their origin in other lands. Long before the Meiji Restoration goods were transported to Japan and along with them came ideas, customs and traditions. All nations divide people into social, economic and political groups. Those of the same mind are drawn to one another, and while that may be harmless enough, purposeful discrimination is ugly and born out of fear. If people will only accept differences, a multiracial society can draw on the wealth of many cultures and be beneficial to everyone, furthermore ageing societies such as our own cannot survive without accepting diversity. Nomura-san, whether you agree or not, you don't have a choice. Itsue has been living alone ever since she divorced. She is a competent woman capable of going her own way. If she is determined to marry and you disapprove, you will never get to see your grandchildren. Your duty is to contribute to your daughter's happiness and to help her raise her family."

Nomura looked down at the table. Tears welled in her eyes and she reached into her handbag to fetch a handkerchief.

"Welcome Chulsoo into your family," Kitamura continued, "and I am certain you will never regret it. You will become proud of your daughter's courage. There will be other social barriers and your support, rather than your criticism, will be essential for her"

As soon as Françoise arrived at Nagoya station she rushed to Itsue's home and blurted out her thoughts on where the stolen statues were, and what they were going to be used for. She spoke so fast Itsue hardly had time to absorb all the details.

"Let me get this straight. You want me to accompany you all the way back to this Sakakibara place and search a museum because your intuition tells you stolen statues might be there?"

"If I don't see it for myself, I'll never stop wondering. You know what I'm like."

"But you have no proof. All you have is a hunch."

"It's more than that. Shigehiro said the museum could have been built for tax reasons, a pilgrimage location or a distraction for tourists travelling to Ise. Maybe all of those things, but Monsieur Moustache knew about art and I'm certain he's the man I saw at the station the first time I went by."

"How can you be so sure it was him? All middle-aged men in dark suits look similar from a distance and all kinds of people drive black cars, not only gangsters."

"I saw him close enough on the plane and not many Japanese men have moustaches and I'm certain I saw that car before... at the airport!"

The phone rang and a high-pitched beep signaled an incoming fax. Itsue watched as the page started to feed from the machine.

"It's from Paris," she said.

A cup of sencha seemed like a good idea to sooth her irate guest and Itsue crossed the room to prepare her best Japanese tea.

"Itsue, think what it would mean if I am right."

"I am," Itsue said over her shoulder. "You'd find statues, stolen perhaps, then what?"

"We'd tell the police, they would arrest those concerned and we'd have stopped fine works of art being sold into private collections."

"Françoise, I can't believe you are being so naïve about this. Japanese police do not act simply on information provided by a French tourist. Gangsters here know the law, and the police tread very carefully when they deal with them. Police may take many months to build a case, especially with organized criminals."

Itsue poured hot water onto the tender crushed green leaves.

"Anyway, what if statues are sold into private hands? Is that such a bad thing?" she asked as she swirled the water around in the pot.

The fax machine gave a final beep and Françoise went to retrieve the message.

"Itsue, you don't understand. Theft of artwork deprives the world of important historical information. Museums are not able to classify data and the public cannot get to see them," she waved the fax in her hand, "and researchers like Georges cannot study them except by private arrangement."

Françoise studied the signature on the fax for a few seconds. It was not from Georges but from his associate Fabrice.

Bonjour Françoise, – Qu'est-ce qui se passe? Hier, la police est venue me poser des questions, demandant la localisation de Georges. Il semble qu'ils ont trouvé des statues sous la garde de Georges à l'Université et on voulait l'interroger. La prochaine chose que je sais,

Georges est arrêté, soupçonné d'appartenir à un réseau international de trafiquants.

La semaine dernière, j'ai entendu un client parler à Georges au téléphone réclamant qu'une statue de Georges figurait sur une liste d'oeuvres volées. Ce client peut avoir dénoncé Georges à la police.

Si tu possèdes des informations à propos de statues volées en provenance du Japon, peut-être que tu devrais revenir en France le plus tôt possible pour parler à la police et aider à libérer Georges. – Fabrice.

Françoise read it through several times.

"Well. It appears some of my hunch is true. This fax is from my husbands' associate Fabrice." Françoise tapped the paper with her fingers. "He says Georges has been arrested on suspicion of belonging to an international smuggling organization. It seems the police came to question Fabrice about Georges' whereabouts, said they wanted to interrogate Georges about certain statues under his care at the university. Fabrice says he overheard a client claim one of Georges' statues was in a list of stolen art works and thinks he may have been the one who reported Georges to the police. He says if I have information about statues being stolen from Japan I should return home as soon as possible and talk to the French police to help get Georges released."

Itsue sighed. Exasperation welled inside her.

"Françoise, even if you are right you can't go around playing detective here in Japan."

"Itsue, please trust me. There are too many coincidences. Smuggling is a lucrative business. Vast amounts of money are involved and it's a major concern to museums all over the world. It is more common than you think. The statues Shigehiro's grandfather made would not be out of place in that imitation Louvre museum. They could be stored there awaiting export, hidden in full view. Since whoever runs the museum deals with replicas they would know shipping regulations and how to avoid them. If those statues were sent to Europe or America they could be sold to art dealers or collectors for several times their Japanese value."

"Françoise, I appreciate you want to help Shigehiro but it's not your problem. Think of what you're saying. Searching for missing statues in ..."

"Sakakibara-Onsenguchi," Françoise interjected.

"... a hot spring I've never even heard of."

Silence ensued. The two women sipped at the *sencha* Itsue had prepared.

"How far is this place?" Itsue asked finally.

Françoise looked sideways.

"An hour... hour and a half."

To Françoise it seemed an interminable time before Itsue spoke again.

"All right. Tomorrow morning. Let's go and..."

Françoise rushed around the table to hug her friend so fast she almost spilled her tea.

"All right... All right... Tomorrow," Itsue laughed.

~~~~~

Seated on the edge of his bed, Yoshihisa studied his feet. As Shigehiro walked into the ward the old man in the next bed coughed loudly and, when Yoshihisa looked up, gestured in the direction of the entrance.

"Here's that young priest to see you again."

"Hello Father," Shigehiro said gently. "I've come to take you home."

Yoshihisa turned to face his son and their eyes met for a short time.

"Please listen a while before we leave," Yoshihisa began, "laying here has given me plenty of time to think." Yoshihisa hesitated, and again looked down at his feet. "Fact is, you knew your grandfather as an old man, and he was good to you, but I grew up in a different era and he was severe to me..."

Shigehiro tried to protest but Yoshihisa held up a hand.

"Please hear me out. I am not bitter. That's how children were raised in those days, but he had time for you that he did not have for me. You were allowed to talk freely with him whenever you were together and I became envious of the attention he gave you. I knew it was wrong, but I could not help it."

Shigehiro remained silent and Yoshihisa continued.

"Please believe me. I truly repent of my actions. I'm sorry the statues have been taken and may never be returned. I'll regret the trouble I caused my father, and you, for the rest of my life. Especially loosing the Blue Buddha, I realise now how important it was."

Shigehiro squatted down and fastened his hands around the clenched fists his father held together in his lap. Yoshihisa looked at his son and tears welled in his eyes.

The old man in the next bed rustled his newspaper and cleared his throat. Shigehiro helped his father gather his belongings and they bade the old man goodbye. As they walked to the exit Yoshihisa stopped and turned towards his son.

"You still want to follow in your grandfather's footsteps?" he asked.

"Yes," Shigehiro replied.

"Go ahead. I won't stand in your way any longer."

二 十 五

September 19th Nara, Mie, Osaka, Nagoya

The following misty autumn morning in the living quarters at Honkomyo-ji in Kasanui Yoshihisa woke with recollections of the previous week still pounding in his brain: the black car, the door beside him wide open, a disturbing laugh, spinning red lights, voices in local accents and the face of the youth who crushed his front teeth. He opened his eyes and stared at the ceiling to rid his mind of these dreadful thoughts. With the pain in his chest and jaw still causing anguish, he began to reflect on how difficult it must have been for Shigehiro to accept becoming the next abbot of Honkomyo-ji, but the temple had been cared for by the Kurosawa family for generations and he had raised his son to be his successor, would it be right to let him pursue his own ambitions?

Yoshihisa had long wanted to explain about the day long ago, when, after reciting the evening's sutras, he had been to the work shed and discovered the hidden Blue Buddha. Yes, he found where it was kept and, aware of its possible value, he planned to use the statue to finance his dream of expanding the temple, but he had not reveled his plan to his family and now could not find the words or the courage to divulge the fact.

At the hospital the previous day Yoshihisa watched Shigehiro's eyes intently as he tried to explain how distressing it had been for him, over the years, to watch his son enjoy the carefree relationship with his grandfather that he himself had been denied. Yoshihisa knew it was common practice for grandparents to indulge their grandchildren, but his father's benign attitude towards Shigehiro gnawed at his very psyche.

Yoshihisa had been comforted when his son fastened his hands around his own clenched fists. It was perhaps a sign of reconciliation after the years of aversion and alienation that had occurred between them. Envy prevented him from appreciating his son's sensitivity towards his father's art. The statues represented an artist's prayers but he failed to comprehend the emotional significance of creative meditation. He was relieved. The fight was over. His son had the right to follow his own dream. He would no longer stop Shigehiro from pursuing his ambitions. He was glad to be back at the temple, and drifted back to sleep convinced that everything would soon be all right.

In the senior advisor's spacious country residence Cheong had lain awake since early dawn. His life as a mobster was proving to be too stressful. The memory of Yoshihisa's cry of pain as Kouno grabbed his jaw and cracked a couple of teeth haunted him. He reflected on the events of the past few days. Yoshihisa began to see through Cheong's scam of getting statues away from temples and Cheong hurt him to ensure his silence. Cheong reasoned it was probably later at the senior advisor's residence, when he was told to interrupt the exporting operations that his world started to collapse. He thought back to the day at the museum when Chulsoo showed up late, and then the audacity to ignore him in the spa. Both incidents angered him. Getting Chulsoo to caddy for him and berating him in the car only resulted in short-lived pleasures.

Cheong wondered when Chulsoo began to think about leaving the organization, and whether his own actions actually forced his nephew's hand. When Chulsoo burst into the office and yanked him from his chair, if not for his stocky build and experience he may well have lost to the youth's strength. Instead, he managed to knock Chulsoo to the floor, but gratification only lasted a few minutes. In the anger of the moments that followed he said too much. Disclosed not only that Chulsoo's father was still alive but also where he could be found.

A few days later, exhausted from searching for his father, Chulsoo again appeared in Cheong's office. Bruises and minor cuts revealed at least one fight with other gang members who followed Cheong's orders and stayed silent about the whereabouts of his brother-in-law. But Cheong had been outraged at his nephew for asking to leave the organization. He berated the youth he nurtured for so long but it was a useless battle. Cheong felt proud to have raised Chulsoo, but filial love is strong and Cheong had seen the resolution in Chulsoo's eyes to live his own life away from demands of the organization. Cheong admired the youth for standing strong and steadfast in his convictions but at the same time, unlike his father, showing respect for the organization. There was no choice but to agree to his nephew's request.

Nevertheless losing his right hand man was troublesome. Cheong had been fortunate to have his nephew guard his back for so many years. Now he would have to promote Kouno to senior bodyguard, but would a distant relative be trustworthy in a crisis? The Oyabun requested Cheong to think up another scheme to get money out of the country and he knew the senior advisor would not accept new ideas unless they were well thought out. Cheong's life was becoming difficult and his mood varied greatly. One moment he grinned as he remembered the fool in Paris that disposed of the statues had been arrested, but the next minute he frowned uneasy as he recalled Georges René de Cotret's wife was also called Françoise like that friend of Chulsoo's woman. He did not like this coincidence. It seemed too ominous.

~

That previous evening, after driving Chulsoo back to the museum, Kouno took a train to Imazato, walked to the Taiko practice hall, and crashed out on an old futon in a back room. Early the following morning he raised his hand to shield his eyes against the glare of a security guard's flashlight. 'Get out of here,' the guard ordered but the moment he recognised Kouno he apologized profusely. The guard left, but Kouno could not get back to sleep. He could not understand why Chulsoo cared so much about that Japanese bitch or the old professor's junk collection. As for himself he much preferred the French chick. He was confused. Chulsoo's arrogance when told to return to Osaka still angered him and now he had lost his lifelong friend. On the other hand there were opportunities to ingratiate himself with Cheong and he figured he would surely soon be promoted to the position Chulsoo previously held.

~

In Nagoya, Chulsoo gingerly cupped his left hand in his right. His aunt, with whom he stayed that night, welcomed him warmly as she always did. The pain from his finger had subsided, but a heavy throbbing still remained. It was like Itsue's words that still pulsed through his brain. Would she and her family accept the loss of his finger as sufficient evidence that he had parted from the underworld? He knew the only real chance of being accepted was through the recommendation of Itsue's uncle and aunt in Nagoya but Chulsoo's reputation was compromised the day he took Kouno, along with Itsue and Françoise, to see Kitamura. That had been a major mistake for he now realised that only Kouno could have given Cheong such opportune information about the statues in that shop. Damn also that he fell asleep in that Oyamada service area. Chulsoo's lateness angered his uncle more than he expected, and was the final straw in his decision to leave the organization. Chulsoo was now a free man. The details of the events that led to his freedom were etched on his mind: the Go board, the white sheet and the thin bladed knife. From the moment he stepped into the senior advisor's house everything happened in a blur. He squatted down next to the Go board, the senior advisor addressed him, he nodded assent and within seconds the end of his little finger, severed from his hand, shot out across the board, then the final warning from the advisor, and now, when he closed his eyes, he could still see the saddened expression on his uncle's face as he and Kouno had left the senior advisor's residence.

~

Uncomfortable on the thin bedding at Honkomyo-ji Shigehiro pondered the events of the past two weeks. His father had loaned out grandfather's statues to make money to build an annex to the temple. The last creation of his grandfather's had been taken from the temple without permission. Shigehiro vowed to find it but the unfulfilled promise weighed heavily on his mind. He had been distracted by his attraction for Françiose, but what disturbed him was Sasaki. Why hadn't Inspector Sasaki filed that first report? As dawn approached, pieces of the puzzle started to fall into place: Sasaki's reluctance to take details, being asked at Nara central police station why he had not reported the situation before, and the attentiveness of the sergeant when he heard Sasaki's name mentioned. All of that left no doubt in Shigehiro's mind that Sasaki had been covering for whoever was behind this, but gave him no clue as to where the statues could be.

~

In the cramped apartment in Nagoya Françoise snuggled down in her futon. Three weeks earlier she had been elated at the prospect of coming back to Japan, but now as she remembered the coarse heavily built man she had nicknamed Monsieur Moustache, she shrank further under the covers. On the other hand she had been able to spend an enjoyable time with her dear friend Itsue and to visit her old history professor who had arranged an introduction to a Buddhist sculptor and in turn, if not somewhat fatalistically, she had met the sculptor's grandson. The young priest immediately planned visits to various temples in the area and Françoise remembered how she first perceived his offer to be her guide as an incursion into her plans. Later however, she had to admit his help had been invaluable, and that she rather enjoyed his company.

Quite what induced her to stay in Nara with him that first night was still a question she pondered. Despite having her luggage and papers spread all over the floor of a business hotel room in Kashihara, she accompanied him to the five-star Nara Hotel. Françoise recollected the pleasant dinner, the educational conversation and his advances towards her outside her room. Why had she pushed him away, she wondered, for there had been six thousand miles between her and a husband who had not shown any interest in her for many months. Whatever the reason, two days later at the Kashihara Royal Hotel she could not hide her fondness for him. Perhaps because of the unspoken sadness of grandfather Hiro's passing or could it have simply been the effect of two bottles of Sauternes?

In the short time Françoise had known Shigehiro he taught her many things, although his explanation of the museum at Sakakibara-Onsenguchi was debatable. The Louvre roofed building and giant Greek statues set in that lonely country valley seemed incongruent with a simple tourist resort. The glimpse of the mustachioed middle-aged man captured her imagination. With her experience as museum curator Françoise knew that smuggling was a billion dollar enterprise and with her new knowledge of how statues were made it was not hard for her to reason how illicit money packed in Buddhist icons would be exported to some other Asian country. The laundered money used to purchase gold bullion that would travel by a roundabout route to eventually end up in the ample coffers of North Korea. The empty statues would be bought by unscrupulous dealers, perhaps sent to Europe or America and sold to collectors. By the time Françoise arrived back in Nagoya she was convinced she had stumbled across a smuggling ring of some huge proportions. Suddenly, recollection of the statues that constantly passed through her husband's antique shop sprang to mind. Could Georges, unbeknownst to her, be involved in this scam?

In the futon next to Françoise, head throbbing from too much sake, Itsue awoke and wiped the tears from her eyes. She had been delighted to see her old friend, but at the same time her hopes of marrying Chulsoo had been dashed to pieces on the rocks of parental disapproval. The previous night, drinking alone in her apartment with tears rolling down her cheeks, she mentally accepted that she had no choice but to agree to her mother's demands. Then last night, Françoise rushed in with her detective story and her desire to investigate this Louvre styled museum. Itsue had drunk more Shochikubai as she tried to explain that the place was either nothing more than a tourist attraction or, if it were not, a place too dangerous for them to go probing around looking for stolen statues. Finally, exasperated with trying to talk reason to Françoise, she agreed to accompany her friend to this strange spa and see for herself. Perhaps the adventure would distract her from thoughts of Chulsoo.

二 十 六

September 19th Sakakibara-Onsenguchi

Itsue parked the Honda at Nagoya station parking lot. Françoise rushed to purchase two tickets for the spa town. Itsue ran to join her and they sprinted to the platform to board the train. Françoise pulled the curtain back from the window to watch the panorama of Japanese countryside. The early autumn sky lent a dramatic blue backdrop to the red and white industrial chimneys of Yokkaiichi and the coastal views of Shiroko. When Itsue spied the fairy tale towers of the love hotels at Tsu, her tangled emotions towards Chulsoo sprang to mind.

At Nakagawa they changed trains and headed westwards towards the inland mountains. Françoise looked out over the empty rice paddies on both sides of the train. Her trip to Japan had gone by so fast and the humid heat of late summer had changed dramatically in the early autumn. The train slowed as it entered a tunnel, emerged from the other end, and stopped at the elevated station of Sakakibara-Onsenguchi. Itsue instantly sought out the Louvre roofed building and the European replicas.

"I thought you said they could be seen from the train."

"They're on the other side of the tracks," Françoise responded as they got off the train. "Wait till the train has gone."

As if in response to her comment the doors of the yellow and white carriages closed and, as the train left the station, Itsue's eyes opened wide at the mysterious sight beyond the low railings of the opposite platform.

"Well, look at that!" she exclaimed. "I've never seen anything like it."

Incongruous in the surrounding farmland stood a square white building resplendent with pyramid-shaped roof like that of the Louvre museum in Paris, and on the corners two immense replicas of Aphrodite of Milos and Nike of Samothrace exactly as Françoise described them. Further up the valley, clearly visible above the treetops, a huge golden Buddhist Kannon with its incessant stare welcomed the two women.

Françoise scampered down the stairs to the exit and Itsue followed. While Françoise asked for directions, Itsue looked over a rack of leaflets that promoted various hotels, golf courses and a hot spring in the area. Itsue showed Françoise what she found.

"See. It's a museum of art reproductions and behind is a Buddhist temple."

"Yes. I know. So it seems," Françoise replied with a glance at the leaflets. "Come on. Let's go! It's just over there."

Françoise walked off across the station forecourt leaving Itsue no choice but to follow. They entered a dimly lit underpass and came out the other side. Françoise stopped a moment in front of a forlorn abandoned restaurant in the middle of deserted paddies and Itsue caught up with her. A billboard on their right displayed an illustration of both museum and temple areas with a sizable parking lot between the two compounds. As they walked across the car park towards the museum, Itsue gestured to the assigned areas for tour buses.

"See, a simple tourist attraction. Hotel and Ryokan owners collaborated in the hope of acquiring more customers."

"You make it sound so innocent, but how do buses get through that narrow underpass?"

"They use a different route. Don't be so skeptical."

Françoise reluctantly agreed, but something on the other side of the car park had caught her eye, a shiny black sovereign president with the registration: 88-88.

Itsue bought tickets from the female clerk and the two friends entered the spacious air-conditioned museum. Minutes later Françoise gave a gasp. On the far side of the room, set in three tiers along one wall, stood Buddhist statues of the kind Françoise had been searching for all over Asuka, Nara and Kyoto.

"My goodness! Itsue," Françoise whispered as they walked over to the statues. "Whoever owns this place possesses unlimited resources. All kinds of sculptures have been collected here and reproductions of this size are very costly."

Itsue wandered off along the row of Buddhist sculptures: Nyorai, Bosatsu, Myoo,[1] then turned off down a row of European sculptures: Nike, Aphrodite, Apollo and others. Françoise however, stood immobile in front of the row of Buddhist statues and began to wonder if they were indeed reproductions. They appeared masterfully crafted. Could they be original works? But why would original works be kept in such a place? Suddenly someone behind her spoke. She turned and saw a man, his cell phone pressed to his ear, step from a room. He flicked off the light and walked away as the door began to swing closed. Françoise, accustomed to dark storerooms at the Cernushi, ducked into the narrowing space and let the door close softly behind her. In the darkened interior Françoise rummaged in her handbag, found her flashlight and turned it on. The beam streaked along shelves high and low and reflected on some golden objects. *Le chat,* thought Françoise as she remembered the cat at Eikan-do. She moved closer and identified four miniature figurines identical to the ones missing from the Horyu-ji exhibition at the Tokyo National Museum. She lifted one of the attendant figurines and weighed it in her hand. Heavy, solid brass and too well crafted to be replicas, they must

(1) Nyorai indicates a being that has entered nirvana. Bosatsu designates an enlightened being still practicing. Myoo are guardians that represent strict spiritual training.

be the originals, but it was too dark to be sure. Without a second thought she dropped the figurine into her bag, grabbed the other two attendants and put them in with the first, reverently picked up the statuette of Queen Maya from the shelf and placed it on top of the others. *Zut!* She couldn't close her bag, she moved back to the door, opened it carefully and slipped out into the museum. Itsue was nowhere in sight, Françoise looked around and finally found her in front of a statue of Venus De Milo.

"Where have you been? I have been looking for you," Françoise whispered. "Let's go to the bathroom!"

"What's going on?" Itsue asked.

Françoise turned and followed the signs to the ladies' room with Itsue behind her. Once inside, Françoise breathed a heavy sigh of relief.

"Takes too long to explain right now. Please. Give me your backpack." Françoise took the backpack from Itsue and squatted to the floor. One by one Françoise took out the statuettes from her handbag and transferred them to the backpack.

Itsue crouched beside her. "What are you doing?"

"I need to put these in your backpack. I can't close my bag with them in it," Françoise whispered as she handed the backpack back to Itsue. "Put something on top of them and don't say a word. I'll tell you outside."

Itsue slipped off her cardigan, placed it on the statuettes and closed the backpack.

"Okay," Françoise said. "Let's leave now."

"But we've only just arrived," Itsue protested.

"I know. But I've seen enough."

They returned to the museum hall and Françoise strode quickly towards the exit. As they passed a middle-aged man, and a giggly young woman half his age, hanging onto his arm, Itsue, curious, turned and stared at them as they sauntered by.

"Come on, Itsue. Let's go!" Françoise urged her friend.

"What's the rush?" Itsue demanded, "These statues are fantastic. I want to see them."

"Maybe another time," Françoise said. "Right now we have to get out of here."

They turned the corner, back into the row of Buddhist icons.

"Itsue, please hurry," Françoise pleaded in a hushed voice as she took Itsue's arm and pulled her towards the exit.

Itsue, caught off balance, began to stumble forward. Her right hand clutched the strap of her backpack. Her left hand flayed the air for support, found an extended hand of a thousand armed Kannon and held on tightly. As Itsue fell to the floor, the Kannon statue pulled off its stand, crashed in an avalanche of wooden arms, broken hands and symbolic Buddhist objects, on the floor beside her. Françoise turned and saw her friend face-down on the floor and the Kannon's torso in pieces around her, but worried as she was of Itsue's well being, Françoise's attention was drawn to the bundles of Japanese Yen notes that had burst from the broken statue.

"Stay where you are!" A guard shouted. Another man appeared at the other end of the room, cell phone in hand.

"Get Cheong down here," the guard shouted, and the man ran off.

Françoise helped Itsue to her feet. The guard indicated a black padded bench in the middle of the gallery and the two women obediently seated themselves on it. Soon the unmistakable voice of Monsieur Moustache addressed Françoise in her mother tongue.

"*Ha, ha, ha, ha. Mon amie de Paris,*" he bellowed as he stepped gingerly over the broken pieces of statue. Another man followed the stocky form of Cheong but stopped a little way off and pulled on a pair of white cotton gloves.

"So you're interested in mediocre replicas?" Cheong intoned sarcastically. "I thought you liked original art objects with more value."

Françoise stared in disbelief at the man she had nicknamed Monsieur Moustache.

"I am responsible," Itsue stammered. "I will pay for anything that…"

"*Urusai!*" Cheong shouted as he raised his hand to strike her, Itsue flinched and he lowered it without touching her.

Françoise regained her composure, flipped open her bag and took out her card case. "Here is my name card. You can send me the bill," she said.

Cheong appeared to reach for the card, instead grabbed Françoise's bag and twisted it from her grasp. Françoise indignantly started from her seat but a powerful hand on her shoulder held her down while his other hand emptied the contents of the bag onto the floor: purse, handkerchiefs, cosmetics and a variety of sanitary and other feminine goods, lay scattered at Cheong's feet. He dropped Françoise's bag on the floor and stared down at the paraphernalia, noted the postcards from the Tokyo National Museum but what interested him most was an open leather photo flip. He picked it up and flicked through the photographs: student days in Nagoya and Paris, Georges and Françoise in India, Chulsoo and Itsue in the photo Itsue had given Françoise in Nagoya.

"Well! You certainly get around, don't you? Madame René de Cotret, and unexpectedly I get to meet you, Nomura-san. This is a surprise! Ha, ha, ha, ha."

The women frowned at each other questioningly.

"I think we'd better talk upstairs." Cheong's voice almost a whisper.

Still holding the photo case, Cheong turned and walked away.

"That's Chulsoo's woman?" he questioned as he passed the man in white gloves.

"Yeah," Kouno nodded.

"Bring them up," he growled and strode off towards his office.

The women gasped as they recognized Kouno, but saw in his expression that he was no longer their friend. Itsue thought it prudent not to speak, she instead squatted down and helped Françoise gather her possessions.

Accompanied by the guard, Françoise and Itsue preceded Kouno up the winding staircase that Cheong had just taken. The spacious room contained on one side a black leather couch and on the other an antique rosewood desk. Kouno indicated for the women to sit on the couch, he then walked across the room to the window. The guard returned to the gallery. Cheong dropped the photo case onto his desk, eased himself down into his chair, and looked at the Hanafuda cards that had been scattered over the desk when he and Kouno heard the sound of the falling statue, and the commotion downstairs. Slowly he gathered the cards, put them in a little plastic case, and placed it on one side of his desk. He then looked up and glared at his two interlopers.

"Madame René de Cotret, a lady who borrows Buddhist statues and puts them in exhibitions for people to come and see. Her museum makes money, but does any of that benefit the people who kindly lent them to her? I think not."

"How come you know so much about me?" Françoise's curiosity overcame her fear.

"Ha, ha, ha, ha." Monsieur Moustache leaned back in his chair. "I know a lot about you Madame, and your husband who tries to teach me how to differentiate between Monet and Manet, between Renoir and Rodin. He thinks I am a thief but, unlike you, statues I find are mine, and I use them help my kinfolk. People who still have to scratch a living from the fields without the aid of modern machinery."

Emboldened by anger Françoise spoke.

"Oh! Now I understand. My husband told me the statues he sells are from India, but they only come through India. You are the source. A man of Korean ancestry who takes advantage of Japan by stealing their art works. The fact that those statues would not exist if your ancestors had not been such excellent artists, and that they are culturally important in the history of your people, does not matter to you."

Cheong, hands on the arms of the chair, pushed himself up, grabbed the photo flip, walked around the desk and crossed the room.

"You think I give a damn about what I take from Japan? You have no idea how Koreans view the history of their country. Japan occupied my homeland and should have paid back what it took, but do you think it has?"

Cheong threw the leather bound flip case into Françoise's lap. Kouno turned from the window while Cheong looked menacingly from one woman to the other.

"Neither of you have any idea how easy it would be for me to have your lives turned upside down." Cheong spoke quietly, but his deep voice, and the proximity of his bulky frame, instilled a fear the women had never known before. "I don't know which of you two found this place, nor what you think you hope to accomplish, but you are messing in something you know absolutely nothing about. You are very fortunate that I know who both of you are, if I did not, your lives would be in very grave danger." He leaned towards Itsue, his face inches from hers, his breath stale with cigar smoke. "You may have a Korean fiancé who thinks you're wonderful, but I don't give a shit what happens to you. Return to Nagoya, forget you ever came here, and never let me see you again." He turned slightly and stroked a forefinger gently down Françoise's cheek. "Perhaps you know Japanese men have a penchant for sadomasochism." He lifted her face and glared into her eyes. "An attractive lady like yourself would be an especially suitable star in a movie that sells rather well." He paused. "Do you understand me?"

Françoise swallowed. Her throat was dry, and she gave a strangled acknowledgement.

"Then go back to Paris, and never ever mention to anyone what you saw here today, because if you do, I know who you are, and I will search you out. Be certain of that."

Cheong turned to Kouno. "Drive these two imbeciles to the station and make sure they catch the next train to Nagoya."

Itsue grabbed her backpack and pushed Françoise towards the door. Followed by Kouno they left. Cheong went to the window and watched as the two women walked across the car park. Scared and silent they got into the back seat of the car and Kouno drove off. Cheong then turned from the window and went behind his desk. Picked up his phone and called a number in Paris.

二 十 七

September 20th Tokyo & Paris

At Nagoya station Itsue and Françoise walked briskly to the parking lot, found Itsue's Honda dutifully waiting for them and drove to the apartment. The journey back from Sakakibara-Onsenguchi had felt like an eternity. After meeting Cheong face-to-face Itsue realized she would never be able to see Chulsoo again, and resolved to tell her parents the engagement was off. Françoise, now certain her husband was involved with Yamamoto, gave up on uncovering the whereabouts of the Blue Buddha.

Exhausted, the two women climbed the five flights of stairs to Ituse's home, slipped off their shoes in the entrance, and breathed heavy sighs of relief. Itsue went to the kitchen cupboard, pulled out the 1.8 liter bottle of Shouchikubai they had drunk from the previous evening and, with a questioning look, held up the two-thirds empty bottle to Françoise who nodded in agreement.

"Well! So that's Chulsoo's Uncle. What an unpleasant introduction that was." Itsue said as she filled two *tokuri* with sake.

"You mean that man Yamamoto is your boyfriend's uncle?"

"Yes. Cheong is his Korean name."

"Oh! Wow, Itsue, I'm truly sorry," Françoise said. "You must have feared for your life."

"It was you challenging him that scared me the most. But I don't regret anything. We took a risk and we got out alive, without injury. What to do next is more important. Those statuettes you gave me are still in my backpack."

"Itsue, you are a treasure," Françoise exclaimed. "I had forgotten all about them."

Itsue took the cardigan from her backpack and stood the statuettes on the table.

"They really are beautiful," Françoise sighed.

"Yes they are, but what are you going to do with them? You can't leave them here."

"Well, I'll have to take them back to Tokyo. Martin will be in for a surprise."

"And when you return to France?"

"Can I stay with Georges you mean?"

"What about Shigehiro?"

"What about him?"

"Come on Françoise. You know what I mean."

"And what about Chulsoo?"

"It's over," Itsue sighed as she brought the sake from the kitchen and poured two choko. Françoise watched the movements of the particles of gold in her cup.

"To celebrate our safe release."

They lifted their cups in salutation.

"*Kanpai*," Itsue downed her drink in one gulp.

"To our fortunes," Françoise added.

~~~~~~

The following day as Françoise sped towards Tokyo on the Shinkansen at two hundred and eighty kilometers an hour, fields of colourful cosmos flashed past the carriage window. Françoise leaned back in her seat and before long, as the Nozomi 700 eased into Tokyo station, checked her watch to make sure there was enough time to pay Martin a visit. *Parfait! J'ai assez de temps pour aller au musée et j'espère que Martin travaille aujourdh'hui,* she murmured to herself. Françoise descended the escalator, exited the Shinkansen line, searched for directions to the Yamanote line and boarded a train for Ueno. Herded towards the exit with the other commuters she came out of the subway into the daylight, and headed across the park towards the Tokyo National Museum.

The two grey suited receptionists recognised Françoise as soon as she walked in. "Ohayo gozaimasu," they greeted her in unison.

"I wonder if I could have a quick word with Martin? I will not keep him long."

"I'll call him," the older woman replied. "Please wait over there."

The woman's marked Japanese accent would have amused Françoise if she'd had more time; instead she went straight to the reception area, hoisted her case onto a seat and had just unzipped it when Martin walked across to her.

"Oh! Martin," she said. "I'm so glad you're here, otherwise I would have been caught trying to smuggle stolen goods out of the country."

Martin frowned. "What on earth are you talking about?" he asked.

"Please, just hold out your hands."

Françoise took the three kneeling miniature figurines from her bag and placed them, one by one, into his hands. She reached into her bag again and pulled out the figure of Queen Maya and held it up for him to see.

"But... How... Where... Where did you get them?"

"I'm sorry, no time to explain," she said as she laid the figurine gently with the others in Martin's hands. "I have a plane to catch at Narita in a few hours. I know I can trust you, so please, just go and put them back in their showcase."

"But you can't just walk in here and give me these. People will think I had something to do with the theft. I'll have to make a report and…"

"I know, Martin. I'm a curator myself, but…" Françoise spoke quickly as she zipped up her case and lowered it to the floor. "…I really can't help you. I'm sure you'll be able to find a way around it." Halfway to the exit she turned and, mimicking the sideways glancing Buddha at Kyoto's Eikan-do, she looked back over her shoulder.

"Don't dawdle Martin, and look after them this time," she mocked.

Martin stared at Françoise's back until the automatic doors closed and obscured her from view. A frown creased his forehead and long sigh escaped from his lips. *"Merci Madame,"* he said, *"Bon voyage!"*

Then, their eyes wide in amazement, the two assistants came over and helped Martin take the statuettes back to the gallery.

The plane left Narita International Airport exactly on time and flight 305 to Charles de Gaulle was smooth and uneventful. No Monsieur Moustache, and no sucking of teeth interfered with relaxation. Fourteen hours later the pilot's announcement comforted Françoise beyond belief.

"Mesdames et messieurs, nous allons bientôt commencer notre descente sur Paris. Redressez vos sièges et bouclez vos ceintures s'il vous plaît. Il est maintenant 15h32 à Paris et la température est de 12 degrés avec un ciel nuageux. Tous les membres de l'équipage vous souhaitent un bon séjour à Paris et espèrent vous revoir bientôt sur un vol d'Air France."

The pilot began the final descent to Paris and Françoise peeped out at the landmarks below. A familiar face at the airport would have been nice but Françoise did not expect such a treat.

Instead she collected her bags from customs and took a taxi directly to her home. As she fumbled with the key in the lock, steps approached from the other side, the door was pulled open and Georges stood there smiling.

"I... I thought you were in custody," she stammered.

"Out on bail. Not to leave the country until after the trial. Scheduled for next month on the fourth. Should go well, four is a favorable number for me. Welcome home!"

He reached for her bag and attempted a kiss but she shied away.

"You've been charged?"

"Yeah. Afraid so."

"Then you do have a hand in statues coming out of Japan."

"You of all people must realise smuggling gives me access to fantastic pieces of art."

"Including stolen works, Georges, and you condone that. How could you do such a thing while married to me? I'm curator of a museum that is dedicated to the protection of Japanese art?"

"Come on, Françoise. You know how it works. It has been going on for years. Treasures are taken by archaeologists and sent to museums, or by locals and sold on the black market. It doesn't matter who buys them."

"I can't believe you said that. Do you really think it's all right for people to sell off national treasures?"

Georges responded with a shrug of his shoulders. "Kept in a museum or in a private collection what's the difference? They still bring pleasure and inspiration to artists who know and really care about them."

"Georges, you disgust me. It's people like you who keep smugglers in business."

"Yes, and you met one of them, didn't you?" Georges smirked. "Monsieur Cheong."

"You mean Yamamoto?" Françoise questioned.

"One and the same, a heavily built man with a dark moustache and a laugh that resonates forever. I understand your friend damaged some property on his premises."

"My God, news travels fast! So you do deal with him."

"Françoise, it is because you are married to me that he released you."

"How do you know all this?"

"He called me. Evidently he saw a photo of us together."

Françoise recalled the scene in the museum when Monsieur Moustache had glanced through the photo flip case.

"How long have you been doing this, Georges?"

Georges grunted sardonically. "Ever since we got married. I met Cheong by chance in Pondicherry when we were there on our honeymoon, and later we set things up."

"So Yamamoto sends the statues to India, you travel to India, collect them and have them shipped to Paris."

"Something of that sort. He fills the hollow statues with bank notes to get them out of Japan and buys gold bullion on the black market that eventually ends up in North Korea. I buy the empty statues from Cheong, ship them to France, and put them up for sale."

"Knowing you'll have no trouble importing them under the guise of university property, you then make a handsome profit over what you pay Yamamoto."

"You make it sound harsh but... yes, that's the basic idea. Once goods are taken from their source no one can prove where they came from."

"You're wrong, Georges. Antiques sold by reputable dealers have a detailed record of where they come from and when they were bought."

"In the major museums of the world they do," Georges countered, "but not on the open market. Hundreds of antiques are sold without ever being recorded, while in other museums countless artifacts await documentation by your overburdened officials. You know that, Historian."

"And you think to avail yourself of my reputation to add credence to your own. You take advantage of unscrupulous thugs who steal from temples and religious institutions. You think you are too clever for anyone to see through your operation but your show is over, Georges. I'm going to leak this to the press."

Georges slapped her face hard. "Françoise, be careful for your own sake! Cheong may have released you, but believe me he is a ruthless gangster with no qualms about who he hurts. His organization depends on secrecy. He will not take kindly to a leak of information."

Françoise held her hand to her face as tears welled in her eyes. "Damn you Georges René de Cotret. You are guilty…"

"As I said, out on bail awaiting trial."

"…and a bastard!"

"Come on, Françoise. If it's the trial you're concerned with, the nature of antiquities makes the issue of ownership a murky affair. The stuff I deal with is seldom reported stolen. It will be impossible for the police to prove a chain of ownership."

"Not if the public prosecutors know what they are doing, Georges!"

Françoise stormed off up the stairs to the bedroom suite. Later, after letting the shower beat on her shoulders for a full five minutes, she changed into her nightwear, seated herself on the edge of the bed and dried her hair. Georges was still downstairs in his study and she hoped he would stay there.

~

After a restless night rolling from one side of the bed to the other Françoise awoke as dawn was breaking through the gap in the curtains. She opened her eyes and stared at the vacant pillow beside her. Whether in her dreams she rolled towards Georges or towards Shigehiro she never ascertained, for neither of them had been in the bed with her. She rose, blinked several times on the way to the adjoining bathroom, looked in the mirror and put a hand up to her cheek. Her trip to Japan had given her an opportunity to discover the unthinkable about her marriage and she now understood just how drastic the differences between Georges and her had become. Her mind finally made up Françoise wrapped her gown tightly around herself and went downstairs to find Georges already at the breakfast table.

"*Mon coeur,*" he said cheerily from behind his newspaper as she entered the room, as if nothing had happened the night before. "After this court case is over, I have some outstanding university research at Pondicherry to finish. Numbers are favourable for you to accompany me." He bit into his toast.

"No, Georges. You go on your own. Then you can concentrate on your illicit dealings."

"Don't be silly. I won't be doing that."

"No!" She spoke as calmly as she could. "I want a divorce!"

Georges stopped chewing, stared at her across the table and slumped back into his chair. Finally he grimaced as he swallowed his mouthful of toast.

"You don't understand. It's just a month. If you don't want to take more leave from the Cernushi, you can stay here in Paris."

"No, Georges. It's you who don't understand. I'm appalled by your attitude, tired of your petty thinking and disgusted with your dealings. I want out of this relationship! We are not compatible anymore. We have different values and ambitions."

He threw the remains of the toast on his plate and stood up abruptly.

"It's because of your trip to Japan, isn't it? You met someone!"

Françoise stared disdainfully at the mess on the table.

"You would think that Georges, wouldn't you?"

"Too damn right I would think that, and it's true, isn't it?" He threw his napkin on the table. "We'll talk about this later." He walked out and slammed the door behind him.

"There's nothing to talk about, Georges," she yelled at the door. "And you'd better not have the trial on the fourth either. It's not an auspicious day for you."

Françoise reached across the table for a cup and poured herself some coffee. Georges had been mistaken. The eighth had been perfect for her to go to Japan. In Judaic symbolism eight is associated with new beginnings, renewal and the start of a new cycle. Georges had not understood the full meaning of the number. Arriving in Japan on the ninth had brought pain but nine was also devoted to heaven and its angels and thanks to the angels Françoise had survived. Georges was tied to his favorite number four. He lived by it. The number that evokes all that is earthy, human and mortal, the number of the created world. The number inevitably linked to death. Françoise's relationship with Georges had died. In Japan she had met a man whose number was three, the number *par excellence* that symbolizes the trinity. St. Augustine, the father of medieval symbolism, linked four to the body or matter and three to the soul or mind. The men in Françoise's life had gone from a four to a three person. Four times three make twelve. Twelve days in Japan, the number of completeness and fulfillment. All in her favor!

二 十 八

One Week Later
September 26th Nagoya & Paris

One rainy evening in late September Itsue returned home from work, parked her car at the nearby parking lot and rushed to her apartment. As she neared the building a spontaneous scream escaped from her lips and her hand went to her mouth. Chulsoo was slumped on the entrance steps; his face buried in his hands and his hair a mess.

"Chulsoo! What on earth has happened to you?"

He opened his eyes, lifted his head a little and stared at Itsue's feet. He gave a wan smile, his cheeks and forehead smudged with dirt, and his breath stank of stale alcohol.

"I found where my father..." His voice trailed off.

Itsue laughed then the laugh turned to tears. Chulsoo was exhausted, defeated beyond hope. Itsue took his grubby hands in hers, held them tightly, and he winced.

"Chulsoo! Your finger! What happened?"

"I had it cut off."

"What do you mean?" she squealed.

"To leave the underworld. So I can have a respectable life with you."

Tears welled in Itsue's eyes as she realised he had undertaken the proof he would have nothing more to do with his uncle. A promise she asked for in the Nagoya Hilton Hotel that now seemed so long ago. Itsue bent down and took his face in her hands.

"You'd better come in and get cleaned up," she whispered.

They climbed the five flights of stairs. Chulsoo squatted in the entranceway to remove his shoes. Itsue went to the bathroom and turned on the heater to fill the bathtub with steaming hot water.

"Go and shower while the bath fills up," she told him. Chulsoo gratefully did as he was told. He closed the dividing curtain of the changing room behind him, left his clothes on the floor and went into the bathroom. He seated himself on the plastic stool and looked in the mirror. He heard movement in the room beyond and the sound of the washing machine. The door behind opened and Itsue stepped naked into the bathroom. He started to turn but she pushed his head back and squatted down behind him, reached for a handful of shampoo, turned the shower onto his head and started to shampoo him.

"You're drowning me," he said through the foam running down his face.

"You deserve it," she giggled and pulled a rough washcloth from the rail and soaped his back. He took the cloth from her and washed his chest and stomach. Itsue rinsed him and ordered him into the bathtub. Chulsoo's knees broke the surface of the water as he soaked. He watched the soap slide down Itsue's delicately curved back while she shampooed her hair. She rinsed herself off, sprayed the steam from the mirror and smiled at his reflection over her shoulder.

"Go on, out! I want to get in the tub."

He obeyed without a word and shut the door gently behind him.

"There is a robe in the other room you can put on," she shouted.

He dried himself and stepped into the other room, took two cans of beer from the fridge, placed one on the kitchen table, pulled the ring tab of the other and relished a deep draft. Itsue came from the bathroom wrapped in a white towelling gown and her hair twisted in a towel balanced precariously on her head, she reached for the beer and like Chulsoo took a long needed draft.

"Now. Tell me what has happened," she said, as she seated herself at the table.

"Uncle Cheong and I came to blows. While we argued he let it slip that my father was alive somewhere in Nishinari. I spent two days there asking everyone where he might be but nobody knew anything. I even got into a couple of fights with some of my uncle's men who had been ordered not to reveal my father's whereabouts. Nobody would help. Then I remembered that even the homeless have a network of underdogs who will pass along information for a price. I made it known that I would pay, and eventually a guy approached me and said he would take me to where my father was. The man led me to the grounds of Osaka Castle, pointed to a man that appeared a little younger than the other homeless men around him, took the money I offered and quickly left. My father was seated on the ground next to a bicycle and some paper carrier bags. Like other homeless men he collects used cardboard cartons and empty beer cans to make the little money he needs to survive. I went towards him and he glanced up belligerently.

"What do you want?" he said. I told him my name and then my mother's name but he would not believe me. He hadn't seen me since I was a schoolboy. I told him about our life in Nagoya and eventually he accepted that I was his son. He got to his feet and embraced me. He asked about my mother and I told him she was well."

"But why does he have to stay there, in those conditions?"

"Support of family members is enormously important for Korean people. Uncle Cheong was angry that my father didn't come to him for help."

"Why didn't your father ask your uncle for help?"

"He didn't want to have anymore to do with Uncle Cheong's activities. Father worked hard to have a decent life away from the organization, that's why we moved here to Nagoya but when he was laid off from his job he feared becoming a burden. He thought that if mother kept her job, she would have enough money to take care of me but that he would be a strain on her resources, so he decided to disappear until he could find other work. Mother however, lost her job and she returned with me to Tsuruhashi. When Cheong was told what father had done, he was furious and had him found and brought back to Osaka."

Itsue took a few moments as she silently took in the situation. "What happens now?"

"I don't think Cheong will stop me from helping father now," Chulsoo replied. "He knows it would hurt mother too much if he did anything to me. In my uncle's eyes father failed to look after his sister and he punished him for that, but it's over. Now that I have left the organization it will be less embarrassing for Cheong if both my father and I are no longer around. Cheong will leave us alone if we keep away. He raised me and I know him well. He is strict but not malicious. If I can find work in Nagoya, I will bring father to live here."

Chulsoo leaned back against the kitchen counter and Itsue stared at him across the table. He loved her and she knew it, and he needed her in order to start a new life. Should she tell him that she had met Uncle Cheong, she thought to herself. No, best not to for now, it would take too long to explain. However, what Cheong said that scary afternoon at the museum proved that what Chulsoo said was probably true. 'Return to Nagoya and never let me see you again,' he had told her. His face mere inches from hers, his breath overpowering. The memory had been etched on Itsue's mind.

"Chulsoo, what am I going to do with you?" she said quietly.

He shook his head lost for words.

"You need someone to take care of you," she prompted.

He frowned. "Would you make *misoshiru* for me every day?" he ventured.

Itsue laughed aloud at the conventional proposal.

"And you want me to wash your underwear as well, I suppose?" she replied.

Chulsoo laughed, crunched the empty beer can in his hand, placed it on the table and walked around behind her chair.

"I'll do whatever I can to make you happy, if you'll be by my side," He whispered.

Itsue leaned back and laid her head on his chest.

"What will you do about your finger?"

"A little toe can be grafted onto the stub. Nobody will notice if I get a good surgeon."

"And your tattoo?"

He placed his hand under her chin and turned her head to face him.

"They are difficult to have removed. If I keep it, I won't be able to go to public baths, but these days a lot of onsen towns accept people with tattoos of this size."

He leaned forward and kissed her lightly on the lips, she held him tightly and their frustrated passions took over.

Late the following morning in Itsue's apartment Chulsoo snored rhythmically. Blankets and sheets bundled around him as he lay among the twisted futons hurriedly dragged from the closet the night before. Itsue arose quietly and went to prepare breakfast, placed everything on a large kitchen tray and took it to the next room. She woke him up and seated together on the bedding futons, they ate, talked, laughed, kissed and fell into each other's arms once more.

Finally, showered and dressed, Itsue picked up her handbag and car keys from the table and steered Chulsoo out the door, down the stairs and along to the Honda. The rain had stopped and it held promise for a clear day. Itsue clicked the door release and

Chulsoo walked around to the passenger's side. He stood awhile beside the car before opening the door.

"Where are we going?" he asked.

"To my parents. I have to introduce you," she answered.

~

On the third floor of the Cernushi Museum in Parc Monceau as the sonorous click of the director's footsteps recedes down the hallway, Françoise reaches across her desk and leafs through the papers the director has just dropped on top of the pile of scattered documents already there. She finds the document she hoped would be there, swivels around to face the computer, pulls the keyboard towards her, saves the report file and opens a letter file. Ten minutes later she prints it out and reads it through.

THE MUSEUM CERNUSHI PARIS FRANCE

September 26th

Dearest Shigehiro,

I am deeply indebted to you for your help during my stay in Japan.

Unbeknownst to me, my estranged husband has been trading in stolen statues for several years. A number of pieces he had recently sold have been traced and turned in to the police. The authorities have requested the Cernushi Museum's help in identifying and ascertaining whom the works legally belong to. I have been assigned to assist them and have just received documentation that a small Buddha of a dark blue hue is among them.

The Buddhist Archive Exhibition at the Cernushi is scheduled for two months in the summer of next year. I wonder if it would be possible for you to be our guest speaker. To have you in attendance in your blue samue would give our exhibition enormous authenticity. The French public would gladly attend short lectures about the statues from someone so knowledgeable as you. I would be happy to arrange your accommodation and to be your host throughout your stay.

Fond regards,
Françoise René de Cotret

Françoise folds the letter, slides it neatly into an envelope, copies the address from Shigehiro's name card, and drops it into the out tray. She reaches down, pulls open the bottom drawer of her desk and rests her foot on its front edge. The metal swivel chair squeaks as she leans back, but impervious of the sound, she gazes up at the ceiling as recollections of the time spent with Shigehiro at Kashihara fill her mind.

"Je me demande comment ce serait d'être mariée à un sculpteur bouddhiste," she murmurs aloud as she wonders how life would be married to a Buddhist sculptor. True, he hadn't proposed yet but he'd get around to it, she'd make sure of that.

Fin

Glossary

Japanese and Korean Terminology

Japanese honorific suffixes.
sama – sir or madam.
san – Mr. or Ms.
kun – a boy or young man.
chan – a girl or young woman.
sensei – a teacher, doctor or professor.

Words for family members.
ojisan – uncle.
ojiisan – grandfather.
obasan – aunt.
obaasan – grandmother.

Other Japanese / Korean words.
Bizen yaki – A rustic brown pottery made in the Okayama area.

Tokkuri and choko – A small pot and a small cup used for drinking warm sake.

Dai-jokki, Chuu-jokki, Sho-jokki – Large-mug, Medium-mug, Small-mug.
Refers to the three sizes of beer mugs used at many drinking establishments.

Kanpai – Cheers! Expression used before drinking alcohol. Lit. 'Drain your glass'.

Itadakimasu – Bon appétit! Expression used before eating. Lit. 'I'm going to receive'.

Gochisosama - Expression used after eating. Lit. 'Thanks for the feast'.

Hanbok - Traditional Korean clothing.

Chogori - The short jacket like top of traditional women's clothing.

Ch'ima - The colorful traditional skirt that flares from under the chogori.

Chijimi – Common type of omelette made with flour, water and garlic chives.

Oyabun - Is the father figure head of an underworld organization, although the advisor, with business acumen and knowledge of legal proceedings, often has equal authority.

Yamabushi - An ancient organization of austere mountain ascetics with roots in both Shinto and Buddhist faiths. Members are noted for hanging over ravines while others hold on to their ankles and demand that they swear to be good subjects.

Burakumin - The word pariah means social outcast. Originally the Indian lower caste's name came from the word for drummer, the original pariahs being drummers. Could it be that the idea of lower castes, burakumin, was introduced into Japan along with taiko drums and Buddhism? The community is still classified as depressed and until recent times both economic and educational privileges were denied to their members.

Zelkova - The main wood used to make Taiko drums. It is an extremely hard deciduous tree that belongs to the elm family.

Trees native to southwest and eastern Asia can reach up to thirty-five meters. Almost all trees are currently grown in botanical gardens and relatively few are known to come from countries of their natural habitat.

Chapter 26 Note (1) - Nyorai indicates a being that has entered nirvana. In English it is that of Buddha, but is not confined to the historical figure of Sakyamuni. Bosatsu designates an enlightened being that represents compassion and guidance. Myoo are destroyers of evil spirits that represent severe training and trail by fire.

Appendix

Museums Temples and Statues in this Book

The Cernushi Museum - Chapter 1

The Cernushi museum in Parc Monceau, Paris exists and has a collection of Japanese art displayed in their permanent exhibition. Françoise is a fictional character, and there seem to be no offices on the third floor.

Honkomyo-ji - Chapter 2

Honkomyo-ji is a small temple in Kasanui south of Nara. The temple and adjoining shrine described in the novel are real but the present residents bear no relationship to the fictitious characters in this book. The Sho Kannon cannot be seen at this temple and of course the Blue Buddha made by Grandfather Hiro is a creation of the authors.

Tokyo National Museum - Chapter 3

Tokyo National Museum in Ueno Park has several exhibitions each year. However the four brass figurines of Queen Maya and of her three kneeling attendants mentioned in chapters 3, 26 & 27 are normally kept at Horyu-ji in Nara.

Ikaruga - Chapter 5

Ikaruga town and the surrounding area north of Asuka and south east of Nara are central to the development of Japanese culture. Many historical temples here testify to the importance religion played in the lives of early Japanese people. The main temple in this area is Horyu-ji easily accessible from Horyu-ji Station on the JR line. Here the seated Shaka Nyorai (Skt: Sakyamuni) the historical Buddha. Flanked by Fugen (Skt: Samantabhadra) and Monju (Skt: Manjusri) who respectively represent praxis and wisdom. Made by a Korean sculptor of the Tori school in the early half of the Asuka period (before 600). The canons of such images were fairly rigidly circumscribed but over the centuries individual styles developed and we can thus follow the spread of such influence. Other temples mentioned in the novel are Matsuo-dera that preserves a mixture of Buddhist and Shinto influences. Yata-dera is a well-kept peaceful temple famous for its hydrangea blooms in June. Horin-ji keeps a beautiful display of Korean style sculptures and Hokki-ji that is built on the site where Prince Shotoku once lived.

Nagoya - Chapter 7

Kitamura Antiques in Nagoya is a fictitious location. However, the statues mentioned in chapters 7 & 8 are easily identified and can be seen in many temples. Reproductions range from small brass statuettes to larger than life wooden sculptures. Fugen Bosatsu (Skt: Samantabhadra) seated on an elephant represents emotion. Monju Bosatsu (Skt: Manjusri) seated on a lion represents intellect.

Asuka - Chapter 10

The Asuka period goes as far back as records go in dating factual Japanese history. Resembling an archaeological dig the area contains temples, palace remains, tumuli, archaeological ruins and unusual carved stones. Tachibana temple, with its statue of Prince Shotoku's horse, is from where Prince Shotoku regularly travelled when going to Asuka-dera to engage in Buddhist studies. Asuka-dera (Hookoo-ji) has a representation of Prince Shotoku as a young man to which sculptors have given a rather feminine appearance. It also houses a rather badly repaired bronze Buddha that appears peaceful when viewed from one side and annoyed when viewed from the other side.

Kintetsu Tsuruhashi - Chapter 12

Even before exiting Kintestu Tsuruhashi station one is aware of the aroma of grilled beef. The Korean market town is home to the largest population of ethnic Koreans in Japan. Famous for its many 'yakiniku' restaurants and 'kimuchi' stalls, here in the hustle and bustle of the narrow crowded alleyways, a short walk from Korean Town, can be found Korean goods of all kinds: kitchenware, household commodities, traditional food provisions and of course the strikingly colorful 'hanbok' costumes.

Nishi-no-Kyo - Chapter 15
Yakushi-ji

Yakushi-ji is currently the head temple of the Hosso sect, which is the second oldest Buddhist sect in Japan. Its two pagodas are known as 'frozen music' because of their rhythmic appearance. Cleverly constructed each pagoda appears to have six floors, but alternate roofs are built onto the outsides of each floor. The bronze ringed roof ornaments atop the pagodas, the *sorin*, are 10 meters high and weigh 3000kg each.

The Grand Main Hall houses a magnificent bronze Yakushi Triad. Made of bronze and dated from the Hakuho Period (645-710) Yakushi Nyorai (Buddha of Healing) sits in splendor on the medicine chest between two standing mirror images of Nikko (Bosatsu of the sun) and Gakko (Bosatsu of the moon). Originally covered with gold, a fire in 1528 left the three of them in their current blackened burnished condition. The medicine chest is of special anthropological interest as it displays artistic styles from several distinct cultures that traveled to-and-fro along the Silk Road: animal designs from China, lotus designs from ancient Persia, crouching barbarians from India, grapevine scrolls from ancient Greece.

Also enshrined at Yakushi-ji are four *Shi Tenno* that show the evolution of Buddhism as it travelled from India to Japan. These four kings were originally ancient Indian Devas and introduced into Buddhist doctrine as guardians of *Shumisen*, the inaccessible mountain at the centre of the universe. The Chinese incorporated them with four Chinese gods who guarded the corners of the world and named them according to the colors assigned to them: blue, red, black, white. The faces of these Shi Tenno have kept these four colors and these colors have become symbols of good luck shown in the tassels hanging on the four sides of the sumo ring.

Toshodai-ji

Toshodai-ji built in 759 and preserved in its natural environment is a world heritage site. The main hall or golden hall has recently been completely rebuilt, an undertaking that took nine years. It was first totally dismantled, repaired, then reassembled and reopened in 2009. The front of the hall with its colonnade of eight pillars emulates Greek design and inside houses three magnificent images: *Rushana-butsu* the Buddha of light, seated on a lotus pedestal of forty-eight petals, and standing images of *Yakushi Nyorai* the Buddha of healing, and of *Senju Kannon* the Thousand-armed Kannon,

Seven Great Temples of Nara - Chapters 15 &18

1: Todai-ji. (East Temple) The majestic eighth century Todai-ji in Nara Park, home of the colossal bronze statue of Birushana Buddha housed in the largest wooden structure in the world, attracts millions of people every year.

2: Saidai-ji. (West Temple) Although somewhat overshadowed by its eastern counterpart, the more aesthetic and secluded Saidai-ji houses two statues designated as Important Cultural Properties as well as other significant statues.

3: Yakushi-ji. Here, in addition to the magnificent bronze Yakushi Triad, one can view an image of Sho Kannon considered by many to be the most beautiful reproduction of the merciful goddess in Japan. (More in this book at Nishi-no-Kyo - Chapter 15.)

4: Kofuku-ji. Located inside the western precincts of Nara Park this temple complex, one of the oldest and most famous, expanded rapidly under the patronage of the Fujiwara family that ruled most of Japan until the 15th century.

5: Gango-ji. Situated a little south of Nara Park, this temple initially occupied a wide area within what is now Naramachi of present day Nara city. A world cultural heritage site, the temple was moved from Asuka and underwent several name changes.

6: Daian-ji. The Nihon Shoki records the founding of Kudara Dai-ji as the predecessor of Daian-ji. Despite earthquakes in 1585 and 1596 that destroyed most of the temple it has managed to preserve several statues designated as Important Cultural Properties.

7: Horyu-ji. Located in Ikaruga, some distance from the other temples, the grounds of Horyu-ji contain the world's oldest wooden structures built around 747. It was the first site in Japan to be recognized by UNESCO as a world heritage site.

Kyoto - Chapter 19

Omuroouchi. This mountain area of Kyoto is a hiking route of eighty-eight temples just north of Ninna-ji. Inspired by the famed eighty-eight temple pilgrimage around Shikoku, monk Sainin had it made in memory of Kobo-daishi. Except for temples numbered one, thirty-six, sixty-five, and eighty-eight, the other eighty-four are no more than small wooden buildings that contain images of faithful Buddhist priests.

Koryu-ji. This temple is located in the Uzumasa area of western Kyoto. Even as recently as the early 1900's this part of Kyoto consisted mainly of farmland with few family homes. Although now developed it retains the look of early postwar Japan. Rich in history, Koryu-ji was established while Nara still reigned as the capital of Japan. The people here, many of Korean heritages, established textile and carving industries. The Korean, Kyoto Chosen Daini Shokyo School, is located to the west of this area.

Miroku. (Skt: Maitreya) This statue of the Buddha of the future or the yet to appear Buddhist messiah is seated with one ankle on the knee of the opposite leg and one finger against the chin in a pensive attitude. Naked to the waist, it is of plain wood although traces of gold lacquer can be seen in the folds across the belly. Another statue in the same pose is also displayed but this figure is fully clothed. The drapery clings to the shape of the body and hangs in regular folds around the pedestal. This style originated during the Chinese Northern Ch'i period in the 6th century and was later seen in Korea and Japan.

Matsuhisa Institute of Buddhist Art

Kayu Matsuhisa the youngest daughter of Matsuhisa Sohrin took on the presidency of the Matsuhisa Buddhist and Religious Art Institute after her father's death in 1992. Her father Sohrin devoted his life to Buddhism and education and imparted his knowledge of carving and engraving techniques to everyone, professional artisans and amateurs alike. His works were kept close at hand for others to study and many are still at the institute. Kayu's grandfather Matsuhisa Hohrin started to engrave at the age of ten, and after a career of seventy years, is said to have created seven thousand Buddhist images. - https://www.matsuhisasohrinbussho.jp

Zenrin-ji - Chapter 22

Zenrin-ji is located on the eastern edge of Kyoto City near to Nanzen-ji and home to Mikaeri-no-Amida the famed looking-back Buddha. Also known as Eikan-do the name is derived from the seventh head monk Eikan (1032-1111) who it was said on February 15th 1082 was walking around inside the main hall chanting nembutsu when the Amida Buddha got down from the altar and began to walk ahead of Eikan. The monk was so surprised he stopped in his tracks whereupon Amida looked back and said, "Eikan you are dawdling." The monk later commissioned a sculptor to create a statue of the Amida Buddha looking over his shoulder to commemorate this event.

Sakakibara Onsenguchi - Chapters 9 - 24 - 26

The museum and temple at Sakakibara-Onsenguchi are real. After a journey of ninety minutes from Osaka Namba on the Kintetsu line one cannot miss the pyramid shaped roof reminiscent of the Louvre Gallery in Paris and the larger than life replicas of Venus de Milo the Greek goddess of love and beauty and the headless winged Nike of Samothrace. The first director of the museum, the archbishop of Houjuzan Daikannon-ji, Yujiro Takegawa negotiated with the Louvre in Paris and procured approval for a sister pavilion. Almost 1,300 replicas were made from original sculptures and the museum opened in 1987. The temple also has a vast collection of sculptures related to Buddhist traditions. - http://www.louvre-m.com

二 十 九

Sometime Later

Shigehiro receives the letter from Francoise. He decides to go to Paris, but after the exhibition returns to Japan where he studies for three years under Kayu Matsuhisa at the Matsuhisa Buddhist and Religious Art Institute in Kyoto. During that time he lives with the author Francis Abbott and they spend many an evening discussing the issues in this novel. Shigehiro's father, Yoshihisa, continues as abbot of Honkomyo-ji and begins the training of priests that will one day take charge of various temples in the Ikaruga area, one of whom will be selected as the new abbot of Honkomyo-ji.

Françiose meanwhile, after her divorce from Georges, decides to quite her job and travel to Canada. Whilst in Ottawa she meets the author Johanne Léveillé who advises her to go back to Japan again. Shigehiro has by then received credentials as a qualified sculptor and well… we'll leave it to you the reader to decide whether Françiose does in fact go to Japan, whether she meets Shigehiro, and whether they marry… or not.

Itsue and Chulsoo, of course marry, much to the chagrin of her brother. To everyone's surprise Cheong turns up at the wedding, (How he found out about it, he would not say.) Itsue's mother, enamored with his excellent manners, invites him back to her home, where he meets Kitamura Sensei and promises to get the two statues returned. Later Cheong unfortunately develops colorectal cancer, probably from all those cigars he smoked, and has to go into hospital. Much to Kouno's distress the group that Cheong headed is disbanded, and Kouno is sent to Yamaguchi.

Martin takes the four statuettes back to his office and calls the museum directors. After explaining what happened, he is reprimanded but the directors have no choice but to accept the return of Queen Maya and her attendants. After the police have been informed, the statuettes are put back on their plinth, where they remain to this day.

Biography

Francis Abbott : Johanne Léveillé

Both of these authors have been immersed in Japanese culture for many years. Through their various work environments and respective interests they have experienced and questioned behaviors of their hosts as well as their own. Curiosity and eagerness to understand the human condition have led to numerous discussions with people in all walks of life.

In 1980, Francis Abbott had the opportunity to leave England and take up a position at a university in Kansai. He has resided in Kyoto ever since. In 1985, Johanne Léveillé left Canada and went to Japan for work. She remained in Kobe for 15 years where she studied the ancient Japanese art of calligraphy. While currently involved with Japanese culture in her home country, she frequently returns for visits to Japan.

Francis and Johanne became acquainted in Japan working at the same university. They started a writers' group, had several magazine articles published and gave presentations. While engaged in this enterprise, the idea for this book was born. Researching the accuracy of details needed for the novel, Francis and Johanne in their separate ways travelled to all the locations mentioned herein, and gathered numerous historical facts, this coupled with personal experiences, shaped this story.

Francis and Johanne treat cross-cultural matters with respect and objectivity, consequently this novel offers a wealth of fascinating cultural information often completely unknown to outsiders.

Malcolm E. Parker PhD

Printed in the United States
by Baker & Taylor Publisher Services